PRAISE FOR *LITTLE BOY LOST*

"*Little Boy Lost* isn't just an engrossing novel; it's one that enlightens as well."

—William Kent Krueger, *New York Times* bestselling author and Edgar winner

". . . Tense, powerful thriller . . ."

—*Publishers Weekly* (starred review)

". . . Trafford delivers . . ."

—*Booklist*

"*Little Boy Lost* is an exciting and thoughtful read . . . Trafford's writing style is brisk and no-nonsense with a dash of introspection and a lot of keen observations . . . tackles some important and tough issues head on . . ."

—*Bookreporter*

". . . A cracker-jack narrative . . ."

—*The Missourian*

GOOD INTENTIONS

OTHER TITLES BY J.D. TRAFFORD

Little Boy Lost

No Time To Run

No Time To Die

No Time To Hide

GOOD INTENTIONS

J.D. TRAFFORD

THOMAS & MERCER

Published by Thomas & Mercer, Seattle

www.apub.com

ISBN-13: 9781542045513
ISBN-10: 1542045517

Cover design by Jae Song

For my family and all the people who choose to serve others.

In re the Honorable James Thompson
California State Board on Judicial Standards
Inquiry Transcript, Excerpt

BOARD MEMBER GREEN: Do you understand that you can be represented by an attorney at these proceedings?
THOMPSON: Of course I understand that, Nick. I'm a judge.
BOARD MEMBER GREEN: And do you also understand that you could exercise your right to remain silent?
THOMPSON: Yes.
BOARD MEMBER GREEN: Even though this is merely a disciplinary hearing, your testimony this morning before this panel could be used as a basis to prosecute you criminally for many things, including, at the very least, obstruction of justice. Understanding that, you'd still like to continue?
THOMPSON: I'm here.
BOARD MEMBER GREEN: That's not what I asked. That's not an answer to my question.

THOMPSON: [Pause] I understand the risk, and I'd like to go forward.
BOARD MEMBER GREEN: Without counsel?
THOMPSON: Without counsel.
BOARD MEMBER GREEN: Very well.

CHAPTER ONE

My life began to unravel the same day I found my mentor dead. I had planned on meeting Judge Harry Meyer early in the morning for coffee at the Tin Cup Diner, a local hangout for judges and lawyers that was close to Oakland's courthouse on Twelfth. A newspaper reporter had called me with a vague message about one of the first child abuse cases I had handled, and I needed Harry's advice.

She didn't give me any specifics, but I knew which case she wanted to talk about. Because I'm a new judge, you'd think I hadn't yet done anything that would merit media attention, but you'd be wrong.

When Harry didn't show at the Tin Cup, didn't return my phone calls, and didn't come to work, I got worried.

"Anything I need to do right now?"

My new law clerk, Karen Fields, shook her head. "Nothing until this afternoon, Judge."

"This my mail?" I pointed to a stack on the edge of Karen's desk.

"Yes, Judge." She nodded. "Didn't look like anything important."

I picked up the stack, which included the new issue of the California State Bar Association's monthly magazine, and put it all in my briefcase.

Then I grabbed my black wool trench coat and went to the elevators. As I rode down to the main floor, I put the coat on.

I was glad I did, because a stiff, cold wind came off Lake Merritt the moment I stepped outside. I buttoned up the coat higher, took a step forward, and braced myself for another blow. The tall trees lining the lakeshore park bent as darker clouds rolled over the redwood hills in the distance. It wouldn't be too much longer until the sun disappeared for the winter, sending the Pacific coast under a blanket of clouds.

I walked to a parking garage about a block away, got into my Range Rover, and drove out of Oakland toward Harry's house in Berkeley's Rockridge neighborhood. Even though it was less than seven miles away, there wasn't a quick route because nothing was quick in Oakland.

I had been to Harry's restored Craftsman so many times, it was practically my own boyhood home. He and my father had been law partners together, and, after my father died of a heart attack, Judge Meyer stepped up as my mother fell apart, met a new man, and eventually moved to Florida. It was Harry who had taught me how to throw a baseball and pitch a tent, and his wife, Mary Pat, kept me fed.

It took twenty minutes to cross town. I drove down Broadway, turned left on College, and then up into a leafy residential area. Harry's house was in the middle of the block. The neighborhood was calm, but an uneasy feeling grew as I approached the house.

Then I saw it.

The front door was wide open. The wooden storm door swung in the breeze. It creaked and banged as I walked up the steps. I noticed when I reached the top that the screen was torn, pushed out from the inside. Then I saw Harry.

He died in the entryway.

A gun lay discarded a few feet away. Harry's body was twisted: legs bent, one hand above his head reaching toward nothing, the other hand—stained dark red—wrapped tight to his stomach. Blood had pooled underneath him.

The air was heavy and caught in my lungs. It was thick and raw.

I couldn't move my feet as I stared at him. I knew Harry was gone. I didn't need to check. The ends of my fingers went numb, then my hands. Sickness rolled up from my stomach, and that's what forced me to move. I turned around, went back outside, and threw up in the bushes next to the house.

◆ ◆ ◆

I don't know how long it took for the paramedics and the police to arrive. I can't tell you who got there first. I don't even remember much of the call itself—what I said or how I said it, whether I was crying and screaming or whether I was methodical and calm. I only remember the lack of feeling in my hands as they shook, and how hard it was to unlock my phone and dial 911. Tapping that stupid code had been damn near impossible.

I must have, at some point, walked down the driveway and sat on the curb, because that's where I was when the officer approached me.

"You Judge Thompson?" The officer spoke with hesitation. He had a baby face and was probably twenty-three.

"Yes." I nodded my head. "I called it in."

"Any reason you were here?"

"I was worried." Then I told the officer about the morning. I told him about our plans to meet for coffee, and how Harry didn't show up or return my calls. "He lives alone now. His wife's in a memory unit—Alzheimer's—and Harry's not young. Thought it could be his health . . . Didn't imagine it was this."

"Anybody who I can call to confirm?" The officer was all business, trying to play it cool, pretending he handled murder investigations all the time.

I didn't take offense. Most murders weren't great mysteries. They were simple. It was usually the person standing next to the dead body

with the bloody knife. Case closed. By focusing on the only person around, which was me, the cop was just playing the odds.

"You can call my law clerk." I searched my phone's contact list for Karen's number. My hand still shook, but not as badly. "She can fill you in. Folks at the Tin Cup also know who I am. They can confirm I was there this morning."

The officer nodded, unsure of whether to treat my candor with thanks or skepticism.

I didn't really care. My thoughts were elsewhere.

◆ ◆ ◆

Police officers continued to arrive. Within minutes, the whole area was cordoned off. A barricade was placed on both ends of the block, and eventually the medical examiner, forensic team, and detectives arrived. That was when the investigation truly began.

From the comfort of my vehicle, I watched them work the scene. Although I could handle the cold wind, I had decided to get inside the Range Rover when an icy rain began to spit down on me.

Theoretically, I could leave at any time. I wasn't under arrest. I was just a witness, but I wanted to stay. I owed Judge Meyer everything.

My wife, Nikki, understood that. Between my law school loans and her loans from medical school, we had been drowning in $200,000 worth of debt. She wasn't making much as a resident at the local hospital, and the cost of living in the Bay Area didn't help. But, thanks to Judge Meyer, who'd helped me become a judge, we had won a little space to breathe. I was now earning triple what I had as an assistant prosecutor.

"Should I come over?" There was some static over the phone. Nikki's voice trailed, sounding as lost as I was. "I can find coverage at the hospital. Somebody can pick up my shift."

"Stay." I fought back the lump that formed in my throat. Telling her what I had seen was hard. It made it real in a way that was different from when I was talking to the cop, more personal. "I've gotta call Karen and check in," I said. "I'll see if they need any more from me here, too. Then I'll let you know what's going on."

I hung up with Nikki and then, forcing myself to keep it together, called my law clerk.

Karen answered on the fourth ring. "Judge Thompson's chambers, how may I help you?"

"Karen, it's me."

"Oh." Karen sounded a little surprised. "A police officer called asking questions."

I told her where I was and what I'd found, keeping it short.

Karen didn't say anything at first. She'd been with me for only a month, but she knew how close I was with Judge Meyer. Under her breath she said, "Unbelievable." Then to me she said, "I'm so sorry, Judge. He was a great man, a really great man." There was another long pause and then a question. "What do you want me to do about your afternoon calendar?"

I emitted a quick, involuntary laugh. I couldn't help it. It didn't matter if the judicial district was large or small. The justice train rolled on. Matters needed to be called. Disputes needed to be heard. The system didn't stop for anybody, not even Judge Meyer. It never stopped.

"How many?" I asked.

"Twenty lines." *Lines* meant the number of cases on any given docket. "All broken babies. No truancy. No juvenile delinquency."

A weight pressed down on me.

We called them *broken babies* for short, even though they weren't all technically babies, nor did they all have broken bones. They were broken in other ways. They were kids who were removed from their homes and placed into the foster care system, broken emotionally or physically by their parent: a three-year-old wandering the halls of an

apartment complex with a diaper that hadn't been changed in a week; a five-year-old found playing in the corner of a meth house during the execution of a search warrant, her mother passed out in the corner; a newborn with two broken legs; a three-year-old with a fractured skull and cigarette burns down her back; a six-year-old with gonorrhea or some other sexually transmitted disease that nobody, especially an innocent child, should have to endure.

It was the science of child abuse. There were pediatricians board certified in the subject, who could determine whether an injury's explanation given at a hospital was consistent with the actual injury.

Unfortunately, every day I was becoming an expert myself. I was learning about how parents could be unnaturally cruel. In less than a year as a judge, I'd learned how to read an X-ray. I could determine by the shape of a fracture whether an adult had broken a child's bone by twisting, squeezing, or using a baseball bat. I knew at what age a baby's skull hardened, and at what amount of torque a leg bone would snap at various ages and under what circumstances. I knew whether a burn was caused by accidentally stepping into too-hot bathwater, or by a parent holding their child's feet in boiling water as punishment.

Me becoming an expert was what Harry had wanted. It was why he called in every favor, why he tapped every connection he'd developed over his long career. It was how he convinced the former governor to appoint me on the governor's last day in office, a process that bypassed the merit selection committee and ignored its recommendation to appoint my former boss, the Alameda district attorney, Nick Green.

Harry Meyer was the former president of the American Association of Juvenile Court Judges. He was a nationally recognized speaker and an authority on child abuse and the child protection system. Nearing retirement, he wanted me to carry on his legacy. I had reluctantly agreed, but I didn't think I'd be on my own so soon.

"Can you move them?" I asked.

"I could reschedule the hearings," Karen said, "but we'd blow the timelines."

All child dependency cases were on a strict statutory timeline. Since Alameda County's child protection agency received most of its money from the federal government, it was audited by the US Department of Health and Human Services almost every year. If the county wasn't in compliance with the federal timelines, then it could be sanctioned or lose its funding entirely.

There were thousands of reports of child abuse and neglect in Alameda County. There were over a hundred kids removed from their homes every month and even more in foster care. In addition to investigating abuse at home, county social workers had to personally look into additional reports of abuse and neglect at the foster homes and group homes. The whole system was collapsing under its own weight. Some would argue that it had already collapsed. Cases that should've taken months took years.

Judge Meyer and I were trying to change that.

"Keep them on," I said. "I'll come back."

"You're sure?"

I wasn't sure, but that was how it was. The system never stopped. Harry wouldn't have wanted me to stop, either. "I'll be in after lunch."

"OK," Karen said. "That reporter called again. Anything I should say?"

The reporter. I remembered the reason why I had wanted to see Harry that morning. "Push her off." I hung up, watching as a detective finished his conversation with the medical examiner and then walked toward me.

He was a big guy. An aged high school football star with broad shoulders and a matching gut. He tapped on the Range Rover's window.

I rolled it down. "Want to come in here and talk?" I asked. "Out of the rain?"

The detective nodded. "Appreciate that." He walked around the front and got in the other side as I rolled up my window. "Much better." The detective held his thick hands close to the hot air coming out of the vent. He took another minute, then turned and introduced himself. "Detective Frank Jarkowski." He held one of his paws out to me.

"Jim Thompson," I said. We shook, and the introductions were done.

"So you're the new judge."

"That's true." I nodded. "Relatively new. It's been about a year."

"Look pretty young to be a judge." Detective Jarkowski eyed me, sizing me up.

I'd heard it before, and I knew the comment was only a test. People wanted to poke me. They wanted to see my reaction. They'd watch to find out if I got defensive or turned arrogant. In short, they were looking for a reason to dislike me.

"You're not the first person to say that." I fell back on the script that I'd developed for this conversation. It just came out. The response and inflection in my voice were automatic, even in these circumstances. "Come back and see me in six months. I'll be fat and bald, just like a good judge should be." I paused for a beat, then delivered the punch line: "I promise you won't be disappointed, or your money back."

Jarkowski laughed, initially sincere, but the rest was forced. It was only a bridge. He had places he needed to go with me, and I wished he would get on with it.

The detective nodded toward the house. "Sorry about that young cop givin' you the business earlier. He's new."

"I don't mind."

Detective Jarkowski nodded, pleased with my answer. "Everything checked out, by the way, with your law clerk and the diner," he said. "But I do want to test your hands for gun residue—not 'cause I think you did it, more for trial."

"Defense attorneys?"

"Exactly." The detective pointed at me, pretending like I was a genius. "When we find the person who did this, I want to be able to show that I did my job. I eliminated you as a suspect, not because you're a judge, but because your alibi was solid and your hands were clean."

"Do you know when Harry died?"

"A couple hours ago, maybe three, but that's not official." Detective Jarkowski reached into the big pocket of his trench coat and removed a sealed white plastic envelope. Inside the Gunshot Residue Kit were four plastic bottles, white adhesive pads, and latex gloves. "Mind?"

I shrugged. "Not at all."

Jarkowski put on the latex gloves. They barely fit over his large hands. "So you knew Judge Meyer well?"

"Very well." I nodded as Jarkowski opened the bottle labeled LEFT PALM. "Harry liked to say that he knew me before I was born."

Jarkowski took my left hand and manipulated it into position. "Any idea who did this?" He stuck the adhesive pad onto the palm and waited a few seconds, then pulled it off and put it in the bottle. When I didn't respond to his question, Jarkowski prodded me. "I know this is tough, Judge, but cases get harder to close the longer an investigation goes. We need to move."

"I know." I held out my right hand. Jarkowski stuck an adhesive pad onto its palm, took it off, and put it in the bottle. Then he repeated the process, switching from the palms to the back of both hands. When Jarkowski was done, he put all the bottles into another envelope and sealed it, then initialed and dated the seal. The process established the first link in a chain of custody.

Detective Jarkowski returned the envelope to his pocket. "Again, my apologies for all this. Just wanna be thorough."

"Understood." I nodded, now watching the medics. They had finally emerged from the house with the stretcher. On top was Judge Meyer's body in a black bag. "To answer your question," I said, "I honestly have no idea who did this. Nobody in particular comes to mind."

I watched as the medics rolled the stretcher toward the ambulance in the driveway. "Harry was a Boy Scout—Eagle Scout, actually. Didn't drink too much. Pretty boring life, but he did terminate a lot of parental rights. Who knows? Maybe one of them held a grudge . . ."

I thought more about it. Over his decades on the bench, Judge Meyer had probably terminated the parental rights of over a thousand people and placed over ten thousand children in foster care. "Actually," I said, "I'm sure a lot of them held a grudge."

Detective Jarkowski nodded as, in the distance, medics opened the ambulance's back door. "You might be right." We watched as they loaded the stretcher with Judge Meyer's body into the back. "I guess we'll find out."

CHAPTER TWO

Before I even entered the courtroom, Karen Fields and another court clerk had everything lined up. The mothers were prepped and sitting in the waiting area. I say *mothers*, because it was rare to see a father. Sometimes they appeared, often wrongly thinking that a warrant would be issued for their arrest if they didn't come to court, but most of the time it was mothers, alone.

Inside, the institutional players were all present and accounted for. Everybody sat in their assigned seats at a long wooden table in front of the bench. If they knew about the death of Judge Meyer, none of them said a word. It was business as usual.

The social worker and the child protection agency's attorney, Sylvia Norgaard, sat on the right. Norgaard, as always, wore a perfectly fitted suit. She had married well, and her outfit likely cost more than the social worker made in a month. There was also the parent's attorney, Sophia Delgado. Delgado was a large woman. Unlike Norgaard, she didn't spend money on her clothes. Instead she invested a small fortune in her nails.

In the middle of Norgaard and Delgado was the CASA, Cherelle Williams. The acronym stood for Court-Appointed Special Advocate.

The CASA, or guardian ad litem, was specifically appointed to advocate for the child's best interests. To some a CASA may seem unnecessary, but in reality, the children the system was designed to protect were often lost amid the chaos surrounding their parents' lives and the attorneys' legal wrangling. The CASA was independent, there to be the eyes and ears of the court.

Karen Fields got up. "We're ready to proceed, Judge." She walked past the attorneys, then out the courtroom door. As the heavy oak door swung closed, we all heard her shout the family's last name three times. Then she came back into the courtroom, walked to her seat, and sat down.

A few seconds passed. The door opened, and a mother came inside. Tanya Neal carried a huge down jacket that made her appear even smaller. It was tough to figure out her age. She'd lived a rough life.

Neal put her jacket on an empty chair and took her seat next to Delgado.

Tanya Neal was too thin. *Heroin,* I thought. Then I pulled Neal's file up on a large computer monitor to my left. Court administration had installed one on every bench in the courthouse when we converted from paper to electronic files.

I clicked a few buttons, glanced at the screen, and confirmed that one of Tanya Neal's issues was, in fact, heroin. Then I turned to her. "Good afternoon." I offered a sympathetic smile, then asked the parties to introduce themselves for the record.

They each said their names, and Norgaard gave a brief synopsis of what Ms. Neal had been doing since her last court appearance. "Unfortunately, Your Honor, Tanya Neal was dismissed from her treatment program for nonattendance and missed four of her last six drug tests." Norgaard looked down at her notes, then back up. "We're going to file a petition to terminate Ms. Neal's parental rights to her four children very soon."

I turned to the social worker and asked if she had anything to add, which she never did, then to Cherelle Williams. The CASA echoed the

concerns raised by Norgaard but spent most of her time talking about each of the children.

"The teenage girls, Neisha and Kayla, are struggling. They're defiant in the foster home, running away and not attending school. The younger boys, Bobby and Damien, are OK. They want to go home, too. I'm trying to get them into sports or something, but the foster parents seem reluctant. For all of these kids, it's the first time in their lives that there's real structure. They're used to living pretty much on their own, raising themselves, doing their own thing. Foster care has been tough."

I clicked a button. A box appeared on my computer screen, and I typed a note in the electronic file. I looked away from the screen and back to Cherelle Williams. "Anything else?"

"The father." Williams shook her head. "He's out of prison now. He's made contact with the older girls through Facebook. I'm concerned about that. Very concerned about that. He's a dangerous man."

Finally it was Delgado's turn. She spoke while her client, Tanya Neal, sat silent. Delgado assured everyone that Ms. Neal would work harder. "She understands that the stakes are high, Judge. If she knows the whereabouts of the father or if the father contacts her or the children, Ms. Neal will let the social worker know immediately."

Ms. Neal remained silent, listening to her attorney. The parents usually didn't talk. Their lawyers were afraid of what they might say; some even instructed their clients to remain silent, like in a criminal case. It kept the hearings moving, which is why many judges liked it. I did not.

Judge Meyer taught me not to give in to the pressure of time. Harry taught me to address every parent directly, even if it made their lawyers uncomfortable. This was their child, no matter what brought them to court. The parents needed to be heard.

Harry told me it didn't matter what was going on in my life or whether I was tired or sick. Good judges set all of that personal baggage

aside and did the job. *Learn to compartmentalize. That is the key to surviving.* And that was what I was going to do, even though I had just lost a man I loved. Even though I just wanted to go home. I was going to do the job, just like Judge Meyer had taught me.

"Ms. Neal," I said, keeping my voice soft. "I'm proud of you for coming to court today. You could've skipped it. You could've stopped coming and stopped trying, but the fact that you're here shows that you care about your kids."

"I do." She trembled. "I want to see them."

"Then you know what you need to do. You need to get back into treatment. You need to go to your drug tests, prove that you're clean, and keep in contact with your social worker so that visitation can be arranged. But we can't do visitation when you're high."

"I will," she agreed, but it was clear she had doubt.

"You heard what the county is going to do. They're filing a petition to terminate your parental rights. If things don't change, then I'm not going to have much of a choice. Your kids can't be in foster care forever."

Ms. Neal nodded.

Sensing the end of the hearing, Norgaard stood and asked that I say the magic words that every judge must say in order to keep the money flowing from the federal government. Specifically, I had to find that the agency had made *reasonable efforts to reunify the child with the child's biological parents*, I needed to *continue temporary legal custody with the agency*, and I needed to determine that placement in foster care was *in the children's best interests*.

I parroted the magic words as required, and then Ms. Neal gathered her gigantic coat. She received paperwork for the next court date and walked out of the courtroom. Although I didn't know it at the time, Tanya Neal was going to disappear, but the case wasn't going to end.

◆ ◆ ◆

About two-thirds of the way through the calendar, that reporter who'd called me earlier, Benji Metina, came into the courtroom. Hearings were open to the public, although the public rarely came. She sat in the back, watching me and taking notes as I worked through the remainder of the afternoon calendar. It was unnerving, but there wasn't anything I could do about it.

As the only Native American reporter at the *San Francisco Chronicle*, Metina was often assigned to cover the casinos and anything that happened on the reservations that dotted Northern California. She also covered the family and juvenile court beat and, lately, wrote more and more investigative stories about local politicians, conflicts of interest, and government failures.

When the last family was called and the calendar was done, Karen gaveled the court to a close. I stood up and gathered my papers. I heard Metina call out my name as I walked toward the door that led to my chambers.

"Judge Thompson," she said, "have a moment for a few questions?"

I didn't stop. I pretended that I didn't hear her.

◆ ◆ ◆

The little red light on my phone blinked. I had messages, but I wasn't going to take the time to listen. I had no intention of hanging around the courthouse. I was sure that by now everybody knew what had happened. They knew Judge Meyer was dead.

I hung up my robe, loosened my tie, and sat in the leather chair behind my desk. The "To Be Signed" basket was filled with a half dozen orders. I removed them, took a pen out of my drawer, and got to work.

When I was done a few minutes later, I took the signed documents out to Karen's desk and placed them in the "To Be Filed" basket. Then I picked up my jacket and left.

I kept my head down and walked as if I were late for an important meeting. Out of the corner of my eye, I noticed a few clerks and an attorney open their mouths, about to say something, but they thought better of it. I somehow made it out of the courthouse without having to talk to anyone.

CHAPTER THREE

Our little rental house was in Laurel, a neighborhood sandwiched between two highways. The area had always been considered relatively safe by Oakland standards, but never fancy. Real estate agents had been touting it as *up-and-coming* for about forty years, but at some point people were going to realize that the neighborhood was never going to change. It was stubborn. The immigrants, hippies, and students weren't going to leave.

I smelled chocolate chip banana bread in the oven as soon as I came inside. It was Nikki's go-to food in good times and bad. Hearing the door close, Nikki, still in her hospital scrubs, came out to meet me.

Neither one of us said a word.

Ten inches shorter than me and not much over five feet, Nikki rolled to her tiptoes and kissed me on the cheek. I hugged her tight. Then we sat down on our cheap futon. Like most of our belongings, it was a remnant from our student days. Nearly a quarter million dollars in student loan debt prevented an upgrade anytime soon.

I took her hand in mine and bowed my head, exhausted.

"I can't believe you went back to work." She leaned into me. "People would've understood."

"Maybe." There was no more adrenaline. "When I got done, I literally ran from the courthouse to the parking ramp. I don't know why. I was crossing the street, and I could tell that the light was going to change, and so I started to run and, when I got to the other side, I kept running until I got to my car. The whole way. I never stopped."

The image of Harry, dead in the foyer, flashed in my mind.

"I was convinced that somebody was watching me or chasing me or . . . I don't know." I shook my head. "Must've looked like a crazy man. Once I got started, I couldn't stop."

"It's OK." Nikki put her hand on my leg. "After what you saw, it's OK."

I closed my eyes and sank deeper into the couch. I was deflated and decided to change the subject. "That reporter was there this afternoon."

"In your courtroom?"

I nodded. "In the back." I shook my head in disbelief. "It can't be good. She wanted to talk to me when I was done, wanted to ask some questions. I'm sure it's going to be about Gregory Ports."

"What'd you say?"

A smile crept over my face. "Nothing," I said. "Pretended that I didn't hear her, deaf."

"Sounds like a good strategy." She nodded. "But probably not sustainable."

"If she ever confronts me on it, I'd like you to write me up a little medical diagnosis for selective hearing loss. If you could do that, it'd be wonderful."

"Certainly."

It felt good to be home, safe. Even though I had already told Nikki the story, I again told her what had happened, from the beginning. She never interrupted me with questions. She let me go, just listening, even when I went off on tangents. I think that I talked for thirty minutes, maybe longer.

When I was done, and she was sure that I was done, she kissed me on the cheek and told me, again, that everything would be OK. Then Nikki took a deep breath, having taken in all the information, and looked at me. "What are you going to do?"

I thought about the question, and I wasn't sure how I should respond. "I don't know." I shrugged. "I feel . . ."

When I couldn't find the word, she found it for me. "Adrift."

I nodded. "I didn't seek out this job. Helping kids wasn't why I went to law school, but Harry showed me. It's important work, and I was learning how to do it. I just . . ." My mind drifted. "I wasn't supposed to do it on my own. We were supposed to be a team."

"But now it's just you." She put her hand on my shoulder. "But you've never been a quitter."

"No," I said. "I've never been a quitter."

"Keep telling yourself that." She smiled. "Because it's true." The oven timer went off. She patted my knee, stood up, and walked back to the kitchen. The oven door squeaked as she opened it. Then Nikki removed her freshly baked loaf of banana bread and put it on the counter. She tested whether it was done by sticking a butter knife in the middle. When the knife came out clean, she set it aside and turned off the oven.

"Want some coffee with it?"

"Sure." I pulled myself up off the couch and walked back to the kitchen. "I'll make the coffee, but only if you put extra butter on my bread."

"That's a deal."

CHAPTER FOUR

When I arrived at my chambers the next morning, Detective Jarkowski was waiting. Nobody else was in the office yet. He sat in a chair next to my law clerk's desk and appeared to be reading one of my bicycling magazines. "Hope you don't mind me making myself at home." He gestured vaguely with one of his giant hands. "Some court reporter let me inside, said you'd be in shortly."

Jarkowski closed the magazine and put it on the small end table. Then he tapped the cover, which featured a storklike couple in spandex. "Always interesting to learn what the skinny people are doing." He then took a deep breath and extricated his large body from the chair. "Got a few minutes to talk?"

"Come on back." I walked past him toward my office. "Got a bench meeting in about thirty minutes, so we should be good until then." I unlocked the door separating my office from the reception area and sat at my desk. "Hope you have some news."

Jarkowski shook his head and sat down across from me. "Not much at the moment. And that's why I'm here."

"OK." I leaned back, unsure of where this was headed. "What can I do?"

"Just talk to me." He offered a smile. It was meant to be encouraging, but it looked more like he was hungry and I was slathered in barbecue sauce. "Everybody says that you knew Judge Meyer the best. So I'm trying to figure out where to go. At the moment, I don't have much, to be honest. You mentioned that there might be a disgruntled defendant or parent or something, but we need specifics. I need a name."

"Well . . ." I shook my head. "I don't have anything more specific."

"Did he mention that anybody was threatening him?"

"No."

"In the past few weeks, did he seem distant or afraid?"

I thought about the last conversation I'd had with Harry. "I don't think he was acting different. At least, nothing stands out to me."

He latched on to my ambiguity. "You don't *think*, or you don't *know*?"

"I can't remember anything specific." The conversation went in circles. "Maybe there was something, but I don't think so. He was just Harry. He was a kind man. I was worried about a case and a reporter. Harry was there for me, just like always."

He waited for me to elaborate, but nothing more came. Finally he surrendered. "Think more about it, and if you come up with something, then please let me know." Jarkowski rubbed his large nose. "Anybody else you know that I should talk to?"

"Harry had some relatives, cousins. I called them last night, just to let them know what had happened. I can give you their names, but I don't think that they'll be of much help." Then I thought about Harry's best friend. "You should also talk to Marshall Terry."

"The businessman?"

I nodded. "He was pretty shaken up when I told him the news," I said. "Marsh was probably Harry's best and oldest friend. I'm not sure how often they got together, but Marsh might know things that I don't know. They served in Vietnam together."

"I'll follow up with him." Jarkowski took out a small notebook from his pocket, and then he wrote down the name. "Anybody else?"

"No," I said. "I'll let you know if I can think of more names."

"That's good." Jarkowski wrote another note to himself. "I appreciate this." He put the little notebook back in his pocket, and then he took the conversation in a different direction. "Another theory is some sort of robbery gone bad, like a guy comes up to the door, the judge answers, and there's a confrontation."

I was skeptical. Most of the thefts and burglaries I'd prosecuted before becoming a judge were petty shoplifting cases or somebody stealing electronics from friends or relatives. Home break-ins of strangers happened while the owners were at work or on vacation. There was usually some planning. Burglaries of occupied homes were unusual. Knocking on the front door and waiting for the homeowner to answer was incredibly unlikely.

"Seems like a stretch," I said.

"I know," he agreed. "But we have to follow up." Jarkowski paused for a moment. "What about money issues? Did Judge Meyer ever complain about getting paid too little, or maybe he liked to gamble?"

"He certainly never complained about getting paid too little," I said. "I know he hated gambling. He never even played the lotto, said it was a regressive tax on the working poor."

"What about debt?" he asked. "Did he buy things he couldn't afford? Did he owe people?"

"He lived a modest life. Harry and Mary Pat were comfortable, but it wasn't as if they went on elaborate vacations or drove fancy cars."

"Are you sure?" he asked. His eyebrow raised. "Some people have told me he had money issues."

"Not that I'm aware of," I said. "If he did, he never told me about them."

Jarkowski bit his lip. He rubbed his chin, likely wondering if he should push me further. Eventually, after several facial contortions, he moved on.

"We should be done processing the house by the afternoon," he said, "and then you can get inside. If you don't mind, Judge, it'd be good if you looked around." He held out his large hands, palms up. It was clear that he needed my help. "You see, there may be things that are important that I don't understand or know are missing. If you could go through any letters, bills, bank statements . . . See if there's something DKDK, understood?"

"Not really. DKDK?"

"Something that I don't know that I don't know. Anything that stands out as odd or weird or doesn't feel right." He sat up a little straighter. "We do as much as we can and follow the leads that we are given. I'd know if a flat-screen television was ripped off the wall, but only you know about missing jewelry or something else. You'll see stuff I don't see. You know things that I don't know that I don't know. DKDK."

"So I can go inside the house?"

"End of the day," said Jarkowski. "We contract with a company called Specialized Cleaners. They clean things up after a suicide, accident, or other death."

"I think that's one of the worst jobs in the criminal justice system."

"Awful," Jarkowski agreed. "The chemical smell in the house is going to be strong for the next few days." He stood up and held out his hand. "Thanks again, Judge, for taking the time to talk with me." He turned and started walking to the door, then stopped. "One more thing," he said. "You know who Helen Vox is?"

The question took me by surprise, and I wondered whether this was the real reason he had come to talk with me so early in the morning. "The prosecutor?"

"So you do know her?"

"Of course," I said. "Everybody knows her. She's been around a long time."

"Does child protection work, too, right?"

"Yes," I said. "She manages the division. Doesn't come to court much anymore. She might fill in when one of the attorneys is on vacation or sick, but her job is more policy and administration now."

"And she was tight with Judge Meyer?"

"Yes," I started to answer, but then stopped. "I guess . . . I don't know what you mean by *tight*."

"Did they socialize?"

I thought about it. "Maybe . . . I'm not sure."

He cocked his head. "Not sure? I thought you and Judge Meyer were close."

"We are . . . or were." I became flustered. "Where is this coming from?"

"You tell me, Judge." Jarkowski began to walk away. "You tell me."

◆ ◆ ◆

After Jarkowski left, Karen Fields came into my chambers with a fresh stack of orders for me to sign. "Morning, Judge." She set the papers in front of me.

"Good morning, Karen." I flipped through the documents. I was supposed to read every word, but I gave up that practice within the first week on the job. They were boilerplate orders. Unique information, such as the attorneys' names and the names of parents or children, was populated by a computer program. Although the people who drafted the rules and statutes likely envisioned something different, those people had never worked in the trenches. They didn't understand the time pressure. They didn't know the volume of cases. So, since the rules didn't specifically require independent thought and detail, none was provided. The statutes merely required a written order, and that's what they got.

I picked up my pen and worked through the stack. Then I gave the signed court orders back to Karen.

"Thanks, Judge," she said. "I'll get these filed while you're in your meeting. Then we have some hearings scheduled later in the morning."

"Anything else?"

Karen shook her head. "No, Judge." She paused. "Are you doing OK?"

"I'll be fine." I offered her a gentle smile. Karen's formality was a sharp contrast to her predecessor, and I was still trying to get used to it. The fact that she showed up on time and worked a full day was also a significant change. "Thank you for asking, Karen."

As she started to turn away, I thought about Jarkowski. "Karen," I said, and she stopped. "Do you know Helen Vox?"

She nodded. "I guess. What about her?"

"The guy investigating Judge Meyer's death asked if they were close, Harry and Helen."

Karen shifted from one foot to the other, looking uncomfortable. "What'd you say?"

"Nothing." I shook my head. "The question just caught me off guard, wasn't sure what I should say."

Karen raised her eyebrows, seeming surprised. "Why?"

"Well"—I paused—"they've worked together for years. What else was there?"

Her face tightened. Karen's narrow lips sealed closed.

"What's going on?"

She looked at her watch, now in a hurry to take care of the orders in her hand. "I better go get these filed."

"Stop," I said as she started to walk away. "I asked you what's going on." I didn't want it to seem like an interrogation, and so I tried to keep it friendly. "It's fine. I'm not mad at you . . . I just want to know."

She turned around with reluctance. "It's none of my business, Judge," she said. "Silly rumors."

"Rumors?" I stared at her. She'd been a law clerk for only a month, and Karen was already more plugged in to courthouse gossip than me. "About what?"

"People talk." Karen looked away, unable to meet my eye. "I guess I thought you knew they were . . . like . . . together."

"Together?"

Karen nodded. "Like for a long time, twenty years or something."

"He's married."

"I know," Karen said. "But lots of people have affairs."

CHAPTER FIVE

Part of me wanted to skip the emergency bench meeting and find Helen Vox. I knew, however, that Chief Judge Patrick Karls expected me to be present. The main topics of discussion were Judge Meyer, filling his vacancy, and managing his cases until the governor appointed his replacement. Everybody now expected me to take the lead, even though nobody was too excited about having me around.

As I walked up the stairs to the meeting, I called Helen. She didn't answer, which was a good thing, because I didn't quite know what I was going to say. At the sound of the beep, I kept it simple. "Call me when you get a chance." I left my cell phone number, exited the stairwell, and turned a corner on my way to the large conference room.

The court administrator, Nancy Johns, huddled with Chief Judge Karls near the door. Nancy was the power behind the throne, and I wondered what she was whispering in his ear. Johns could make a judge's life miserable, and without Judge Meyer's protection, I wondered what she was going to do to me.

"Judge Thompson, have a minute?" Johns asked as I walked past them into the conference room. She waved me back over. "I'm glad you're here." Johns put her hand on my arm. "We're very sorry for your loss. If there's anything we can do . . ."

"Nothing right now," I said. "I'm still trying to wrap my head around it, but thank you."

Chief Judge Karls nodded. "I'm in shock. My condolences as well."

"I appreciate your thoughts and prayers." It was all I could manage to say, but neither Johns nor Chief Karls seemed to mind. They had provided the requisite moment of sympathy, which had allowed them to politely return to the business of the court. That was the real reason why Johns had called me over.

"We'll need to figure out a sustainable plan to cover Judge Meyer's cases until the governor names a replacement," Karls said. "We'll also need to discuss what you'd like to do—"

"Whether you want to continue in child dependency or not," Johns chimed in, saving the chief from having to go into details. "From a professional development standpoint, I'm curious whether or not this is the right assignment for you."

I nodded but didn't say anything. It was the first time anybody had ever suggested I rotate off and stop handling cases of child abuse and neglect. It wouldn't surprise me if Johns knew about Benji Metina and was already trying to do some damage control. She was always planting seeds.

"There are some other issues that need to be addressed as well," she said.

"Other issues?"

Johns touched my arm again. "Nothing to worry about right now." Her eyes narrowed. "We'll talk, maybe next week." She exchanged a look with Karls, then turned back to me. "Your former law clerk," she whispered.

"Billy?" I was confused. "What about him?"

"We'll talk about it later."

"OK." I turned back toward the conference room. "But let me know." I walked away, figuring the less I pushed the better.

A few judges milled around the coffee and bagels at the back, and others were already seated. There were four large oak tables arranged in a square. The space felt like a fancy high school cafeteria. The judges had sorted themselves into various factions, each surely thinking they were superior to the others.

There were the judges with ambition. There were judges just a few years from retirement, waiting for the day they'd be eligible for a full pension. Then there were the academics, the institutionalists, the bleeding hearts, and the lock 'em ups. And last but not least, there were the golfers.

I didn't fit into any of the groups, so I made my way toward a neutral corner at the far end of the room, where I could sit by myself. A couple of judges looked up from their iPads, gave me a look of pity, and continued scrolling through their e-mails. Lawyers weren't known for their interpersonal skills, and judges, due to their isolation on the bench, seemed even more socially stunted.

The certification of Judge Meyer's vacancy came first on the agenda. It was a quick overview about process and scheduling concerns. Chief Karls then asked me if I knew anything about the funeral arrangements. It was the first time I had ever been called upon to say anything at a bench meeting.

I managed to shake my head and stutter out a response. "I'm meeting with the funeral home today. Should have more information to share either this evening or tomorrow."

"Thank you." Chief Karls jotted down a note on his agenda, then looked back up at me. "And does his family want us to robe and process down the aisle?"

The *family* would be me. Judge Meyer and Mary Pat had tried but couldn't have any children. I was as close as they had to a son. Unfortunately, Nikki and I were having the same difficulty starting a family, but we hadn't given up yet.

“The procession . . .” I thought about the long tradition of judges attending a memorial service in their black robes. It purportedly started with the death of Queen Mary in 1694. She was credited with creating an independent judiciary. All the judges in England had arrived at her funeral wearing black robes, as a symbol of mourning. Before her funeral, judges wore robes of various colors. Both the black robe and the funeral procession had become a ritual that continued.

“I assume he would want that.” I looked at the solemn faces around the room. “Judge Meyer loved this bench. He loved his job. So I’ll get the details and make arrangements for us.”

“We’ll need a room to robe,” croaked one of the judges near retirement.

“Of course,” I said. “I’ll make sure there is a space for us to put on our robes and store our things.”

“Thank you, Jim.” Chief Judge Karls made another note on his agenda, and the meeting moved on to scheduling. Senior judges were going to be hired to assist the bench while everyone waited for Judge Meyer’s replacement, and a heated discussion ensued related to whether the senior judge would handle Judge Meyer’s child dependency cases or whether another judge would be willing to take on the assignment.

After an hour, it was clear that there were no volunteers to take Judge Meyer’s assignment. Judges wanted to hold criminals accountable or manage large class-action lawsuits. None wanted to terminate parental rights and put kids in foster care.

For the foreseeable future, it was just going to be me.

◆ ◆ ◆

“Hey.” Judge Gary Perillo touched my shoulder as the meeting ended. He was a thin man with large glasses. Perillo resembled a squirrel, and I wondered whether he’d have fewer friends on the bench than me if he

weren't an excellent golfer. "So sorry about your loss. I know you two were close."

"Thank you for your thoughts." That had now become my standard response, and nobody seemed to be asking me for anything more.

Perillo looked around, checking to make sure that we weren't overheard. "Got a call from that reporter at the *Chronicle*," he said. "Just wanted you to know she's been calling people."

"Benji Metina?"

Judge Perillo's eyes widened. All judges, including me, had a great fear and suspicion of reporters. Even the Supreme Court of the United States had refused to allow photographs or video recordings of their proceedings, because they were afraid their hearings would be *misunderstood*.

"She's been asking about Harry and his friends, people he hangs out with," Perillo said. "And she's been asking about you, like your reputation and how you got appointed to the bench at such a young age."

"What'd you say?"

"Nothing really." Perillo looked around again. "Nothing to tell." He waited as a few other judges walked past us. He watched them, and, as his head tilted, the curve of his lenses magnified his eyes to the size of tennis balls and then back to normal again. "But something's up. It doesn't sound positive." Perillo took a shallow breath. "I'd just watch yourself. There are folks here who weren't too happy you got the job, you know?"

"It's been a year since the appointment," I said. "Isn't it time to let it go?"

"These people have long memories. They're patient, and it's like a sport to them. Everybody assumed it was going to be Nick Green. Some of the judges really like that guy. They had written recommendations for him and everything." He leaned closer, conspiring. "Personally, I think he's an arrogant showboat."

"Good to know."

"Have you called her?"

I shook my head. "No. I just want it to go away."

"Well, it won't." Perillo sounded certain, and then he looked away, thinking. "But maybe that's changed now. Maybe with Harry gone, she'll back off. Seems like it'd be in bad taste, you think?"

"Maybe." I patted Perillo on the shoulder. "Thanks for the heads-up."

CHAPTER SIX

Karen Fields had somehow managed to convince another judge to cover all my afternoon calendar. She told me it required begging. She had played the sympathy card, repeatedly, and payback would be expected. I didn't mind. An afternoon off allowed me to make funeral arrangements with Nikki and visit Mary Pat at the memory unit.

At a stoplight on the way to the Chapel of the Chimes, I checked my phone to see if Helen Vox had returned my call. She hadn't, and I thought about calling her again, but the light turned green.

As I drove past a row of new townhomes on Piedmont, I saw the chapel's pale stone and red roof in the distance. I'd give Helen a day before dropping by her place unannounced.

◆ ◆ ◆

Nikki met me at the door, and we went inside. The Chapel of the Chimes was like a Mediterranean villa, filled with light and air. Designed a hundred years ago by California's most renowned architect, Julia Morgan, the structure was timeless. She captured the aspirations of a community that was still in its infancy and gave them an easy place to find peace.

I think that was what Harry liked most about it.

Harry had told me that he had gone to a jazz concert in this chapel with Mary Pat shortly after she was diagnosed with Alzheimer's. It was a beautiful night. The music was uplifting. They spent time after the concert wandering the chapel's many gardens, hand in hand. The sky was clear, and somehow the stars had fought through the city's light in order to be seen. "It was the perfect ending," Harry had said. A few weeks later, both of them went back and made funeral arrangements.

It was hard for me to rectify that image of Harry and Mary Pat holding hands in the moonlight with the idea that he was having an affair with Helen Vox. Harry and Mary Pat were the perfect couple. They were the parents that I wished I had. With my own father gone, my mom pushed me away. I think it was painful for her to look at me. I looked too much like my dad, a constant reminder of her loss.

I found myself wrapping my arm tighter and tighter around Nikki as we walked together. I pushed the conflict aside. For now, I needed to ignore my disappointment and doubt in Harry.

The funeral director, a middle-aged man in a dark suit, was waiting for us. After brief introductions, he led us through a maze of hallways, sitting rooms, and small courtyards with bubbling fountains. Despite the twists and turns, the chapel was relaxed. Most walls were covered with art, most shelves filled with ornate urns.

We eventually arrived at the director's office in the back of the building. It had a large window that overlooked the chapel's gardens, an area specifically designed for families to spread the ashes of loved ones.

"Please sit." He pointed us to the chairs across from his desk, then opened a drawer and removed a folder. "Luckily, you don't need to worry about making too many decisions." He opened the folder and glanced at its contents. "Judge Meyer and his wife were very specific about what they wanted."

He pushed the folder across his desk to me. "This is your copy," he said. "Obviously it outlines Judge Meyer's wishes, but funerals are also about the living." He paused and looked sympathetically at both

me and Nikki. "To the extent that you need something different, you shouldn't be bound by this. These were his wishes, but sometimes the grieving process of family and friends demands something different."

I picked the folder up off the desk. "I'll look it over, but I'm sure it'll be fine."

"And Mrs. Meyer," he said. "Is she able to participate?"

I looked at Nikki, then back at the funeral director. "I don't think so. She may be able to attend, but that's all. She won't be speaking."

◆ ◆ ◆

We managed to get a table for a late lunch at Nikki's favorite café. We sat in the back. Aunt Mary's Café was a casual place that catered to the locals, but whose mix of Southern and Southwestern food had developed a following beyond the Temescal neighborhood.

A waitress brought Nikki a frittata and set a large plate in front of me. It was a grits waffle with a large piece of fried chicken on top. "Thank you," I said as the waitress walked away.

I picked up my fork and studied my ridiculous lunch. "This should be good for my heart."

She smiled. "Very healthy."

We ate in relative silence. When Nikki was done, she was ready to talk. "You've been quiet." She pushed her empty plate away and took a sip of her Arnold Palmer. "Thinking about the funeral?"

I nodded. "A little. If we're not going to have a visitation, we should have some photos or something."

"I can't imagine you want to go back to the house to get them."

"You're right." I thought for a second. "But it'd be good to have something. I also talked with Jarkowski this morning. He wants me to go through the house and see if anything's missing or stands out."

"Like what?"

"Anything," I said. "Seems like they don't have a clue."

"Nothing?"

"Not really." Then I thought of Helen. "He mentioned the name of an attorney this morning."

Nikki looked skeptical. "He thinks an attorney did it?"

"I don't know." I raised my hands in defense. It wasn't my theory. "She's a longtime prosecutor, manages the child dependency unit for the county attorney." I thought of all the times I'd seen Harry and Helen together. They just seemed like colleagues, nothing particularly intimate between the two. "I asked Karen about them, and she said everybody in the courthouse thinks they were having an affair."

"Harry?" Nikki laughed. "An affair?"

"I know," I said, mirroring her disbelief, "but that's what Karen told me, and Jarkowski was asking about her. I really can't imagine it."

"Were they even that close?" Nikki asked. "I'm not sure you ever even mentioned her name."

"Didn't seem important." I now wondered whether I didn't tell Nikki about Harry and Helen because I knew there was more to their friendship. "They're both passionate about kids and child protection. They went out to eat sometimes, maybe a drink after work. I know they presented together at conferences and stuff, cowrote a few law review articles, that sort of thing . . . I don't know."

Nikki pointed at me. "You believe the rumor, don't you?" I hesitated with a response. "I can't believe it."

CHAPTER SEVEN

After dropping Nikki off at home so she could change and work the late shift at the hospital, I got back in the car and headed out of Oakland toward Rheem Valley.

When I was growing up, Rheem Valley was filled with nothing but pear orchards. For many years, topography had prevented it from being swallowed up by the city. Steep hills and valleys initially blocked Oakland's sprawl, but over time the desire for subdivisions was too great. Long commutes became acceptable, and people were willing to spend obscene amounts of money for more space, so the orchards were gradually replaced.

I parked in front of the Walker Assisted Living and Memory Care facility, a simple beige building with white trim, located down the road from Saint Mary's College. Mary Pat had lived on the ground floor of the east wing for ten years.

I walked through the lobby, then down a hallway to where all the residents with Alzheimer's, dementia, and traumatic brain injuries lived. The door was locked to prevent the unit's residents from wandering off.

I pressed a button, and a nurse opened the door a few seconds later. She smiled and led me to a small reception desk, where we talked about

who I had come to see and she checked whether I was an authorized visitor.

As the nurse clicked away on the computer, I looked for Mary Pat. The common area was filled with chairs and several small tables. Some residents were playing cards, others drinking coffee and reading. On one wall was a large television. Four people sat on a sofa. Two of them were asleep. The other two stared blankly at the screen.

The opposite wall was a large glass window—floor to ceiling—that provided an unobstructed view of the Las Trampas Regional Wilderness. Mary Pat knitted a scarf in one of the six rocking chairs lined up near the window.

The nurse pushed a waiver and permission form toward me and handed me a pen. I signed the form without reading it and walked over to Mary Pat with my newly issued visitor badge.

Mary Pat turned and looked at me. There was a flash of recognition, then nothing.

"Mary Pat," I said. "It's me, Jim Thompson."

Her eyes narrowed. "Jimmy?" She studied me. "Little Jimmy Thompson?"

"That's right."

Mary Pat shook her head. "No." But a smile crept across her face as some distant memories connected with the present. "You've grown into quite a man. It has been a very long time."

I smiled. I wasn't going to challenge it, even though she was wrong. I'd visited her regularly since Harry decided that it wasn't safe for her to live at home anymore. "How are you feeling?"

"Fine." She looked out the window. Her pleasant expression faded. "But I'm ready to go home."

"I know." I put my hand on hers and pulled up an empty rocking chair. "I've got some bad news to share, Mary Pat, and I'm not sure of the best way to go about it."

"Don't tell me that I can't go home." She was now irritated. "I keep telling everybody that I'm ready to leave. All my things are packed. I'm ready to go. And if Harry thinks he can send you here to do his dirty work . . ." She folded her arms across her chest and kept looking out the window. "Well, you tell that man he needs to come and get me out of this place."

"It's not about whether you're staying," I said. "It's about Harry."

"Harry?" She turned to look at me. "What's wrong with Harry?"

"There was an incident at the house," I said. "Nobody knows what happened, exactly, maybe an intruder . . . I don't know, but there was a confrontation in the entryway, and Harry was shot."

"Shot?" She shook her head in disbelief. "My Harry, shot." She examined me. It seemed she wasn't quite sure anymore whether or not I was little Jimmy Thompson. "Is he OK?"

I shook my head. "No. He isn't."

"Oh my." She covered her mouth. "I need to get to the hospital. I need to see him."

I reached out and squeezed her hand as my stomach wound tighter. "He died, Mary Pat. He died, and I just went to make the funeral arrangements this afternoon."

"You?"

"We've got everything set for Friday," I said. "I'll make sure there's transportation for you to come. You'll be brought to the chapel, and then you can sit with Nikki."

"I don't understand." She pulled her hand away from mine and started to cry. "Nikki?" A nurse came over to see if I needed assistance. I declined, choosing instead to just sit with her. I wanted to ask whether Harry was ever worried or threatened. I wanted to ask her about Helen Vox, but she was too upset, and I didn't have the nerve.

It took another five minutes for Mary Pat to calm down. She wiped the tears from her eyes and resumed staring out the window. "I'm sorry," she said. "I just really want to go home."

"I know you do."

"I keep telling everybody here that I'm ready to go home, but they won't let me. I'm all packed. Everything is packed and I'm ready, but they won't let me." She turned from the window and looked straight at me. "What you must think of me." She forced a smile. "And who are you?"

"Me?"

"Yes," she said. "If I'm going to cry in front of somebody, it's best if we introduce ourselves."

"Mary Pat," I said. "It's me. I'm Jim Thompson."

"Little Jimmy Thompson?" Her expression brightened as the broken memories connected again. "It's been so long." She took a deep breath and studied me. "Well, you have grown into quite the man." She smiled, but soon her eyes narrowed. "But if you were sent here by Harry, you tell him that he needs to come here himself. He can't be a coward and send you to do his dirty work. You tell him that if he wants me to stay in this place, he needs to come here himself."

CHAPTER EIGHT

Helen returned my call as I drove home. I didn't have to explain. She seemed to know why I had called and kept the conversation short. "I don't want to talk about it on the phone. I want to meet in private." She paused. "I have some personal items at Harry's house. Maybe we can meet there . . . I don't want to go back to the house alone."

I didn't want to be there alone, either, but I kept that feeling to myself. "That's fine. Nikki's at work." I checked my watch. "I'll meet you at seven and I'll bring my key."

"Sounds good," Helen said. "But I have a key, too."

◆ ◆ ◆

When I arrived later that night, Helen was already there. She sat alone in her car. I pulled up behind her and parked. As I got out of the Range Rover, Helen got out of her car, too.

We met and walked together up to the front door. Neither one of us spoke as I put the key in the lock and opened the door. The front foyer was clean, as promised by Detective Jarkowski, but the smell of chemical disinfectant was even stronger than I had expected.

"Give me a minute, will you?" Helen walked past me. "I just need a little time." She touched my arm and crossed through the living room toward the bedrooms, leaving me alone.

I gave Helen her space and wandered through the rest of the house while she stayed in the master bedroom. I looked for something missing, but, except for the chemical smell, the house seemed just as it always had. I didn't see any items taken or disturbed. Nothing clicked as unusual.

After fifteen minutes, I decided enough time had passed. Helen and I needed to talk.

I stopped in the doorway, knocking twice on the doorframe so that I wouldn't surprise her. She was sitting on the bed, her back to me. Clothes and toiletries were gathered in a stack. I assumed this was what she had wanted to collect.

She wiped a tear from her eye as she turned. "Oh, Jim." Helen shook her head. "What a mess I've made."

I looked at her with sympathy and walked over to the bed to sit next to her. "How long?"

"About eight years." Helen folded her hands together and placed them in her lap. "I think Mary Pat had been at the Walker for two years when it really started. I know it's awful." Her eyes hardened, as if she were judging herself. "I never wanted to be the *other* woman, but Harry and I had been so close for so long, and then he was alone and I was alone, and it happened."

Helen wiped away another tear and looked me in the eye. "You have to believe me. People are saying that we were together for ten or fifteen years, maybe more, but we didn't start until *after* Mary Pat was sick. I'm not that type of person, Jim. He's not that type of person."

She tried to take a deep breath, but it was jagged, catching twice. "Harry was a proud and private man. We talked about it, but he just couldn't bring himself to disclose our relationship to anybody, especially the chief judge, and so we just went on."

I understood where Helen was coming from. When judges had friendships with the lawyers that appeared in front of them, the ethical lines were unclear. Judges were allowed to have friends, but at a certain point the friendship created the appearance of bias and impropriety. Unlike friendship, however, the rules about a lawyer appearing before a judge while in a romantic relationship were clear: it was prohibited. No exceptions.

"You were the supervisor," I said. "You didn't need to go. Why didn't you just assign somebody else to cover Harry's hearings?"

"I tried," she said. "And it worked most of the time, but when we were short-staffed for whatever reason, I had to cover the calendars." She looked at the floor, still at fault but now trying to rationalize. "It was part of my job, and I was good at it. I liked it."

I had more to say but let it pass, deciding instead to get to the point. "Helen." I turned to her. "Why did you want to meet here?"

"I have some personal items." She looked over at the things she had collected. "I didn't want to sneak in and take them without somebody knowing . . ." Her voice trailed off with a tremble. "I also wanted to tell you what happened that morning."

CHAPTER NINE

"Harry was worried about you," Helen said. "He was worried about all of us, the different government agencies and the court, but he was especially worried about you. That reporter from the *Chronicle* had filed requests with the county for all sorts of child protection data. I've been reviewing what was going out as a response, and I know it isn't going to look good. We're not much different from any other program anywhere else in the country—overwhelmed and underfunded—but that doesn't matter. Metina wants a big story, and good news doesn't sell."

She stared out the dark window.

"Originally she was focusing on Harry," she continued, "some of the speeches he's made and the policies he's championed. The argument is that he and the county are putting kids at risk. That it's dangerous to try and reunite children with their biological family and keep them in the home." She turned to me. "But now your case is going to be a big part of it."

"Greg Ports?"

"It's got everything Metina needs to do something sensational." She turned away from me. "We were up late talking about you and that

case." To herself: "It was tragic, totally unexpected, and not your fault." Then back to me: "I had some wine, and we went to bed. With the help of some pills, I was out pretty quick."

Helen avoided looking at me as she continued. "I knew that you two were meeting early in the morning, so I didn't think too much of it when Harry got up. I can let myself out and I have clothes here, so I'd just get ready for work on my own and lock up—it wouldn't be the first time. I think I may have rolled over in the morning when Harry got out of bed, but we didn't speak. I know we didn't talk. When he left the room, I went back to sleep."

Her eyes filled with tears. "Then I heard the shot. I knew what it was. It was so loud. It jolted me awake. I was scared, nearly screamed, but I choked it back. I didn't want anybody to know I was here."

She bent over and put her face in her hands, then shook her head back and forth, rocking. "I was frozen. You replay it in your head, thinking of all the things that you could've done. Run out and see who did it; get a description of the car or something pulling away. I could've done so many things, but instead I just stayed in bed. My heart was pounding out of my chest. I just sat frozen."

She took her hands from her face, sat straight up, and turned to me, her eyes desperate for my affirmation. "I'm sorry, Jim, but I didn't do anything, and that's the problem."

I put my hand on her back, comforting her. "You didn't call the police?" I knew the answer, but I wanted to hear her explanation.

"No," she said. "When I was able to move, I thought about it." She sighed. "But there was no phone in the room, and my stupid cell phone was in the kitchen, charging."

Helen stood and started pacing. "I went out, and I saw Harry on the floor. He wasn't moving. It was quiet. I turned away from him, and then I went to get my phone but stopped." She laughed. "I don't know why. Maybe I'd been a prosecutor too long—afraid

of the questions that were going to be asked, embarrassed by all the courthouse rumors being confirmed true, maybe a little concerned about being a suspect. I don't know." She shrugged. "In the moment, I decided that I didn't have any information to share. I didn't see anything. I didn't know anything. I just heard a gunshot. That's it. And so I got dressed and left."

CHAPTER TEN

In re the Honorable James Thompson
California State Board on Judicial Standards
Inquiry Transcript, Excerpt

BOARD MEMBER GREEN: Did you file a report with the California State Board on Judicial Standards related to Judge Meyer's relationship with an attorney that regularly appeared before him?
THOMPSON: Harry was dead. I don't think the board has jurisdiction to punish dead judges.
BOARD MEMBER GREEN: Are you being flippant with me? Because this is a very serious matter.
THOMPSON: Is that a rhetorical question?
[Pause]
BOARD MEMBER GREEN: So did you file a complaint against Judge Meyer?
THOMPSON: As the board would know from their own records, the answer to that question is no. I don't think I have an obligation to do so.
BOARD MEMBER GREEN: What about the rules of professional responsibility? Did you file a complaint related to Ms. Vox with the State Bar of California?

THOMPSON: No.
BOARD MEMBER GREEN: Why not? You were aware of a serious ethical violation, and you didn't do anything?
THOMPSON: I was more concerned with the criminal investigation.
BOARD MEMBER GREEN: Yet, you didn't immediately contact Detective Jarkowski, either?
THOMPSON: I did not. I knew that Ms. Vox was going to do it.
BOARD MEMBER GREEN: How? How did you know?
THOMPSON: Because I told her, either you call Detective Jarkowski or I will.

I didn't like anybody who sat across the table from me. There were two judges and a *community member*. A complaint had been filed, and they were the ones charged by the Board on Judicial Standards to investigate my conduct.

The judges were Herschell "Hershey" Feldman from Sacramento and Pamela Nitz from San Francisco. Both of them had left big law firms to join the Superior Court, taking a substantial pay cut in the process. As a result, they considered themselves to be martyrs for justice. Their proclamations of self-sacrifice grated. *Nobody had ever given up so much for so little.* Talk to them for more than five minutes, and I guarantee that they'll somehow remind you of all that they'd given up.

Then there was the community member. Judges did not want a true community member investigating alleged violations of the professional code, and so the Board on Judicial Standards typically selected an attorney. In this case, the board selected Nick Green. He was the current district attorney for Alameda County, which covers Oakland, Berkeley, and the sprawling communities to the south and east of San Francisco. He was also my former boss.

When I had first started at the prosecutor's office, straight out of law school, Green had been one of the managers of the criminal division. He was pretty decent. Green oversaw minor criminal cases, and

then he personally handled the big stuff. Sometimes he was an asshole, but he was on the side of angels, so his arrogance was forgiven within the office. Then he handled a mother-daughter double murder, and things changed.

Green got camera time on one of cable television's *real crime* shows. He was portrayed as the square-jawed, relentless prosecutor fighting a schlubby and unethical defense attorney. It was great television. Green loved the attention. When the show was done, he didn't want it to stop. That's when he turned ambitious.

Green rose to become the deputy district attorney for all criminal prosecutions, then chief deputy district attorney for the whole county, and then he got elected to the top job. It was all going according to plan, until I ruined it. When I was appointed judge, I had taken his spot on the bench.

Now Green wanted nothing more than to take me down.

Judge Feldman and Judge Nitz didn't have much love for me, either—believing that I hadn't paid my dues or earned my position—so they were more than happy to allow Green to take the lead and provided support only when needed.

Green obliged.

He peered down at me over his half-rimmed glasses. He looked smug, but I knew the glasses weren't real. I knew this for a fact. Green had started wearing them about seven years ago, back when we were still working together. He wanted to look older and more distinguished for television. When he had accidentally left the glasses in a conference room, I couldn't resist. I had heard the rumors. I picked them up and put them on, checking—they were fakes.

The hearing lurched forward. Green pounded on me for another hour. He repeatedly asked the same questions about whether I filed an ethical complaint against Judge Meyer or Helen Vox, but he modified the wording just slightly each time. It grew tiresome after fifteen minutes and painful after twenty.

Toward the end of this line of questioning, even Judge Feldman looked uncomfortable, and Judge Nitz did nothing to hide her boredom. Her mind appeared to have drifted far away from the proceedings. She didn't look at me. Instead she fiddled with her diamond Vacheron Constantin watch, a memento from her days gleefully billing California's largest polluters $600 per hour for her advice on how to avoid state and federal environmental regulations.

Green's approach didn't surprise me. Lawyers had a tendency to go on too long. All of us grew up watching attorneys on television and in the movies. Starting with Jimmy Stewart as Mr. Biegler in *Anatomy of a Murder*, then Andy Griffith as Matlock, and even Tom Cruise as Lieutenant Daniel Kaffee in *A Few Good Men*. They had the power to melt witnesses under their clever and powerful questions. In real life, confessions rarely, if ever, happened, but that didn't stop Green from trying.

He paused, looking down at his notes. Then he took another run at me. "So even though you have a duty to report Helen Vox under the rules of conduct as both a judge and a lawyer, you did not file such a report?"

I looked at Judge Feldman, and I thought I detected a slight roll of the eyes and perhaps even some sympathy. Then I looked back at Green. "As stated before"—I paused, trying to remain calm and not patronize—"I believed that the criminal investigation took precedence, and I didn't want to interfere with it at any point. So I decided to wait, especially since Judge Meyer had passed. Under the circumstances, there was no ongoing ethical violation. You can second-guess that decision now, but that was the decision I made at the time. The rules do not have a specific time requirement. There is no deadline I was under to report her to the attorney licensing board."

Green shook his head, feigning disgust with my answer. It was almost convincing, and if there were a jury, I might've been concerned.

But we were just in a conference room. No audience was present to appreciate Green's performance.

He sighed, then bent over and pulled a large brown folder from his briefcase. He set the folder down before him and removed a new stack of documents. "Let's now talk about the articles by Benji Metina and the death of Gregory Ports."

I knew it was coming, but it still upset me. I tried to mask the mixture of my concern, nerves, and anger. "Of course." I nodded, still deciding whether I was going to be completely honest.

CHAPTER ELEVEN

After Harry's death, the work of the court continued for the rest of the week. His funeral was scheduled for Friday afternoon. Although I had asked for only that afternoon off, Nancy Johns intervened. She hired a retired judge from San Jose to cover both my morning and afternoon calendars. "Nobody wants to come in for a half day," she had told me. "It's easier to find somebody to cover a full day."

I took her at her word, but in hindsight I wondered whether she knew that the *San Francisco Chronicle*'s article was going to be published soon. I could see her wanting to keep me away from the court, making it less likely for me to run into Benji Metina.

In bed that morning, unable to fall back asleep, I felt something wet brush my hand. Then there was a lick. I looked down, and Augustus whimpered at me. I told people he was a purebred mutt, but, as Augustus cocked his furry head and emitted a little yodel, he resembled a large retriever.

"Want to go on a walk?" I reached out and patted Augustus on the head. "Suppose it's better than being here." I pulled back the sheets and got up. In the dark, I fumbled for the closet door, opened it, and turned on the light. On the floor were a pair of jeans and a sweatshirt. I changed, turned off the light, and went back over to Nikki.

She was half-asleep. "What's going on?"

"I'm taking Augustus for a walk."

Nikki sat up. "Are you OK?"

I began to answer but stopped myself. "I'll be OK." I touched her shoulder, encouraging her not to worry. "Just a lot on my mind. It's fine." I knew that I didn't sound convincing, so I bent over and kissed her forehead. I left, deciding to spare her all the thoughts tumbling through my head.

Augustus was content to sit by the door as I prepared for our early-morning outing. I eventually found my hat and gloves and located my keys. Augustus wagged his tail as I attached the leash to his collar, and we went outside.

The sunrise had turned the sky a burnt orange, but it'd be another hour or two before Oakland woke up. Augustus pranced toward a bush, did his morning business, and hopped into the Range Rover for our little adventure.

I stopped at a coffee shop for a latte and a muffin before driving to Joaquin Miller Park for our walk. As we wound up Skyline Boulevard, Augustus seemed to recognize where we were going and got even more excited.

"Easy." I patted his head and parked at the Sequoia Bayview Trailhead.

A few morning runners were gathered at the picnic tables, stretching. By the time I got Augustus out of the Range Rover, they were gone, and we were alone.

This part of the park was more urban utilitarian than unspoiled Thoreau. Even as we got farther from the trailhead, we were more likely to see a free-range plastic bag than anything with fur, but it was quiet, and we were alone.

Augustus pranced along, exhibiting all the traits that people love about dogs. He was oblivious to Harry's death. He wasn't concerned with whether parents reengaged with treatment and kids went to school

or what fathers were doing after their release from prison. He didn't mind that my competence was about to be questioned and public humiliation seemed certain. I gave him food and let him chase tennis balls. For him, life was good.

We walked together a mile farther, toward a dozen lesser used trails that broke off in various directions. I picked my favorite, and Augustus and I zigzagged down a steep slope over to a narrow path that ran along a creek. This path was more natural and provided the isolation that I wanted.

As Augustus investigated the assorted ferns and thimbleberry, I took in the redwoods. We walked for another half mile, and then a smell took away my breath. It was faint, carried on the breeze, but it hit me hard. It was the same raw odor that had greeted me in Harry's foyer.

Stuttered images flashed through my mind: dead on the floor, a pool of blood, a gun, Harry's hollowed face, a silenced scream, Jarkowski talking to me through the window, the black body bag on the stretcher.

Since that morning at his house, I had tried to be strong. Much to Nikki's dismay, I had ignored the shock and kept moving forward, but now everything rushed at me. The smell triggered the memories. I was vulnerable and afraid. I felt sick.

I looked for a place to throw up, and then I saw the source. Black and gray fur was scattered under a nearby tree. An opossum's carcass had been ripped open, likely a hawk's early-morning breakfast. Black flies had already found it, the early stages of rot and decomposition.

I swallowed, keeping everything down, and kept walking.

I tried to think of who could be responsible, but nobody came to mind. I tried to think of a reason someone would've killed Harry, but I had nothing. Our life together was always me talking and Harry listening. The focus was always on my hopes and my problems, and Harry was the one giving the advice. With shame, I realized that we never really talked about him. His fears and disappointments were always presented in the past, a lesson for me to learn from rather than a revelation

of his actual state of mind. Our final conversations were not different. Instead of him talking about Mary Pat or retirement or challenges at work, we discussed me.

◆ ◆ ◆

The night before Harry was murdered, we had a brief discussion. Before confirming plans to meet at the Tin Cup, I had told him my secret. He was the only one who knew. It was something that I'd never tell anybody else, not even Nikki.

The truth was that I had no actual memory of Gregory Ports or his case.

None.

Like every Superior Court judge, I had hundreds of cases come before me every week. A judge's job was to decide and move on. Gregory Ports's case was no different. It was sad, but every child protection case was sad. What brought Gregory Ports into the system wasn't special or particularly egregious. Cases like his came and went. The only difference between Gregory Ports and the thousands of other cases churning through the Alameda County Superior Court was that Gregory Ports was dead.

I had discovered this fact only after receiving an e-mail. Given that it was an invitation to something called a Fatality Review Committee, I had known that it was significant, but I didn't yet understand its connection to me or anything that I had done.

There were going to be representatives present from every government unit and agency responsible for child protection. People from both the state and county were going to come, and I was asked whether I would be willing to participate.

At first I thought it was an honor to be asked. It wasn't uncommon for judges to be invited to participate on various task forces and advisory committees. I initially figured I was selected because somebody

wanted to integrate the new judge into the system. Eventually, though, I suspected that this was not an honor at all.

"Hey!" I remember shouting at my law clerk at the time, Billy Pratt, from my chambers. "Do you know who . . ." I paused. I looked at the e-mail on my screen, then asked, "Do you know a Gregory Ports?"

From the other side of the wall, Billy shouted back at me. "Case or attorney or what?" This was before Billy was fired and I'd hired Karen Fields to replace him. I remember the interaction because, for the first time in weeks, Billy was actually at work when I needed him and relatively responsive to my request.

"I think it's a case."

"OK," Billy said. From my chambers, I heard his keyboard clack. "Give me a second."

While I waited, the uneasy feeling grew. A few minutes later, Billy was in my doorway holding a sheet of paper. "This is the case," he said. "Looks like you handled it on one of your first days flying solo, Judge."

"What happened?"

Billy scratched his chin as he silently read the case summary, a chronological list of the relevant memoranda and orders filed. He flipped to the end. "Looks like you dismissed it, boss." His eyes narrowed on the page as he continued reading. "Kid was removed by the previous judge and put in foster care, and then you sent the kid home."

◆ ◆ ◆

I sat on a fallen log by the creek. I set Augustus loose to play in the water and skipped rocks, thinking about how I could figure out who murdered Harry and what I'd do to them. I'd like to say that I trusted the legal system to handle it, but I knew too much.

Then I thought about the coming media storm and my options. Quitting seemed like an easy solution, especially with Harry no longer available to guide me. A peremptory strike before the newspaper

article was published would mute the criticism, but it'd also create more problems. It'd appear to be an admission, and who would hire a disgraced judge? I'd be a pariah in the legal community. Nick Green would never allow me to come back to the Alameda County Attorney's Office, and no law firm would touch me. Then there were the student loans. Unemployment wouldn't make them go away; it'd just make them even harder to pay off.

Confronting Benji Metina was another option. Rather than run from her, I could give her access. Maybe if she saw me handle a few cases competently, her attitude would change. She'd see that there often weren't any good solutions, only the least bad of several bad alternatives. Talking to her was a risk, and it could make matters even worse.

I could also gut it out, keep my head low, keep quiet, and go about my work. News cycles change. People will talk about it for a day, and then there'll be another crisis . . . maybe.

CHAPTER TWELVE

That afternoon, the judges gathered in one of the many nooks within the Chapel of the Chimes. All of us wore our black robes. Most were gathered in groups of two or three, like crows on a rooftop, waiting.

An attendant informed us that the funeral was about to start, so we lined up in order of status and seniority. Members of the federal judiciary were first, then the California Supreme Court, then the California Court of Appeals, and then the Superior Courts.

As a member of the lowest court as well as the judge with the least seniority, I was last in line. I waited as the others filed into the chapel, and then it was my turn.

I entered the chapel with a knot in my stomach. I knew it was my imagination, but I felt like every person in the chapel was staring at me. I took deep breaths as we made our way down the aisle. I allowed my eyes to drift to the ceiling and take in the aspirational space. I told myself that this was Harry's day. I needed to focus on Harry.

Three rows were roped off near the front, and the first judges to enter had already sat down. I followed the line forward and settled at the end of the row. I looked to my left and saw Nikki sitting next to Mary Pat. Next to them were two large nurses from the memory unit. They were ready to assist if Mary Pat acted out. I hoped that wouldn't

be necessary, but nobody knew what Mary Pat would do when people began to talk about her husband's life and death.

Two rows behind Mary Pat was Helen Vox, dressed in black. Her white hair and sharp jawbone were striking. She sat perfectly erect and proud. Her presence was a declaration. She wasn't going to be shamed.

Music began to play. Even without amplification, the notes drawn by the string quartet were crisp, the acoustics in the chapel perfect. From the back, an urn containing Judge Harry Meyer's ashes was carried down the center aisle. The urn was a large hand-thrown clay pot in muted blue, green, and dark purple, beautiful and humble at the same time. It was encased in glass atop an ornate wooden carrier.

Four men served as pallbearers, two on each side. Members of Judge Meyer's extended family followed.

Harry's pastor from First United Methodist of Berkeley welcomed those in attendance. He told a few stories about Harry's love of fishing, and then he introduced Marshall Terry.

If a movie director sought somebody to portray a US senator or the president of the United States, it would be Marshall. He was tall and thin, with a square jaw and a full head of silver hair. Pursuant to Harry's instructions, he provided the first eulogy.

"Good afternoon. My name is Marshall Terry, but my friends call me Marsh, and I had no better friend in this world than Judge Harry Meyer." He spoke with total confidence, telling stories about Judge Meyer as a young man. "We met in Vietnam, both of us too stupid to dodge the draft. And it was in a rice paddy somewhere in Quang Ngai that we promised each other that if—and it was a big if at that point—we got out alive, we'd be brothers forever. He promised that if I came with him to college that he'd help me through it, and he did."

Marsh smiled. "Now keep in mind that Harry and I weren't exactly the same. Let's just say we have different temperaments, but Harry was always good to me. He saved my life on multiple occasions. The first few were in Vietnam, and then the last time was twenty-five years ago.

That's when he picked me up, and I asked him, 'Where's the party?' And he said, 'AA.' It wasn't easy, but I have sobriety and my life because of Judge Meyer."

Marsh looked at Harry's urn. "I love you, buddy."

Then he stepped down as the minister returned to the pulpit and introduced the chief justice of the California Supreme Court. Unlike Marsh Terry, she wasn't personally picked by Harry to give a eulogy. Harry would've been embarrassed, thinking such a show would be pretentious. It was, however, a request to me by Chief Karls, and, after some hesitation, I decided that Harry deserved to be honored in such a manner.

Even though she didn't have a significant personal connection to Harry, she was there as a spokesperson for the judiciary, and it was important for Harry to be recognized. I wanted people to hear about the various committees that Harry had served on as well as the many awards that he had received. Rumors had swirled since his murder, and this was my little way of rehabilitating the man I loved.

When the chief justice finished her remarks, the string quartet began to play again—"Amazing Grace." Harry loved that song, and it didn't surprise me that he had chosen it to be played during his funeral. It was a song of redemption, the blind having recovered their sight.

We all could use a little redemption.

Once "Amazing Grace" concluded, it was my turn. I stood and walked to the podium, then removed my typed remarks from my pocket. I felt that knot in my stomach again. When I looked down at the words, my vision blurred with tears. I wiped them away and looked out at the audience. Their faces were long and somber.

Judge Harry Meyer had impacted countless lives. He was a generous soul. Of course, I wasn't alone in experiencing his kindness.

I looked at Mary Pat and forced a smile, wondering what she was thinking. Did she know why she was present? Who I was? What was happening? Behind her, Helen Vox clutched a handkerchief in her

hand. She knew that I was looking at her. Helen held my stare and nodded, giving me some of her strength.

I looked again at my typed remarks. I told myself to just start reading, and that's what I did. "Thank you all for coming. As you know, Harry Meyer was more than a colleague to me. He was a mentor, he was a friend, and he was the father I needed so badly. I feel lucky that he opened his heart to me." The tune of "Amazing Grace" floated through my mind. "Many times I was lost, and Harry Meyer was the one who ensured that I was found. I will forever be thankful for his strength and guidance."

CHAPTER THIRTEEN

After the funeral, I dropped Nikki off at home and went to pick up a pizza. The sun had set by the time I got back. Augustus was in the front yard rolling in a pile of dirt, and Nikki sat on the front step drinking a glass of wine.

I started to relax, but the feeling didn't last. My cell phone rang as I got out of the Range Rover. With the box of pizza in one hand, I answered with the other. "This is Jim."

There was a crackle on the other end of the line. "This is Chief Judge Karls." He cleared his throat. "I looked for you after the funeral today, but we didn't connect. The words you spoke were lovely, very nicely done. The whole service was nicely done. I can only hope that people remember me half as fondly as Harry when I pass."

As I unlocked the gate, Nikki got up from the front step. "Thank you, Chief, I appreciate that." I handed the pizza to Nikki, and she pecked me on the cheek before turning and walking back up the sidewalk and into the house. Augustus smelled the food and followed closely behind her.

I stayed outside. "I'm about ready to eat." I wanted to move the conversation along. "Is there anything I can do for you?"

"Yes," said Chief Karls. "I'm calling for some other reasons."

I knew that, but waited for him to lead.

"We need to meet tomorrow morning," he said. "My apologies."

"Tomorrow is Saturday," I said, stating the obvious.

"I know, but I've been told that the newspaper is running that article tomorrow. We need to discuss it before Monday."

Chief Karls assured me that the meeting would be relatively quick. He even gave me permission to dress casually. Not that I was planning on wearing a suit and tie to a 10:00 a.m. weekend meeting, but now the chief had blessed something that I would've done anyway. He was a benevolent leader like that.

"You have to take this seriously, Jim," he went on. "I heard that Benji Metina will not be kind. There are going to be a lot of eyes on you now." He paused. "I'm sorry this is happening so close to losing Harry, but it is what it is."

It is what it is, I thought. *What a stupid phrase.* "If you want to meet, I can meet."

"We'll go over some options. Nancy Johns will be there, of course."

"To do what?"

"To help you." Chief Karls was losing his patience. "When you look bad, Jim, we all look bad. This is bigger than you. We need to protect the district." He hung up, not waiting for my response. Chief Karls was done talking.

◆ ◆ ◆

When I got inside, I found Nikki sitting at our kitchen table, a 1950s chrome-and-Formica dinette set she had bought at a consignment shop shortly after we moved in. It was the only table that would work in our tiny kitchen.

Nikki picked up a piece of pizza and put it on her plate. "Who was that?"

"The chief." I grabbed a ginger beer and a plate and sat down at the table across from her. "He wants to meet first thing in the morning. That newspaper article is coming out." I wanted to scream, but I held steady, checking my emotions as I grabbed a slice of pizza. "I'm sure it's going to be the first of many meetings."

"I'm sorry," she said. "What time?"

"Ten." I picked a small piece of sausage from my slice and tossed it to Augustus. The dog had somehow anticipated the treat, catching it in midair and gobbling it down. "I'm thinking we can go over to Harry's house after. Start cleaning it out. It's gonna take a while."

"I can do that," Nikki said. "I don't work tomorrow, but Sunday is going to be a long day, double shift." She told me about a guy who came into the emergency room the night before with four plastic Coke bottles stuck to his toes. After inserting his toes into the top of each bottle, he couldn't get them out. "I didn't understand it," she said, "and then a nurse told me it was a sex thing." She smiled. "Like, he was a dude who likes his toes to get sucked, but he couldn't find somebody to do it." She was trying hard to improve my mood, and it was almost working.

"That's absurd."

Nikki got up, took her plate to the sink, and came back over to me. "I did some Internet research and it's true—it's an actual kink." She kissed the back of my neck, then put her hand on my cheek and made me look up at her. "Do you want me to suck your toes?"

I laughed. "I think I'll pass on that one."

With my mind elsewhere, she forced me to be present. She kissed my lips and took my hand. She took me back to the bedroom and turned off the lights. In bed she kissed me again, gentle at first and then harder. "It'll be OK," she said as she straddled me. "It'll be just fine."

CHAPTER FOURTEEN

It was the second day in a row that I'd gotten up before the sun. Even Augustus wasn't ready, and he was usually ready for anything. The dog lay still on his blanket in the corner. His head rested on his front paws. With one eye slightly open, Augustus watched me crawl out of bed and leave the room.

Even he didn't want to get up.

In the living room, our old rolltop desk sat piled high with junk mail, bills, and random things that didn't have another home. In the middle of this stuff was a cheap computer. I wondered whether I should get a cup of coffee first, but I knew I couldn't wait that long. I needed to see it. Delay wouldn't make things better.

I also didn't want Nikki standing over my shoulder. I didn't want her studying my reactions, worrying about me.

I typed in my password, then clicked onto the Internet. A few seconds later, the website for the *San Francisco Chronicle* appeared. A narrow black bar across the top provided the temperature. Below it was the newspaper's iconic banner, and then the headline:

THE BOY WHO SHOULD HAVE LIVED:

Dangerous Policies, Lack of Funding, and Inexperience Blamed in Tragedy

I scrolled down. A picture of Gregory Ports filled the screen. The little boy smiled at the camera, his eyes bright as he played with a plastic truck at his foster home. Next to Gregory was a picture of me, the official head shot from my profile on the court's website. I was wearing my black robe in front of a mottled blue background. To the extent I had wrinkles, all were digitally erased, resulting in a picture that made me look more like a kid on the eve of his high school graduation than a Superior Court judge.

I scanned the article, and it didn't take long for me to find my name:

> Although everyone agrees that there are few legal matters more important than a case related to the abuse and neglect of a child, Judge James Thompson was assigned to handle child protection cases despite having no formal training, no experience as an attorney with child protection laws, less than ten years after graduating law school, and being just thirty-three years old. "When there's an opening in child protection, you go down the list of the willing and able," said Frank Bell, a former guardian ad litem who is now retired. "It's a tough assignment, and most judges are either unwilling to do it or don't have the skills to understand poor families that are in total crisis. Sometimes you don't get the rock stars."

> An attorney who would only speak anonymously for fear of retribution stated, "I'm not saying Judge Thompson is a bad guy. He seems nice enough, but when the governor appointed him, it raised eyebrows. The governor bypassed some very qualified individuals that were recommended by the merit selection committee. Occasionally things like this work out OK. In this instance, it was an obvious mistake." Many in the courthouse have nicknamed Judge Thompson "The Kitten."
>
> "The guy is just in over his head. He comes into the courthouse or you see him walking down the halls, and he looks like a lost kitten. That's how he got the nickname. Somebody says they saw him walk into a closet by accident, thinking that it was a conference room." The attorney laughed. "Don't know if that story is true, but it sure sounds about right."
>
> Another attorney who regularly appears in front of Judge Thompson also agreed to speak on the condition of anonymity. He stated, "I don't think the governor really understood what he was doing and who he was getting. The governor must have owed Judge Harry Meyer a huge debt or something, because his appointment was pretty crazy. And now we're all stuck with him."

I stopped, unable to read any more. I had suspected courthouse gossip. It came with the job, but it was another thing to see it made

public. Every time somebody googled my name, that story would appear. A story about a young, unqualified judge whose incompetence resulted in a child's death. I was "The Kitten."

I scrolled down the page. It was another article about Harry's murder. After repeating the basic details and ongoing police investigation, the article pivoted to the memorial service. Although it contained many nice quotes about Harry, it also suggested that both the Court and Alameda County Social Services were under scrutiny and under renewed public pressure.

I pushed back my chair and closed my eyes, and I thought about what I would say to Chief Karls and Nancy Johns.

◆ ◆ ◆

All the judges' chambers in the courthouse were the same, except for the chief judge's office. His was twice the size. Nancy Johns and Chief Karls both sat near a window overlooking Lake Merritt. Even though it was Saturday, Chief Karls was, as always, dressed in a fitted suit, a crisp white dress shirt, and an expensive gold-and-blue tie.

In contrast, I was wearing jeans and a vintage White Stripes T-shirt.

"Please shut the door behind you and have a seat." Chief Karls pointed to the empty chair across from him. He thanked me for meeting on such short notice and on the weekend, as if I had a choice, and began with a poor attempt at empathy as I sat down. "How are you holding up?"

"Fine." My posture stiffened, and my teeth clenched. I wasn't going to bare my soul to them or anybody else in the courthouse. "Like you said yesterday, it is what it is."

"Right." Chief Karls appreciated the fact that I was quoting him back to him. "Only so much you can control." He tried to be reassuring, but the man operated within a very narrow band of emotions. I pitied his children.

After checking his watch, the chief decided that his brief talk from the heart should conclude. “Well, if you need anything, you know you can come to me.” He was now ready to move on.

“I appreciate your concern, Chief,” I said. “What is it that you wanted to talk to me about?”

Chief Karls glanced at Nancy Johns, then back at me. “Couple things.” He looked down at a roster of the district’s judges and their current assignments. “We need to discuss your rotation.”

“What about it?”

“I’ve asked Nancy to explore other options.”

“You want to take me off child dependency?”

“It may be best.” He kept it vague. “I’m not trying to say that you did anything wrong, Jim. Please don’t think that . . . but we need to be thoughtful. What are the needs of the bench at this moment? What is best for you?” He didn’t wait for me to respond. Instead he posed a more direct question: “Have you ever thought about whether you actually want to continue handling these types of cases?”

“It’s what Harry wanted,” I said, which was true. “I made a commitment to him.”

“Well, I know that Judge Meyer had many plans and ideas, but that doesn’t mean he was right. There are plenty of different assignments: criminal, civil, family, probate, commitments.” He looked at Johns, as if seeking confirmation that he was going in the right direction. “It’s true that you were assigned to child protection, because that was what Judge Meyer wanted, but now we have more flexibility.”

“Meaning he was murdered.”

He held out his hands, resigned. “I’m trying to be respectful, Jim. I’m not looking for a fight. But the truth is that you didn’t sign a contract. You’re not bound to what Judge Meyer wanted you to do. You can be whomever you want.” His expression turned to sympathy. “With the article and the coming fallout, it’s every judge’s nightmare. I’m just putting this out there and seeking your thoughts.”

"It'd look bad," I said. All the reasons why I didn't want to quit were the same as the reasons why I didn't want to be reassigned. "Seems like an admission that I did something wrong, like I'm being punished."

Chief Karls brushed away the obvious. "Like I said, that's not my intent."

"Maybe," I said. "But it creates a perception."

He sighed, frustrated that I wasn't making it easy for him. Then he changed the direction of the conversation. He'd planted the seed, and I was sure he'd return to it later. "I've heard that the governor is making an announcement later today." He rolled his eyes, as most judges do when discussing politicians. "This creates some further issues."

"It'll keep it in the news," added Johns.

"Plus," Chief Karls continued, "Benji Metina isn't done. Based on the data requests submitted by the newspaper, I don't think this is going to be a single story, more like a series, one a week, maybe months."

"Figured that." I didn't mention my conversation with Helen Vox.

"Nancy has been making calls," Karls said. "I believe that Metina and the *Chronicle* want to push back on many of the ideas and reforms that Harry implemented over his tenure. There's some professor at a little private college that wants to make a name for himself. They're going to say Judge Meyer advocated for policies that kept kids in dangerous situations. That he was more focused on parents' rights, as opposed to the well-being of the children. And they're going to say you're carrying the torch now that he's gone."

"That's not true," I said. "Harry highlighted the trauma experienced by kids in foster care. He was one of the first to research the outcomes of kids removed from their homes. He just wanted more balance. He wanted to ensure that the removal was really necessary."

"I know." Johns leaned in, pretending to agree, although I doubted she had an opinion. "But the argument goes that you were simply following Harry's lead by putting Gregory Ports back home, and that's why he died."

"Returning him to his mother was the recommendation of both the county and the guardian ad litem." I felt my anger rise. "I didn't do anything on my own in that courtroom. We're all partners. The agency and the guardian ad litem are the ones who were working the case every day, not me. They made the recommendation. You listen to the professionals and make a decision. That's what judges are supposed to do."

"And that's the other theme of these stories." Johns looked at Chief Karls for permission to continue, and he consented to her taking the lead. "I really don't want to be a gossip, but they're asking questions about how closely Harry was working with county social services and, specifically, Helen Vox. That perhaps"—she searched for a less dramatic way to talk about Judge Meyer's affair—"perhaps the institutions were not as independent as they should be."

"Even if it ends up being nothing," Chief Karls chimed in, "it just looks bad."

I pointed at them. "And, are you two going to defend Harry?"

They didn't respond.

"He's not even around to defend himself," I said. "We need to defend him. The county and the district have made tremendous progress under his leadership. You were both at the memorial service yesterday. You heard about his service and recognition."

Chief Karls held out his hands, both slowing me down and pushing back on any responsibility for the mess. "It's out of my control, Jim, and I'm not sure that picking a fight with the media is the right thing to do, anyway." He looked at me like he was a teacher with an uncooperative student. "It's a dynamic situation. This is all unfolding, and we don't have all the facts. I don't want to make a statement or rush into a fight without all the facts."

I stood. "So you're just going to let Harry's reputation be ruined?"

"I didn't say that." Chief Karls didn't like to be challenged.

"It sure sounded like that was exactly what you said."

Johns intervened. "Why don't we wind down." She looked at Chief Karls for confirmation, and he nodded his approval. "I know Chief Karls has some other work to do." She looked at me. "Judge Thompson, why don't you come down to my office. I can give you the phone number of the court's director of media relations, and I also need to talk to you about your former law clerk."

CHAPTER FIFTEEN

Nancy Johns's office smelled like cigarettes. Even though California had long been smoke-free, a stale odor hung in the background. Johns claimed that it had been absorbed into the walls and carpet, and that multiple attempts to remove the smell had been unsuccessful over the years. The truth was that Johns still smoked a pack a day, and she didn't always go outside to take a puff.

"Judge Thompson, please have a seat." She pointed at a chair in front of her desk, then walked around to the other side and sat down. "May I be honest with you?"

Whenever somebody asks that, it's never good. "Sure. You can be honest with me. I'm sure you've seen it all."

"Maybe not all." Johns nodded her head slowly. "But certainly enough." Her eyes narrowed and her face tightened. Johns had worked at the courthouse for over thirty years. She was protective of the institution. She knew its vulnerabilities, and, at the moment, I was its biggest threat. "You're smart, and odds are that you can survive this. But you have to play it right. You need to listen, and you need to watch yourself."

"I think I am."

"No, you're not." Johns shook her head. "If you were watching yourself, you'd start to build some relationships with your colleagues. Right now you don't have anybody in your corner. You need to diligently take care of your cases. No more vacation days or long lunches with your wife." She removed a pack of cigarettes from her desk drawer, daring me to say something. "You're going to continue to *be* in the news, but try not to *make* news, if you know what I mean. Don't seek it out. Don't do anything stupid." She rolled the cigarette between her fingers and tapped it twice on the pack. "And we also have to take care of your former law clerk."

"I haven't heard from him since I let him go."

"Well," she said, "I have." She opened a folder on her desk. "He's got a lawyer, and he's claiming that he was wrongfully fired. The letter states that he should have been given medical leave to address his anxiety, depression, and chemical use."

I took the letter. "He never asked for it."

"But," she said, "his lawyer claims that he did."

"That's not true." I scanned the letter and put it back on the desk. "He never told me anything about that."

"Did you suspect it?"

"Truthfully?" I hesitated. "Of course I suspected it, but I didn't think it was my place to ask him. I thought that would only create more problems."

"You're right. It's private. If you had asked, we'd be sued over that and not this." With disgust, Nancy Johns returned the letter to her folder. "People have seen him with that reporter from the *Chronicle*. You should be aware of that."

"You think he's talking with her?"

Nancy Johns's face hardened. "I know he's talked with her. Who do you think nicknamed you 'The Kitten'?"

CHAPTER SIXTEEN

It was late that morning when Nikki and I arrived at Harry's house. The smell of chemical cleaners still lingered inside. Nikki turned on the lights and opened up some living room windows. I let Augustus go out back, then walked through the rest of the rooms, surveying a life cut short, while I pulled back the blinds and opened windows to let more fresh air inside.

I returned to the living room and looked out the big picture window. Augustus sprinted from one end of the yard to the other. My former law clerk was very much on my mind since talking with Nancy Johns.

He'd had an unpaid externship with Harry during his last year in law school for school credit. The economy was still in the tank when he graduated, and I felt sorry for him. Judge Meyer gave him a decent recommendation, and Billy Pratt was hired.

Only today had I learned how big a mistake that was.

"Want to start with the kitchen?" Nikki asked from behind me.

I pushed Billy Pratt out of my head. "We have to start somewhere."

"Exactly." Nikki gave me a little hug. "Disposing of moldy food will take your mind off things." She smiled and went out to the Range Rover for some boxes.

I grabbed an empty garbage bag from underneath the sink and opened the refrigerator. The food was in various stages of rot. The worst had likely turned before Harry died, but the extra week had made things worse. Holding my nose, I removed the lid from a Tupperware container and dumped some green meatloaf in the garbage bag.

"Here we go."

◆ ◆ ◆

I was taking sacks of garbage and recycling outside when Helen Vox called. She thanked me for speaking at Harry's funeral and asked about the article. "Are you doing OK?"

"I think you know the answer to that." I opened the lid of a large plastic garbage bin at the end of the driveway. "It's been hard." I dumped the heavy bags into the bin. "I was called into the principal's office."

"Today?"

"This morning," I said. "Chief Karls and Nancy Johns told me the articles are going to continue, just like you said. You and Harry might be the subject of one."

"I figured," Helen said. "I got a call from my boss as well. We're supposed to meet Monday morning, first thing." She paused. "Are you home?"

"No." I opened a green recycling bin and threw a bag of newspapers and magazines inside. "I'm at Harry's place, cleaning up." I walked back toward the house. "It's been a while since I've read the will, but when his wife got sick, Harry had showed it to me." I paused, momentarily lost in the memory. "I'm in charge of his estate, so I think it's on me to get things in order."

"Need some help?"

I avoided a direct response. "Nikki is here. She has the day off."

Although Helen was one of the few who understood how I felt and what I was going through, it didn't feel right to have her come to the house again. "Did you call Jarkowski yet?"

Silence, then Helen told me she hadn't. "It's the weekend."

"I don't think that matters." I got to the front step and opened the door.

"Tomorrow," Helen said. "I'll call him tomorrow."

"OK." I walked inside and paused at the place where he died. A chill ran up my spine. "Either you call him or I will."

◆ ◆ ◆

After dinner, Nikki started on the bathrooms and bedrooms. I went to Harry's office. Ever since I was a kid, I loved his office, with all its books and mementos from a lifetime of law. Packing up his things would be bittersweet.

I started with Harry's files, looking for life insurance policies, tax forms, and bank statements. Jarkowski's suggestion about money issues had piqued my interest, and, as the executor of Harry's estate, I needed to get a handle on his finances regardless.

A small file cabinet sat in the corner. I knew that Harry kept the key to it in his desk's top drawer. I unlocked the file cabinet and started sifting through the papers.

In the very front was a folder with Harry's last will and testament. I removed it and set it aside. Afterward I found copies of his last six tax returns and less important things like canceled checks, old credit card bills, and receipts for various home repairs.

Whenever I found something relevant, I set it aside for later. The remainder went into a paper sack to be shredded.

At the back was a plain manila folder. The folder itself was empty, but there was writing on the inside flap. Harry had written down the websites, user logins, and passwords for various online accounts. I wanted to get to a computer and see what they were all about, but I could handle that later, from home.

After the file cabinet was done, I turned my attention to Harry's bookshelf. It covered the entire wall and was filled with biographies of Abraham Lincoln, business leadership books, and classic literature.

A smile came to my face when I saw the row of Leo Tolstoy's *Anna Karenina*. I had once asked Harry why he had five copies. Harry looked at me with a tinge of pity, because to him the answer to my question was obvious.

"They aren't the same book, Jim," he said. "Each translation from Russian to English is different, and it's interesting to see how a particular translator interprets the greatest work of fiction ever written."

So that was my answer.

I would keep all the copies of *Anna Karenina*. I set them on a small table near the door, next to the stack of financial documents and the manila folder with the passwords. Then I finished boxing up the remaining books to be sold or given away.

I wanted to keep every book, but I didn't have room in my tiny house. I could bring them to my chambers, but displaying hundreds of books that I hadn't actually read would be pretentious. It wasn't who I was. I had grown up a survivor, not an intellectual, and I'd come to terms with that. Learning for pleasure was something that other kids did. For me, I learned to get the job done.

Nikki knocked on the doorframe. "How's it going?"

"It's going." I stared at the bookshelf, now dusty and devoid of books. "I'm ready to go home."

"Me too."

I walked around the desk and pointed at the stack of paper on the floor. "Can you grab that stuff? I'll grab the books."

She stepped inside and scooped it all up, including the manila folder. I reached for the stack of Tolstoy, each version of the book nearly a thousand pages. As I slid them off the table, the pile became unwieldy, and the top two editions fell to the floor.

I jumped back, trying to avoid a broken foot, and a third escaped. As the third book hit the ground, it opened, and some old photographs fell out.

CHAPTER SEVENTEEN

I kissed Nikki good night, and she pulled the covers up to her chin. As I walked to the bedroom door, I heard her roll over to face me. "Sure you don't want to come to bed?"

I looked back at her. "Is that a proposition?"

"No," she said. "In case you didn't notice, I had attempted to remove any romantic connotations from that question." She laughed. "I'm not twenty anymore. I need sleep, and so do you."

"Our days of trading sex for sleep are over, huh?"

"Pretty much."

I nodded and turned away. "I want to look at a few things from Harry's house first, maybe twenty minutes. Then I'll come to bed."

"Promise?"

She was taking care of me, which I appreciated. "I promise." I walked out and closed the bedroom door behind me.

I went to the desk in the corner. Next to the computer was the stack of *Anna Karenina* translations, the financial documents, and the folder with the passwords. On the very top were the photographs that had fallen from the book: three school photographs and one family photo. From the haircuts and style of clothes, I figured they were about twenty years old. The school photos were the standard educational mug shots:

mottled blue background, forced smiles, and a flash that left the color slightly overexposed.

The first picture was a boy. He was about seven, with brown hair and a gap between his two large front teeth, and he wore a Teenage Mutant Ninja Turtles T-shirt. He seemed excited, like he was ready to jump off the stool and run around the room.

The second picture was of a girl, about eleven. Her hair was flat and a little tangled on the ends. Her eyes were withdrawn and drooped at the edges. She was too young to wear makeup, but even if she did, it wouldn't have been possible to hide the dark circles under her eyes.

The third picture was of a teenager. It was hard to tell how old she was. She had large blonde hair, curly, that framed her chubby cheeks. She offered no full smile, just an annoyed smirk. She was already *beyond* school pictures. It was obvious what she was thinking: *Next year, I ain't showing up for this.*

The last picture had all three of them together on an old couch. The boy on one end. The preteen on the other. In the middle was the eldest, holding a new baby. The ages and style of clothes suggested that the group picture wasn't taken much before or after the school photographs. The only difference was the smiles. The smiles were real.

I turned the photographs over, and there was no writing on the back. No names. No dates. No location. Along the top edge of each photo was a small tear, like they had been tacked onto a bulletin board and ripped down, or something like that.

I took a final look at the photographs and set them aside; then, I began working through the list of websites and accounts in Harry's folder. It didn't take long for me to get bored, and so I went to the Action7 website. Perhaps, deep down, that was what I had been planning to do all along.

I knew I should have just ignored the circus, but that's tough to do when you're in the center ring. I clicked on the video replay of the Gregory Ports story.

A car advertisement flashed on the screen, promising low interest and no payments until next year for an off-road vehicle that will likely never go off-road. When the advertisement was done, the anchor for the Action7 news team hyped the story. A photo of Gregory Ports appeared, the same photo on the *San Francisco Chronicle*'s front page. Then came the breathless narration from Action7's investigative reporter, Charlotte Nichols.

"Gregory Ports was a boy whose life was cut tragically short. Now serious questions are being asked about the judge who handled the matter and the agency that advocated for his return home."

Images of court documents spun across the screen as Nichols built the case against me. Each document had a sentence highlighted, which the reporter read with a cold, clinical voice. Although the sentences were boilerplate, she presented them in a manner that seemed to objectively prove my incompetence. Then the executive director of End Child Abuse California, a nonprofit organization I'd never heard of, condemned my reasoning and judgment.

The reporter transitioned. "The death of Gregory Ports and Alameda County's poor track record are very concerning to Governor Lamp, and he's ready to make California safe for the littlest among us." A video clip began to roll of the governor standing behind a podium. The head of the California Department of Social Services was by his side, looking serious with big red glasses perched on the end of her nose. Behind the governor were victims of child abuse, foster-care-reform advocates, and state legislators.

All nodded in agreement as Governor Lamp declared, "Never again." He must have sensed the emotion in the room and that this was likely the only coherent thing he had said during the press conference, so he repeated the line even louder. "Never again." Then the people applauded.

CHAPTER EIGHTEEN

Sunday was a waste without Nikki there to ensure that I did something productive, and Monday morning came quick. She squeezed my shoulder and turned on the lights. She had just gotten home from the hospital after working all day on Sunday as well as the overnight shift. "You going in today?"

"Do I have to?" I rolled over and opened my eyes. She stood there with a cup of coffee, and I pushed myself up. "The nectar of life." I pointed at the mug, confirming that it was for me, and took it. "What time is it?"

"A little after eight."

My eyes widened as I looked at the clock for confirmation. "I overslept."

"Yes, you did," she said. "You must have partied pretty hard yesterday without me."

"You weren't supposed to know about that." I played coy, both of us knowing that there wasn't any party, just a depressed guy surfing the Internet and allowing his personal hygiene to deteriorate as others discussed his incompetence.

I took a sip and put the coffee cup on the nightstand. I forced myself to pull the sheets away, exposing myself to the cold, and swung my feet over the bed's edge.

"You gonna make it?"

I looked at her, my mind growing sharper. "I think so."

"It's a miracle." She turned and walked back to the living room. "Did you find anything interesting?"

"Online?" I said, raising my voice a bit so she could hear me in the other room. I wasn't going to tell her about the fifty times I replayed the governor's press conference while I was supposed to be reviewing Harry Meyer's electronic accounts and bank statements. "Not really. It was all pretty regular. Harry bought groceries and paid his utilities just like everybody else."

◆ ◆ ◆

I got to the courthouse late. I'd like to say it was a little after nine thirty, but it was actually much closer to ten. The courtroom was full of lawyers, clients, and other interested family members. They had been noticed to arrive at court for their hearing about the time I was still waking up. I checked my watch again. I hoped the time was wrong, but it wasn't. Then I hung my jacket on the coatrack, grabbed my robe, and hustled to the courtroom.

Karen was waiting for me in the narrow hallway that ran behind the courtrooms.

"People aren't too mad, are they?"

"They've all had a chance to talk, so that's good." She turned and went into the courtroom, and I was alone in the hallway. It was like being backstage before the curtain rose. The performance would soon begin, whether or not the actors, including me, were ready.

I closed my eyes and recited a brief prayer that Harry had taught me on my first day. *Lord, give me the vision to see the good. Give me the patience to listen. Give me the knowledge to do what's right, for whatever I do is done to the best of my ability.*

As I finished and was about to enter the courtroom, a bailiff gently tapped me on the shoulder and coughed. "Excuse me, Your Honor."

I turned. "Yes?"

"Can I talk to you about one of the people who are out there?"

"I'm running late."

"It'll be brief."

I looked around. "You want to talk here or someplace else?"

"Here is fine." He looked at his sheet of paper, listing cases scheduled for hearing that morning. He flipped to the third page. A name had been circled. "It's the dad." He pointed at a highlighted line on the calendar.

"What's the case?"

"In the matter of the children of Tanya Neal," he said. "State filed a petition to terminate. Looks like this is the first admit-deny hearing."

The name kicked around in my head. It sounded familiar, and then I remembered the woman with her puffy jacket. Procedurally, she was nearing the end. Child dependency cases were a two-step dance. The first part removed the children from the home and placed them in foster care. This triggered the government's obligation to provide services and to try to reunite the family. If the agency believed those efforts were unsuccessful, they took the second step, which was a legal petition to terminate the parent's rights.

The agency's attorney, Sylvia Norgaard, had told the court that they were going to file the paperwork, but I was surprised the termination petition came so fast. "Is she here?"

"Don't know," he said, "but the father, guy named Peter Thill, is out in the lobby, pretty fired up. The social worker says he was making

some threats yesterday. He wants his kids back, today, and if he doesn't get them back, says he just might hurt somebody."

"Pretty vague."

The bailiff nodded. "That's true, but"—he removed some folded pieces of paper from his back pocket—"if you take a look at his social media posts, you'll see why we're concerned."

I started reading the posts, mostly typical stuff, but then there were links to articles about the *child protection industrial complex* and conspiracy theories about social workers getting paid to *snatch* kids and sell them to parents wanting to adopt.

I turned the page and saw that he'd posted the link to the *San Francisco Chronicle* article about Gregory Ports. Beneath the article, Thill wrote: "My judge."

I looked at the bailiff. "You get a warrant for all this?"

He shook his head. "The social worker said it wasn't necessary. It's all public. Idiot doesn't understand the privacy settings."

"Or doesn't care." I looked at the final sheet of paper. Thill's last status update was a picture of a gun, box of bullets, and roll of duct tape lying on a bed. Above the photograph, Thill wrote, "Ready to go."

I handed the papers back to the bailiff. "What's your plan?"

"We made security aware. He had to go through some extra screens, in addition to the metal detectors. So we're confident he's unarmed. And we've got an extra deputy in the courtroom."

I nodded, looking over the bailiff's shoulder toward the courtroom door. "Are you going to charge him with anything?"

"Nothing to charge him with yet," he said.

"Really?"

"That's what the prosecutor says." The bailiff took the copies of the Facebook pages from me. "He got a good talking-to from us. He said he was just blowing off steam, you know?"

"I guess," I said. "Tell the clerks to call it first. I want to get him out of here."

◆ ◆ ◆

The tables were more crowded than usual, because all four children were in attendance. Plus, there was the Alameda County social worker and her attorney, Sylvia Norgaard; the guardian ad litem, Cherelle Williams; Sophia Delgado; and Peter Thill with his new court-appointed attorney.

Benji Metina sat in the back. Her presence unnerved me. Our eyes met. My jaw clenched, and I forgot what I was going to say. My mind was blank, and my mouth went dry. Instead of showing her that I could handle the job, I was "The Kitten." I looked around the room, lost. The silence grew more awkward. Perhaps only seconds passed, but it felt like hours. Doubt filled me. Maybe I wasn't suited for the job. Maybe I should take Chief Karls's advice and transfer to another division.

Karen saw it all and saved me. "Judge," she whispered. "Ready?"

I turned to her and nodded. Karen called the case and gaveled the hearing to a start. The tension was higher than usual, and the presence of the extra bailiff did not help. If my mind wasn't going to allow complex thought, I decided to start simply. "Good morning, everybody." I kept my voice deliberately soft, ignoring Benji Metina and finding a rhythm. I tried to appear calm as my eyes met each of the people in attendance. The kids already seemed bored, but Peter Thill was wound tight.

Although I'd usually allow the county and the tribe to go first, I decided to start with Thill's attorney. "Mr. Thill, I see you have an attorney sitting next to you."

Bob Finley rose up from his chair. He was a veteran attorney who could politely be described as *weathered*. Finley had represented parents in child dependency and termination hearings for decades. His thinning hair was bleached and always three inches too long. He had a narrow thumb ring and two large gold rings on each hand and looked more like an aging rock star than an attorney, but Finley knew what he was doing. I figured giving him a chance to speak right away might defuse the situation.

"Thank you, Your Honor. I'm Robert Finley, and I've been appointed to represent Mr. Thill in this matter."

Thill looked like he was going to spring out of his seat, but Bob Finley gave him a harsh look. "My client enters a denial to the petition to terminate his parental rights, and we'd like to set this matter on for a pretrial."

I looked at Karen, who announced the date of the pretrial hearing.

"Anything else?" I asked.

"Yes, Your Honor." Finley looked down at his client. It was clear that he was already annoyed by Peter Thill, even though he'd only represented him for less than ten minutes. I could tell that Finley didn't want to make the request he was about to make, but it was an effort to build his relationship with Thill. "My client would like his children returned to him immediately. Says he has some housing lined up and that the kids want to be with him."

"When you say *lined up*, does he have housing, or is he looking for housing?"

"He is currently staying at a friend's house."

I shook my head. "The request is denied. I don't know much of anything about you, Mr. Thill, since you've been incarcerated during most of these proceedings. Nobody from the county has come out to look at your home, and the fact that you're just staying there for a little while isn't stable enough to justify the disruption of your children's current foster care placement."

Thill mumbled under his breath. "I need a real attorney." He stared at Bob Finley with the same hatred he'd directed at me. "This whole thing is a setup." Thill slammed his hand down on the table, and the bailiffs moved in closer. Each bailiff looked at me and waited.

"Mr. Thill." My voice went even softer, forcing Thill to lean toward me in order to hear what I was going to say. "I know you're upset, but I can't send the kids home with you today."

Thill pointed at Finley. "He told me to just sign away the rights to my kids." Thill shook his head, then looked at his kids, all of whom were on the edges of their seats. "I ain't gonna do it. I love them. They love me. They want to be with me, not in no foster homes. I need a lawyer who's actually gonna stop this."

"If you want a trial, you will have a trial, but I can't reassign you a new attorney. His job is to give you honest advice in private—sometimes advice you don't want to hear—but then be your advocate at any trial."

"I love you, Dad!" the younger boy, Bobby, shouted. The older boy, Damien, said the same thing, and then the teenage girls, Neisha and Kayla Neal, joined. It was a full rebellion.

"I just want to be with you, Dad," Kayla said.

Thill turned away, looking at the floor, his hands balled into fists.

"Why don't we take a break," I said. "The attorneys can come see me."

◆ ◆ ◆

The attorneys dutifully filed into my chambers. When the chairs were filled, Karen rolled in a third. I looked at Thill's attorney. I liked Bob Finley. He was a good advocate, but he wasn't a sucker. I had no doubt that he had told Thill to voluntarily terminate his parental rights given his violent history and convictions for criminal sexual conduct and kidnapping. It was unlikely Thill was going to win, and there was little reason to waste everyone's time.

Getting to the point, I asked, "Any chance he'll cool off?"

Finley shook his head. "Don't think so, Judge." He looked at the other attorneys, then back at me. "Plus—and I don't say this lightly—I don't really feel comfortable meeting with him in private anymore." Finley didn't provide any more detail, and he didn't have to.

"I understand," I said. "The bailiffs have expressed concerns about comments he's made in the courthouse, and the social worker has also seen threats posted on Mr. Thill's Facebook page." I paused. "Of course

I want everybody to get home safe at the end of the day, but we have to go forward."

I turned to Sophia Delgado. "Have you heard anything from Ms. Neal? Do you know where she is?"

Delgado shook her head. "No calls back. I checked the jails, nothing."

"What do you want to do?"

"Ordinarily she'd be in default and the case would be over, but since the father is back in the picture, I'd like to enter a denial and see if she shows up at the next hearing. There's really no prejudice—"

Karen Fields stuck her head in. "Excuse me, Judge, but I think we have a problem."

I looked at the attorneys. Each of them seemed as surprised as I was. Then to Karen I said, "What is it now?"

"The two older girls," Karen said. "They told the social worker that they needed to go to the bathroom, and . . . looks like they ran."

CHAPTER NINETEEN

Thill smirked through the rest of the hearing. He basked in the chaos that everyone knew, but could not prove, he had created. My guess was that Thill and his girls had arranged a place to meet. The girls had not spontaneously run. The whole thing had been planned, and there wasn't anything I could do about it.

I looked to the back of the courtroom. Benji Metina sat, waiting. Her little notepad was open, and she was ready to write down every word I said.

"Mr. Thill." I looked at him. "If Neisha or Kayla contact you or you learn where they are, then I order you to contact the social worker assigned to the case immediately and turn them over to child protection. Do you understand?"

"I do, Your Honor." He smiled. "I'll get right on that."

"I'm sure you will," I said before Karen Fields banged the gavel down a few times and called the next case. Thill got up from his chair and walked out of the courtroom with a strut. I knew that my order was meaningless. I could issue dozens of orders citing legal precedents and laws every day, but they were just pieces of paper. If a person didn't care, it didn't matter, and Thill didn't give a damn about what I said or did.

◆ ◆ ◆

Since I got started late, there wasn't much time for lunch between the morning and afternoon calendars. Karen brought me a sandwich while I sifted through e-mails, although I didn't ask her to, and she wasn't required to feed me. It might have been pity.

I can't imagine that she enjoyed her weekend, either. It couldn't have been fun to have family and friends ask her if she was really working for the judge in the news, the one responsible for a dead boy. It's not something young lawyers wanted on their résumé.

Thirty more families were processed in the afternoon. Some parents edged closer to reunifying with their children. Others were stuck. Each was given a hearing and had to sit around a table as outsiders discussed the intimate details of their lives and struggles.

It was after five o'clock when the afternoon calendar finally ended. The institutional players had already started packing up their laptops and files as the clerk announced the date of the next review hearing and an Order to Appear hummed out of the court's laser printer.

I left for my chambers. As I got out my key, I noticed a picture somebody had taped to the door: a gray kitten with white fur on its chest with little black stripes. Its ears were folded back and down, and it looked up with sad eyes. Below the picture was the meme: "You Eated My Cookie."

Great, I thought. *Gossip about "The Kitten" has now escalated into teenage bullying. I'm sure somebody is having a good laugh. It's junior high school all over again.*

I removed the picture, unlocked the door, and walked back to my office after hanging my black robe on the coatrack. Mail needed to be read. Orders sat in my "To Be Signed" basket, and a half dozen other items sat in my "To Be Reviewed" basket. Without even logging on to my computer, I knew there were likely twenty or thirty new e-mail messages, even though I had managed to get caught up on them during my brief lunch break.

I ignored it all. I placed the kitten picture on my desk and walked over to the window. Below me, some birds fought over a stale sandwich that hadn't quite made it into the garbage. My mind ground through its daily purge. This was the part of the job that nobody talked about: the decompression. In the public speeches and even among friends, being a Superior Court judge was always *an honor* or *challenging, but rewarding*. Rarely did judges admit that the honors and rewards were few.

The day-to-day life of a judge consisted of pushing dozens of cases through a system. The happiest judges were the oblivious ones. They were the intellect workers, not the intellectuals—smart enough to get the job done but lacking curiosity about the system itself. Ignorance was bliss, and at times I wished I were one of them. Judge Harry Meyer, however, hadn't allowed that.

Karen interrupted my trip down the mental rabbit hole. "Are you OK?" She was in the doorway. I didn't know how long she'd been watching me.

"I'm fine," I said, but I wasn't convincing. "Come on in and have a seat."

Karen nodded and did as instructed while I walked around my desk and sat down. I waited for her to get settled in the chair across from me. "Karen," I said, "if you want to look for a new job, I wouldn't blame you."

She shook her head. "I'm not looking for a new job. I just started this one."

I could tell that the thought had crossed her mind, and I'd be worried if it hadn't. "Well, if you do, I'll give you a good recommendation. Not sure what it'd be worth, but I won't stand in your way." I picked up the cat picture and slid it across the desk. "What do you think? Somebody taped it to our door."

She looked down at it, then up at me. "At least it's a cute kitty."

"You're right. It could be worse." I laughed and took the picture back. "Not sure how, exactly, but it could be."

"You'll be fine," Karen pronounced, sounding eerily like Nikki and not like somebody who's supposed to be my subordinate. "Anything else you need me to do before I go home?"

"Maybe," I said. "Do you have Billy's contact information?"

"Like what?"

"Phone number would be best," I said. "Maybe e-mail if you've got it."

Karen seemed hesitant. "You're not going to call him, are you?"

"He's spreading rumors about me."

"Yes." Karen was direct, and I appreciated her loyalty and her not minimizing the situation. "He was fired. Of course he's going to say things, but calling him seems like a bad idea."

"I understand," I said. "But he's also saying he was wrongfully terminated. I want to talk to him about that and about Judge Meyer."

"In that case," Karen said, "you should definitely not call him."

I wasn't ready to give up quite yet. "Maybe."

"Judge . . ." Karen looked at me, concerned. "With all due respect, that is a very bad idea. You're a smart man. You shouldn't do it. With the governor's task force and the media scrutiny, it's just going to be trouble. He could record the conversation. He could make up something. Who knows what'll happen."

I took a breath and let it go. "You're right. Forget it."

"I will." Karen was serious. "It's all going to blow over. Just wait."

"I'm not so sure."

CHAPTER TWENTY

The parking garage was dark and mostly empty by the time I got there. I took the elevator up to the third floor, got out, and saw my Range Rover at the far end of a row of vacant spaces. As I got closer, I saw a compact woman in jeans and a white dress shirt.

"Judge Thompson," she said. "You've been working late."

My hand tightened on my briefcase's handle. The *San Francisco Chronicle* reporter stood at my car door.

"Ms. Metina," I said. "You know it's not safe loitering in Oakland parking garages after dark."

"I'm touched that you care." She put her hand to her heart. "But I think I can handle myself." Then she came toward me. Metina had a digital recorder. "I've been trying to speak with you for some time, Judge Thompson."

"You know the rules," I said. "No comment on pending cases."

"But you'd agree that Gregory Ports is not a pending case." She planted her feet and held the recorder closer to my face. "That case ended when you dismissed it, and even if it didn't, the case certainly ended when Gregory Ports died." She studied me, waiting for a response. When I didn't give one, she continued. "I think the public would like to hear your thoughts."

"I don't have any comment." I attempted to sidestep her, but she didn't move. "Please, I'd like to go home."

"I understand." Metina waited, examining my reaction and studying my mood. "It was a rough day," she said. "A father is threatening to kill you, and two of the kids are now missing."

"I don't have any comment on that, either."

"What are you going to do without Judge Meyer's help?"

That question got to me. *What was I going to do without Judge Meyer's help?*

I didn't answer. I made another attempt to pass her, instead, but she didn't move. My frustration grew. Everything was falling at the same time. As the pieces came down, I couldn't catch every one. Something was going to crash. Something was going to break. "Please, excuse me or I'll have to call the police."

"The police?" Metina smiled. "Come on, Judge, people should hear your side of the story." She stepped aside, finally allowing me to get to my car. "I'm ready to talk when you are."

I opened the Range Rover's door and got inside. As I tried to stick the key in the ignition, my hand shook, no doubt the combined result of adrenaline and anger. It took a few tries, but I got the key in and pulled out of my parking spot. I stopped after five feet. I looked at Metina in my rearview mirror.

I'd had enough. I was tired of being blown around.

I loved Judge Meyer. I respected everybody who had told me to simply ride things out, but I wasn't going to sit back. I wasn't going to hide. If things were going to crash, then I might as well exert some control over when the pieces fell.

"Ms. Metina," I called out the window.

"What is it?" Metina looked surprised. She walked toward me.

"How about an off-the-record conversation?"

"Off the record?"

I nodded. "After we do that, then maybe we can discuss if there is anything appropriate to put on the record."

She smiled. "You're smarter than they give you credit for."

"I think that was a compliment," I said. "And—as an unsolicited suggestion—this conversation is going to go much better if you stop insulting me." I unlocked the doors and nodded toward the passenger side. "Come around and hop inside. We'll go for a little drive."

◆ ◆ ◆

I got on Webster Street and began driving to the island. "Where do you want to start?"

"Off the record?"

"Everything is off the record until I say it isn't."

Metina's mood changed. She still had an edge—a journalist's skepticism—but the possibility of my cooperation altered the dynamic. She had been hunting me, and I had been running. Now the chase was over, and I'd gotten some power back. I wasn't in control, but I could impact the direction.

"Why don't you tell me about the mother?"

"Sheila Ports?"

"Yes."

"I think you know all about that." Although I wasn't involved in the case from the beginning—I handled only the final hearing and didn't remember the case—I'd read the file multiple times. It was tragic but not significantly different from the others on my caseload.

"I want to hear it from you," Metina said. "That's what I want to know. That's what people want to know."

"I'm not so sure people really want to know. They want me to say something so that they can attack me." Traffic slowed, and I turned on my headlights as we drove into the Webster Street Tube. It was a tunnel

connecting Oakland and Alameda Island. About a quarter through the tunnel, I decided I needed to play along.

"Sheila Ports was an addict," I said, "and, like a lot of addicts, she eventually ran out of money. Once an addict runs out of money, they do inexplicable, desperate, and often horrible things to get their next fix. That's the nature of addiction."

"And that was how Gregory got hurt?"

"His mother was known. She was poor, bipolar, and addicted and therefore surrounded by men who were ready and willing to take advantage of her. Say what you want about a married businessman going to a strip club or some guy paying for a blow job. These guys were and are different. They are predators. They live deep in the shadows. They talk. They share stories, give one another tips."

"And they abuse little boys?"

"They do whatever they want." As we came out of the tunnel, it took a moment for my eyes to adjust to the light. The two lanes multiplied into four, and I stayed right as they split apart. "In exchange for a little food or some cash or some crystal meth, they'd take her and/or take Gregory and . . . you can fill in the blanks."

"Then he was removed by the agency and placed in foster care."

"Ironically, Sheila Ports wasn't doing too bad when Gregory was removed, comparatively." We crossed Atlantic Avenue. "Somehow she'd found a bed for her and her son at the Bethany Hope Mission. The social workers at the mission had connected Sheila with a county mental health worker. She got some meds, an injectable that lasts a month rather than the pills she'd have to remember to take every day. Her mind was clearer than it had ever been in the past ten years."

I stopped at a traffic light. "That day, the day Gregory was placed in foster care, Sheila had walked into the emergency room with pride. She was trying to be a good mom, and she was impressed with herself that she had noticed Gregory wasn't sleeping, and that she knew a doctor needed to examine her son's congestion and stomach pain."

"And that's when the doctor saw the bruising?"

"Exactly." The light turned green, and we continued down Webster toward Shoreline Drive. "During the examination, he lifted Gregory's shirt to listen to his breathing. That's when the doctor saw the bruising and scars. There were eight distinct yellow bruises, four on each side, where a person had grabbed Gregory and squeezed so hard that the fingers had left marks. Then there were the small cuts, mostly healed, and the scars from cigarette burns near the boy's buttocks."

Parking spots were rare near the water. I got lucky and spotted a car pulling away from a spot on one of the side streets. I made a quick turn, pulled in behind, and shut off the engine. "The doctor was a mandatory reporter." I turned to Metina and finished the story. "So he asked Sheila to wait while he filled out some paperwork, and that's when the police were called to do the removal. That's how Gregory was put into foster care."

"And then you sent him home."

"You make it sound like he was in foster care for a day," I said. "Gregory Ports was in foster care for almost nine months. Nine months for us may not seem like much, but through the eyes of a child, nine months is a long time. The mother seemed stable. Everybody who spoke at the final hearing agreed to reunify the family, and they knew the case best. I had been on the bench only a week. I was a new judge, but the recommendation made sense. That's when and why I sent him home."

"And then he died."

"You're right." I opened the door and took a step out. "That's when he died," I said, shutting the door.

◆ ◆ ◆

We walked to the path that ran parallel to Shoreline Drive. Another twenty yards down, we found a park bench to sit on.

"They still haven't caught the man who did it," I said. "The mother doesn't remember anything. She says she was passed out when Gregory was beaten so badly that his brain swelled, which ultimately killed him." I watched as a sailboat crossed in front of us, and then the men on board lowered its anchor for the sunset. "I don't know if she really doesn't remember, but I believe it. Just one more layer of tragedy."

"Would you do anything differently?"

"Of course," I said. "If you can predict the future, you can always make the right decisions. If the foster parent would've spoken up, if there would've been somebody raising some concern about her sobriety, but there wasn't any of that. When all the recommendations from all the parties are to reunite the child and dismiss the case, it's not realistic to think that a judge is going to do his own thing."

"But that's the culture that Judge Meyer developed, right?"

"That's not fair." I watched as another sailboat joined the first one. The edges of the sky had darkened to a hazy orange. "The government has a pretty bad record of messing with families, especially poor families and families of color. There are lots of kids that are reunited, and it's fine. The family isn't perfect, but it's a family. It's good enough. We can't have millions of kids in foster care forever. There's not the money and there aren't enough people willing to adopt."

"What about that guy in court today? Certainly you're not going to let him have his kids back."

"I can't talk about a pending case." I thought about all the kids that morning. Tanya Neal and Peter Thill's children were in full rebellion against the social workers and the court and demanded to go home. It didn't matter that Tanya Neal was an addict and missing, or that Peter Thill was a convicted felon and considered extremely dangerous. They wanted out of the system.

"Parents have constitutional rights," I said. "Kids have constitutional rights, too. You can't just break up a family. You need to give them an opportunity to be heard. It's the rule of law."

"Do you think Judge Meyer followed the rule of law?"

I stopped watching the sailboats and turned to her. "Is there something you want to tell me?"

I thought I noticed a smirk, but I wasn't sure. *She knows something,* I thought, *something I don't know.*

Metina changed the subject. "What are your thoughts about AFC Services?"

"I haven't really thought about them." And that was the truth. AFC Services provided parenting assessments, psychological assessments, skills coaching, and some emergency housing to families involved in the child protection system.

"Do you know whether it's a for-profit or nonprofit?"

"I always assumed it was a nonprofit," I said. "Marsh Terry started it, because Harry was frustrated that nobody was willing to work with parents who had their kids in foster care. It was sort of a favor."

"And do you know how they got their contract with the county?"

"I don't. It was before my time." I looked at the sky and wondered where this was going.

"They've been around a little over ten years, and during that time, the county has paid them millions of dollars."

"That doesn't surprise me," I said. "Nobody works for free."

"You're right. Nobody works for free," Metina said. "Especially not Marshall Terry." Metina crossed her legs and leaned back, taking her time before moving forward. "Tell me," she said. "Do you think Judge Meyer's murder had anything to do with me?"

"You?" I shook my head, surprised and confused. "Why would it have anything to do with you?"

"I'm not sure." Metina gently offered her theory. "Not long after I started asking questions, your mentor ended up dead." Her intelligent eyes studied my reaction. "Do you think it was coincidence?"

CHAPTER TWENTY-ONE

The next day, I got to work early. Karen was usually there and had the coffee brewing by the time I had arrived, but it was a different morning. I woke up with a sense of urgency. The conversation with Benji Metina kicked around in my head.

Even though I never went on the record, I was glad that we had talked. I was no longer running from her. I'd gotten a sense of where she was going, and I wasn't afraid. Metina asked good questions, and, in the process, she had broadened my own search for who killed Harry.

There were the photos found in Harry's office, but now I needed to think more about Marshall Terry. Even though he was Harry's best friend, we didn't socialize much, and our interactions were mostly superficial. All I knew was that he had become wealthy investing in San Francisco real estate, and he had helped Harry by starting AFC Services.

Prior to AFC Services, many of Harry's thoughts about the child protection system were merely theories. Harry believed that parenting was, in part, a skill. If that skill was lost through the generations, then it needed to be taught. AFC Services gave Harry an opportunity to prove that his theories were correct. I had never considered how much Marsh Terry had profited from the experiment.

As I dug through my briefcase for my office keys, I heard a cough as someone approached from behind.

"Hope this ain't a bad time, Judge."

I turned and saw Detective Jarkowski. "No." I smiled. "I may be the first person to say this to you, but I'm glad you're here." Once I finally found my keys, I unlocked the door and led Detective Jarkowski into my office.

"Read about you in the newspaper." He slowly lowered himself into one of the two wooden chairs in front of my desk, and I wondered whether he would fit. "Tough stuff."

"It'll be OK," I said, choosing to keep my own doubt and insecurities private. "It's part of the job."

The detective nodded. "That's a good attitude."

"So what do you need from me?"

"Couple things." Jarkowski's mustache twitched to the side. "Got a call from Helen Vox. Talked for a while. She's giving a full statement later this morning."

I nodded, but I tried to keep my expression neutral.

"She told me you encouraged her to come forward."

I hesitated, unsure if that was actually something she told Jarkowski or whether he had merely guessed. "I did." Figured there was no sense in denying the truth. "And I'm glad she called."

"I'm glad, too. Before I talk to her formally, it'd be nice to know exactly what she said to you."

"Detective, I don't think you need to worry about Helen Vox. She's not a killer."

"I'm not saying she is or isn't." He looked slightly offended. "Just want to do my job and explore the possibilities. Rather not walk blindly into a meeting."

"I get that." I checked my watch, wondering how much time we had before Karen would arrive. I wanted to talk with Jarkowski, but I

also didn't want to start the calendar late again. I figured that we had fifteen minutes or so.

I looked up at Jarkowski. "Helen and I met at Harry's house," I began simply. "She had some clothes and toiletries there, and she wanted to get them back."

He nodded, and then I told him about Helen's affair with Harry as well as everything else she had told me about the morning he was killed.

When I was done, Detective Jarkowski asked a few follow-up questions and seemed satisfied. Then he switched directions. "When you were at the house, either with Ms. Vox or later, did you find anything?"

"Not really." I shook my head. "I started to clean, but I didn't get that far. I found a bunch of account passwords and financial statements. I also found the will and tax documents. I've started sifting through those now. Nothing groundbreaking."

I didn't have a good reason to keep secret the four photographs that had fallen out of the book. I should have told Jarkowski about them. He was the detective. I was not. Deep down, however, I think I wanted to be the hero who put the puzzle pieces together. As irrational as it sounds, I believed I might find redemption in Harry Meyer's death. If I could find who killed him, I'd prove my value. Maybe I wouldn't be "The Kitten" anymore. My good deed would absolve all sins. I'd be allowed to return from exile.

"Any valuables stolen?" Jarkowski asked.

"Not that I know of." I thought about my conversation with Metina and decided to share it. "When I spoke to the reporter, she asked me if her articles might have something to do with Harry's murder. She also asked me about Marsh Terry."

Jarkowski considered the information, likely deciding for himself how much he wanted to share with me. "It's certainly possible," he said. "But Marsh Terry was in New York at the time, meeting with a bunch of bankers. So then we'd be talking about a hit job or something." He

shook his head. "I don't see that. Happens in the movies, but not so much in real life."

"She also made suggestions about the contracts between the county and Marsh Terry's company," I said. "Like they were improper."

"That's interesting." Jarkowski filed the information away. It was as if he already knew. "Well, keep looking." He got up from his chair and walked toward the door, then stopped in the doorway and turned around. "Did Judge Meyer ever tell you how he pays for that place where he's got his wife?"

"Walker Assisted Living?"

He nodded. "That's it. I was talking to a buddy, and he said those places cost a fortune."

Jarkowski didn't make the connection between the contracts and Harry's finances, but it was certainly implied. "He never mentioned it," I said, which was the truth. "Maybe Harry had insurance or something."

◆ ◆ ◆

The morning calendar was filled with truants, kids who missed an excessive amount of school without a valid excuse. Although the law allowed only six unexcused absences per year, this morning's truants had anywhere from seventy-five to a hundred and fifty absences. These kids, in short, didn't go to school, ever.

Phone calls from teachers and the principal didn't work. Social workers and even the county attorney had tried to intervene, but that didn't improve their attendance. The kids continued to skip school, so now they were in the court system. Somehow a judge was going to fix a problem that nobody else, with better relationships and better training, was able to fix.

It made perfect sense.

I worked quickly through the docket, dispatching pithy inspirational quotes along with threats of being removed from the home and

being placed in foster care or an inpatient, residential facility. Parents were informed that they could be criminally charged with contributing to the delinquency of a minor and put in jail, even though they never were. And the rest were ordered to get an updated chemical health or mental health evaluation and take their medications.

This was what the justice system had come to: hauling parents and kids to court, making them wait all morning, and then ordering fourteen-year-old girls to take their antidepressants and sixteen-year-old boys to stop smoking weed and playing video games all day.

Justice.

Karen handed me a stack of orders to sign. The orders reflected the things that I said at each hearing. All of them were computer generated after a few text blocks were added, depending on the circumstances. There were about thirty text blocks of boilerplate legal and factual findings, and I've never encountered a case that required a new one to be written.

I signed the orders and handed them back to Karen.

"Thank you, Judge."

◆ ◆ ◆

The afternoon was more of the same. After I had heard all the cases and signed another stack of orders, I went back to my chambers and responded to various e-mails, mostly by deleting them. When I glanced at the clock on my bookshelf, it was already four in the afternoon.

I tried to think of additional work, but I drew a blank. I'm sure there was an order to review, new appellate decisions to read, or administrative duties to attend to. I simply wasn't motivated enough to seek them out.

Ever since Jarkowski left that morning, Harry had been on my mind, and there was only one person who I could talk to about him. I loved Nikki, but she wasn't going to be able to tell me about the

photographs, Harry's finances, and how the county selects its service providers.

The person I needed was Helen Vox, and I figured that she might feel the same way about me. We'd both seen Harry's violent end, and we were both now under fire at work, misunderstood and questioned. Even if Helen couldn't provide answers, we could grieve together.

◆ ◆ ◆

I waited for Helen at a picnic table on Adams Point. Not far from the courthouse, it was the largest park on Lake Merritt, with a boathouse, an elaborate bonsai garden, and a fairyland for children.

It was nice to be outside, though the air was crisp and I had to keep my hands in my pockets. The park was active. Runners, walkers, and kite flyers appeared to outnumber the homeless for once. As the late afternoon transitioned to the evening, that would change.

Helen arrived a half hour after I'd called. I almost didn't recognize her. She was dressed casually in jeans, a sweater, and a knee-length coat. She noticed the look on my face and explained.

"I'm on vacation." She forced a smile.

I stood up and gave her a little hug. "Well, that's good. You look relaxed."

"Thanks. It's sort of good, sort of not good . . ." She hesitated, as if weighing how much detail to provide. "My boss strongly encouraged me to take some time off." She looked at the ground, shaking her head. "I had hundreds of vacation hours in the bank, and he told me that I should use some of them and think about retirement."

"I'm sorry," I said. "Hadn't heard."

"Intellectually I don't blame them. I messed up, but it still hurts." We began walking along the path that circled the lake. "Been at that office for over twenty years. I'm union, so they can't fire me very easily, but they can move me out of the child protection division. I can be sent

to the basement and tasked with contract review until I die. Maybe it's just time to retire."

"Funny you should mention retirement," I said. "Because I've been thinking about retirement myself."

"Let me guess," Helen said. "Nancy Johns and Chief Judge Karls want you to take a break and possibly move out of child protection."

"How'd you know?"

"Because they had been trying to get Harry to do that for years." She stopped and watched a man try to untangle his kite from a nearby tree. "It has to do with staffing and performance metrics. They don't like how slowly the cases move through the child dependency system, and I think Chief Karls didn't like how prominent Harry had become. I think he was jealous."

Nikki was working another overnight at the hospital, so dinner tonight would be with Helen. We decided on a tiny Ethiopian place that probably sat fifteen people at most and where we weren't likely to be seen by anybody we knew. Ethiopian food was an acquired taste. I'd never seen another lawyer or judge eat there, which was one of the restaurant's greatest selling points. It made me smile just thinking of Chief Karls ripping off a piece of the spongy injera bread, scooping up the goat meat with it, and trying to get everything in his mouth without sullying his silk tie.

About halfway through dinner, I passed her the four photographs I'd found. "These are what I mentioned on the phone. I found these in Harry's library."

She flipped through the photographs quickly once, then she took her time, studying each one. When she was finished, Helen looked up, her expression a combination of disappointment and confusion.

"I'm sorry, Jim." She handed back the photographs. "I've never seen these before. Don't recognize those kids, either."

"Harry never mentioned them?"

"Never."

"OK." I put the photographs away. "Thanks for looking."

She nodded as our waitress stopped by, refilled our drinks, then disappeared. "If I had to guess, I think they were probably all foster kids, probably aged out of the system now."

"Why?"

"The tears at the top of the photos," she said. "All the photographs had those tears." She took a drink of her soda and then, since it was clear I wasn't following her, explained. "Based on the age of those photographs, it was back when we had paper files. We didn't shift to electronic files until 2005. Back then, a clerk would plop this big thick file down on the bench in front of the judge. Harry started making the social workers provide photographs of the kids involved in each of the child protection cases. He made the court clerks staple them to the inside of the folder."

Helen smiled at the memory. "Harry didn't want the judges, including himself, to forget why we were doing this. That the cases weren't just a stack of paper. They were real kids. He wanted a reminder. My guess is that he tore those photos out of a file for some reason."

"That sounds like Harry," I said. "But why these?"

She shook her head. "Who knows?"

◆ ◆ ◆

On our way back to Adams Point and the courthouse, Helen pointed out a new hipster bar, a former auto-repair shop that now featured reclaimed wood tables and brick walls accented with shiny corrugated sheet metal. Some urban lumberjacks and women with various piercings and tattoos sat out front sipping craft cocktails.

Helen's eyes lit up. "I think I see a pool table."

"You want to play pool?"

She nodded. She didn't seem happy or excited, more like somebody who just found out she was going to die in thirty days and wanted to do something spontaneous and out of character. *Why not? The end is near.*

"Just don't start a fight while we're in there, OK?"

She smiled. "You never know."

The twentysomethings watched us as we entered and walked toward the pool table. For a moment, they looked suspicious and even confused by our presence, but they didn't say anything. Everything was cool. Perhaps they figured that Helen and I were just being ironic.

Helen dug into her purse. "Here are some quarters. You rack while I get a couple beers."

"I'm starting to get worried about you."

"Don't waste your energy." Helen smirked. "I'm too old to have somebody worry about me. I'm on the cusp of retirement, you know?"

As she went to the bar, I put the quarters in the slots, and the balls released with a crash. I found the plastic rack and placed the balls inside. By the time I was done, she was back with two Metropolis lagers.

She set them down on a tall table. "These were recommended."

I looked at the bartender, a skinny man with a white T-shirt and handlebar mustache. When our eyes met, he smiled and emitted a little laugh. I think he thought we were on a date.

"Are you going to break or what?" she asked.

"Awful sassy, Ms. Vox."

"I've always been sassy, Judge Thompson." She handed me a pool cue and little blue cube of chalk. "Let's get to it."

We played the first game without saying much, but by the second game and after another round of beer, both of us were more relaxed. I told her about my off-the-record conversation with Benji Metina the night before and my conversation with Detective Jarkowski that morning.

In return, Helen told me about giving the police a statement.

I was surprised. "You didn't have an attorney?"

"Why would I need an attorney?" She sank the six, then moved onto the number one. Helen lined up the shot and sent the yellow ball off the far rail and almost into the side pocket. Even though she missed

the shot, she was a much better pool player than I had thought. I wondered what else I didn't know about her.

I took a sip of beer and evaluated where the striped balls were situated on the table. "I think I'd want an attorney, that's all. Sort of a safety blanket." I hit the cue ball into a clump of balls on the side, hoping for some slop. Nothing sank.

"Well," she said, "you haven't had an attorney when you've talked with the detective. So why should I?" She'd gained confidence as the game went on. She bent over the table, pulled back, and knocked another ball into the corner. Then she went for another and sank that as well.

"You're making it look easy."

She looked up at me with a smile. "Nothing is easy." She lined up another shot and gently edged a ball into the side pocket. She was about to hit another when she stopped and looked at me with sad eyes. "Can I ask you a terrible question?"

"Terrible?" I leaned back against the wall. "What do you mean?"

"Forget it." She leaned over, pulled her cue back, and hit a clump of balls in the far corner of the table. Nothing went in.

She sighed, then retreated as I walked up to the table to figure out my best shot. Unlike Helen, I had plenty of balls remaining on the table to choose from. "What is it?" I asked. "Go ahead."

Helen took a sip of beer as she shook her head. "It's going to make me sound awful."

"Awful?" I stopped and looked at her. "What is it?"

"Harry's will," she said. "Have you read it?"

"It's been a while," I said. "I have it, but I haven't read it recently. With the funeral and everything else, it hasn't been a priority."

Helen nodded. "That's fair." She started to say something but stopped. "I just . . . I don't know." She shook her head. "Harry and I had been together for almost ten years." I could see her mind drift away, sorting through the memories. "I know that I wasn't Mary Pat. I

wasn't his wife. I knew going into it that I would never be the love of his life." She looked at the ground. "But since he died, I've just wondered whether, you know, he remembered me or something."

"Like how?"

"I don't know." She pulled out a chair and sat down. "We had plans, you know? We talked about leaving here after retiring, traveling, maybe doing some consulting." She finished her beer. "I guess . . . I told you I never thought of myself as the *other* woman. I thought maybe Harry would show that in some way."

◆ ◆ ◆

By the fourth game, we were pals. I could now see why Harry had fallen for her. Helen's moment of self-pity had passed. She was tough, but you could tell she had heart and a wicked sense of humor.

"Jarkowski wanted me to look at Harry's financials." I was now sitting on one of the nearby stools and slightly intoxicated. "Know anything about that?"

Helen shook her head. "That wasn't really something we talked about. Obviously we weren't married, so paying bills and the mortgage wasn't really something we shared." Helen lined up her next shot. "Any idea where Jarkowski is going with all this?"

"I have no idea." I watched as Helen went on another three-ball run, sinking one after the next. Her game had not deteriorated at all. In fact, I think she was getting better the more she drank. "I think he's just fishing for information because they have no leads."

When she eventually missed, she stepped back, and I walked up to the pool table and began to line up a shot. I hit the cue ball, and I watched as it completely missed the green striped ball where I had been aiming. I bowed my head in shame. I was getting waxed in public by a sixty-three-year-old woman.

"Well"—Helen stepped back up to the table—"Harry wasn't a gambler, played by the rules, and I don't remember him ever even talking about money. It just didn't motivate him. He had a house and a comfortable life. I don't think he cared about getting rich or having more. He loved what he did."

"What about paying for Mary Pat? Jarkowski was wondering how he was paying for that." I thought about the cost of taking care of her at the Walker. "Aren't those places ten or twenty thousand a month?"

"I don't know. I assumed they both had long-term care insurance. Harry once asked if I had some, thought I should get insurance just to be safe."

"The reporter asked about Marsh and the government contracts," I said. "She wondered if that had anything to do with what happened to Harry."

I noticed her body stiffen. "Of course she did." Helen looked at the pool table, then stood up and looked at me. "I'll tell you what I told my boss." Her tone had turned sharp, defiant. "Everything we did was done in the open and followed county procedures. Just ask Metina—I gave her box after box of public requests for proposals, bids, contracts, and evaluations. Marsh and Harry's friendship was no secret, and so the county was especially careful to wall Harry off from the selection process and review. It was all documented and approved."

Helen turned her attention back to the pool table. She bent over, lined up her shot, and knocked the eight hard into the corner pocket, putting me out of my misery. "To spin that into some elaborate conspiracy is crazy."

◆ ◆ ◆

The temperature had dropped another ten degrees, so our pace was faster on the way back to Adams Point. As we got closer, I thought

about Peter Thill and his odd courtroom behavior and vague threats. "Did Harry ever talk about his cases with you?"

"Believe it or not, we tried to avoid talking about specific cases," she said. "But we talked about work. I won't deny that."

"What about death threats?"

"Oh, that." She chuckled. "That's part of the job."

"Anything specific?"

"Not that I can recall," she said. "Jarkowski asked me the same thing, and I told him that I couldn't remember anybody. Harry tried to be tough, like those things didn't affect him. He'd say something like, 'Looks like I have another one after me.' And that would be it."

"Do you think any of his former law clerks would know?"

Helen shrugged. "Maybe."

We arrived at the picnic table where we had met a few hours earlier. I was about to thank Helen for meeting with me and for the conversation when she jumped in first.

"It might be in the journals," Helen said softly, thinking out loud. She looked at me. "Harry kept a journal. Did you know that?"

◆ ◆ ◆

After taking Helen to her car, I walked back to the courthouse. It was late. The courthouse was dark, but my magnetic pass card gave me twenty-four-hour access. I swiped the card, and the door unlocked.

Harry Meyer's chambers was located one floor above mine. He was alive the last time I had been up there. I wasn't sure what I'd find. The investigation was ongoing, and part of me expected to see police tape or at least a sign that directed people to stay out.

When I got to the door, there was nothing. I looked through the window, and the office appeared quiet. The shades were drawn. Everything was normal, as if its occupants merely went home for the day.

All judges were provided an additional master key that opened most of the doors within the courthouse. I took mine out, unlocked the door to Harry's chambers, turned on the lights, and went inside.

The layout of Harry's chambers was the same as mine: an outer area for the law clerk and whatever court reporter had been assigned to work with the judge on a particular day, plus the judge's personal office in the back.

I was surprised at how normal it all looked and felt. Magazines and legal journals were stacked on a small table next to a chair for guests waiting to meet with the judge. A few files were still on his law clerk's desk.

I walked back to Harry's office, turning on the lights. This space was also frozen in time: photographs of Mary Pat hung on the walls; books, trinkets, and awards that Harry had collected over the years were on the shelves; a fresh notepad and pen were placed on the desk as if waiting expectantly for Harry's return.

There wasn't any indication that Harry had been murdered. The violent images of his death that haunted me every night when I tried to go to sleep or surprised me during the day contrasted sharply with the quiet of the room. I felt unease, and I began to have second thoughts. Surely Jarkowski would have already searched Harry's chambers, and I began to feel foolish for being there.

I walked behind Harry's desk and studied his bookshelf, finding nothing but California statutes and old case reporters. I turned and opened his desk drawers, and they were all empty. Their contents had been removed. If the journals had been there, they would have been among the first items placed into evidence.

Suddenly feeling tired, I stepped away from the desk and sat down on a leather couch on the far side of the room. I closed my eyes, put my hands behind my head, and leaned back. I thought about the journals. Harry was a private man. Like the photographs, he wouldn't just have them sitting on a bookshelf for anyone to see. He'd be discreet.

If I were Harry, where would I keep them?

I knew they weren't at his house, and I thought it would be unlikely that Harry would keep them out in the open. They were too personal. If they contained his private thoughts, he wouldn't want them on his shelf. Keeping them in a desk drawer, although more discreet, also didn't feel right.

I opened my eyes, sat up, and looked around the office again. My fingers drummed on a small side table. The table had a lamp and old wooden top—one of Harry's boyhood toys. I fiddled with it while thinking about the journals. Then I spun it, and the blue and red painted lines blurred together until ultimately wobbling to a stop.

I did it again, but this time it was too hard. The top spun to the side, over the edge, and onto the floor. I got off the couch to pick it up, and, while on my knees, I really noticed the end table.

I remembered Harry talking about building it. He was fourteen years old, and he built the end table to earn his woodworking badge for scouts. Harry called it his *Hardy Boys table.* I ran my finger along the side, and I laughed when I felt the string.

I pulled the string, and the front wooden panel of the end table fell open.

Inside there were five of them. Each thick, leather-bound, and filled with Harry's private thoughts, musings, and frustrations. If he was afraid, this was the place where he would write about it. If the kids in those photographs were important, this was likely where I'd learn why.

Thirty years of life.

CHAPTER TWENTY-TWO

Augustus greeted me at the door when I got home that night. He'd been alone while Nikki had been at work and I had been out. He wasn't a happy dog. As I turned on the lights, he ran to the back door, barked, and circled.

"I know." I closed the front door and walked toward him. "I was out too late. Sorry about that, buddy." I unlocked the back door and let Augustus into the yard. As he surveyed the fence, I carried the journals over to our rolltop desk and set them next to the computer.

I went to the kitchen, emptied some ice cubes into a cup, and poured myself a large glass of water. If I was going to be in any condition to work the next day, I needed to rehydrate. I drank half the glass, refilled it, and looked out the back window. Augustus seemed content, so I left him outside and went back to the desk.

At the moment, I was too tired to start reading the journals. I still needed to think through how I'd approach them and take proper notes. I was not, however, too tired to look at Harry's will, even though I'd been procrastinating since getting it from Harry's home office after his funeral. My conversation with Helen had made me curious. It seemed like Harry would have acknowledged her in some way, but I wasn't sure how.

Harry's tax returns and other important documents were in a cardboard box under the desk. I pulled it out and removed the folder containing Harry's will.

No surprises. The main document was just as I had remembered. Harry had appointed me the executor of the estate. Proceeds from his life insurance policy and the sale of the house were put into a trust for Mary Pat, along with the majority of Harry's other assets, like his retirement account, health savings account, and 401k.

I skimmed through it, then turned the page to the addendums.

In most states, including California, there was the ability to designate certain items for family members and friends through a personal addendum. A person could designate a painting over the fireplace to their granddaughter, for instance, because it depicted a lake where the granddaughter learned how to swim. The addendum was intended to be flexible, less formal, and easily changed. Although pictures, furniture, and jewelry were the most common items distributed through such a document, California law didn't restrict the size and nature of what could be given.

I took a sip of water and began to read the two-page addendum. Harry had several money market accounts, and he gave one to the American Association of Juvenile Court Judges. Another he distributed equally to his church, First United Methodist, and the Oakland Nature Conservancy.

The estimated value of these two accounts was not specified, but it wouldn't be hard to figure out. He had listed in the document the name of the financial institutions, account numbers, and even the contact information. I was also confident that the websites, usernames, and passwords were written on the manila folder I had found.

I saw my name as the beneficiary of the third and final money market account. Harry had occasionally hinted at *a little something* for me and Nikki. This was usually when I'd been complaining about student loan debt and our inability to buy a house. Like the other two bequests, Harry had listed the name of the institution, account number, and contact information.

A mix of emotions filled me after I saw my name in his will. Part of me was excited about the possibility of making some small progress toward paying off our debt and, perhaps, taking a little vacation up the coast with Nikki. Then I felt guilty. It just didn't feel right.

I'd trade anything to have Harry back. The ability to make a few extra payments to Fannie Mae came nowhere near filling the void.

I turned the page and read the final provision. I had expected it to give something to Helen, but it didn't. The last designation was a standard designation. It simply directed the executor of the estate to give any and all unwanted personal items and furniture to charity. Underneath, there was a signature block. The blanks were filled in with Harry's illegible, looping handwriting, followed by his signature.

I noted the date.

Harry's personal addendum to his last will and testament was signed two weeks before his murder. I wondered if there had been another one. It seemed likely. Perhaps a previous version included a final gift to Helen, but I'd never know.

◆ ◆ ◆

Augustus barked to come back inside. I got up from the desk and went to the back door, thinking about how and when I was going to break the news to Helen. I wasn't sure whether she was expecting something or whether she merely wanted to be remembered. Beyond the romantic, she and Harry had worked closely together for decades. It seemed like she just wanted acknowledgment.

I opened the door, and Augustus trotted back inside, content and ready for bed. I looked at my watch. It was late, but I wasn't tired anymore.

I went back to the desk and pulled out Harry's manila folder, the one with the websites and passwords. I flipped to the first page of

Harry's personal addendum to his will, the page that listed the three money market accounts.

I read the provision related to me, then looked for the corresponding information on the manila folder. The money market account was held at Pacifica Financial Canyon Bank. I went to PFC's website and typed in the login name and password.

Since the website didn't recognize my computer, a security question popped up. It asked for the place where Harry was born. I looked down at the folder. In the corner, Harry had written *Questions*. Beneath it, he had written *Klaus*, which was his mother's maiden name. Then he had written *Simpson Street*, which was the street where he had grown up. Last, he had written *Sacramento*. I knew that was the place where Harry was born, and I typed in the answer to the security question.

The screen changed to the bank's customer account page. Harry's name was in the upper right corner, along with the last five digits of the account number. Beneath it was a graph, charting the account balance and return on investment over the past ten years, then a list of the five most recent account transactions and the balance.

I read it twice, sure I had misread the number the first time. Then I read it again and realized it was for real. Harry's money market account had a balance of just over $6 million, and now, according to his will, that account was mine.

I leaned back in my chair. Then I looked around to see if somebody was watching me, but I was alone. Not even Augustus cared about what I was doing.

I stared at the screen. I read it again, stunned. This couldn't be right. Harry Meyer wasn't from a rich family. His grandparents were Irish immigrants. His dad worked for the state government as a midlevel accountant. His mom stayed home. And Harry himself was a good lawyer but from a different era.

He and my dad had a general practice on Tenth Street next to a dry cleaner. They took whatever walked in the door. In his day, there wasn't

specialization. There weren't seven-figure class-action settlements, and lawyers didn't charge $600 per hour. He made a decent living, but not much more. Then Harry became a judge, and he was comfortable but never rich.

I reached into the cardboard box and pulled out Harry's most recent tax return. I looked at the first page, and I knew right away that none of the money deposited into the PFC money market account had been declared. His income was too low. His taxes only reflected his judicial salary.

I flipped through the remaining pages. There was nothing in his tax return addendums and attachments that indicated that Harry had a lucrative side business, rental properties, or investment income. I put his tax return back in the box, then turned to the computer.

The account page was still up. I clicked on the transaction history. Every month showed electronic deposits ranging from $10,000 to $60,000. There were also periodic withdrawals, but the amounts taken out were relatively small.

I clicked on each one to get further detail, but nothing useful came up. I saw only a routing number for the deposits—no name, source, or reason given for the electronic fund transfers. And apparently the bank had issued cashier's checks for withdrawals. Names for the checks' recipients weren't available online.

I stopped.

Whatever was going on, it was certainly unethical and likely illegal. Given the timing and a complete lack of any explanation, it also looked like I was involved. If there was a scheme, it appeared as though I was in deep. Maybe Harry wasn't as concerned about his legacy as I thought. Maybe he wanted me to become a judge simply to continue whatever scheme he'd orchestrated, or maybe he hadn't orchestrated any scheme. Besides the money, I didn't have any proof of that.

I looked over at the stack of journals piled on the corner of the desk. Maybe they contained the answer.

Harry, what the hell were you up to?

CHAPTER TWENTY-THREE

In the morning, I should have waited a few hours for Nikki to get home from her overnight shift. Then I should have told her everything. I should have shown her the will, as well as the journals, and revealed our new millionaire status.

But I didn't.

I got out of bed, showered, shaved, and got ready for the day. I wasn't, however, going straight to work. I grabbed two of Harry's journals, which I'd read if I had time after the morning hearings. Then I took a copy of the will, and I put everything in my briefcase.

Checking my watch, I figured that I had just enough time to drive to the PFC branch office on Foothill Boulevard.

◆ ◆ ◆

When I arrived, the bank had just opened—no lines. Smiling, I walked up to the counter with my paperwork and explained that I was the executor of Harry Meyer's estate. I told the clerk I had questions about some specific transactions.

According to the name tag, her name was Barb and she'd worked at PFC for three years. "That's something my manager can help you with,"

she said. "Let me get your name and account number. Then have a seat over there." Barb pointed to a small alcove with a row of wooden chairs, a table filled with magazines, and a large fish tank.

I checked my watch again, wondering how long I'd have to wait. I was due in court in an hour.

Ten minutes later, the manager came out to see me. He was friendly and eager to help. Either he was highly caffeinated or had looked up the account and seen Harry's balance.

"Mr. Thompson." He held out his hand. "Nice to meet you. Judge Meyer was an excellent customer, and I'd be happy to help you with any questions related to his account."

He led me back to his small office, where he sat behind his desk and pointed to the seat across from him. "So what can I do for you?"

"Well"—I sat—"I was reviewing the account information last night, and it appears that Harry withdrew money by asking for the bank to issue a cashier's check."

The manager typed some information into his computer and soon confirmed what I was saying. "You're correct."

"I couldn't tell online who the cashier's check was issued to," I said. "Like who got that money?"

"Let's take a look." He fiddled with the computer's mouse. "Well"—he raised his eyebrow—"looks like he issued all of those checks to himself."

"Himself?"

The manager nodded. "That's correct."

"Why would he do that?"

"I don't know." He looked at his computer screen again, confirming that the recipients of all the checks were the same. "Perhaps he was cashing them someplace else or depositing them into a different account at a different bank." He turned his attention back to me. "It's unusual, but it's his money." Like a good banker, he knew it wasn't his job to be curious. "Do you need any other information?"

"Yes," I said. "It looks like he gets large electronic deposits each month from the same person or place, and I was wondering who was sending Harry the money."

Since I hadn't asked him to close the account, the manager was still eager to please. "I can find that out for you." He seemed to type and click forever. "OK," he eventually said. "Looks like the deposits are being made by something called Red Rock ABC-5555 LLC." He wrote the name down on a sheet of paper. "Some sort of company."

He handed me the piece of paper. "I hope that's helpful."

"It is," I said. "Thank you."

◆ ◆ ◆

I was undeniably late, by any definition of the term. Even though I wanted to research Red Rock ABC-5555, whatever that was, and see if it was mentioned in Harry's journals, people were waiting. I texted Karen as I stepped into the elevator on the ground floor, and she was there when the doors slid open on the third floor. She greeted me and led me through a side door, and then down the narrow hallway behind the courtrooms. Karen had my robe hanging on a coatrack, ready.

"Thank you." I zipped up my robe and took a deep breath, orienting myself. "What am I looking at?"

Karen handed me a ten-page printout of the morning's cases. "Twenty lines," she said. "Including the Tanya Neal and Peter Thill case."

I rolled my eyes. "Wonderful."

"And that reporter you love is sitting in the back. Benji Metina has been waiting all morning. She wants to talk with you when you're done."

"Any other good news?"

"Nope," she said. "Just those two things."

"Is everybody in the courtroom?"

She nodded. "I figured you'd want to call Tanya Neal and Peter Thill first."

"Correct," I said. "Let's get them done and out of here. And if there's a lull in the calendar, can you order me a sandwich for lunch?"

"A Reuben?"

I smiled. "You know me."

◆ ◆ ◆

Everyone stood as I entered. I gestured for them to sit down and took my seat. The tables in the courtroom were less crowded than last time, because the two eldest children, Neisha and Kayla, were still on the run. The younger ones, Bobby and Damien, were there, as well as the lawyers, social worker, and guardian ad litem. Peter Thill sat at the very end, next to Bob Finley. They each stood, one after the other, and stated their names for the record.

"As you all know, we're here for a pretrial hearing," I said, starting easy. I looked at Tanya Neal's attorney, Sophia Delgado. "What is the status, Ms. Delgado?"

She stood. I couldn't help noticing that Delgado's nails were now painted a bright aqua color. "Your Honor," she said. "I still have not heard from my client, Tanya Neal. This is concerning." Delgado looked at the county attorney, Sylvia Norgaard, then back at me. "Once again, I know that ordinarily you'd find my client in default and terminate her parental rights today. And once again, I'm begging for the court's indulgence. My understanding is that this case is otherwise unresolved and that Mr. Thill will be seeking a trial date. I ask that you simply set the trial date, and if my client does not show up, then certainly it would be appropriate to terminate her rights at that time. The state is not prejudiced at all by this delay."

"Thank you, Ms. Delgado," I said. "That is my intention if the case does not resolve." As Ms. Delgado sat down, Bob Finley stood. "Mr. Finley," I continued. "It sounds like we're going to trial."

Finley nodded. "That's correct." Annoyed, he looked at Peter Thill. "My client is not ready to agree at this point."

"Very well." I looked at Karen. "Court date?"

Karen announced the court date she had negotiated with the parties before the hearing. The trial would start next week.

"Any outstanding discovery issues?" I asked.

Both Delgado and Finley agreed that they had all the documents, exhibit lists, and witness lists they needed for trial.

"Anything else?"

"There is, Your Honor." It was now Sylvia Norgaard's turn. I knew this was when the hearing was likely to blow up, and so did Metina. I saw her sitting in the gallery, scribbling into her little reporter's notebook. As Norgaard began to speak, Metina leaned forward in order to hear better.

"As you know, Neisha and Kayla ran during our last hearing. The county believes that they are in contact with their father." Norgaard paused and looked at Peter Thill like a mother shaming a child. "There was a recent picture of all three of them posted on Facebook. I'd like this court to place Mr. Thill under oath and question him regarding the location of his daughters. If he's uncooperative, I'd like him to be found in contempt and placed in jail."

Finley was on his feet before Norgaard had finished. "I object to this. No crime has been committed. I haven't seen this purported Facebook post, and even if he did post a picture of him and his daughters, maybe it's an old picture. What's to say it wasn't taken a year ago?"

"Because your client was in prison a year ago." Norgaard shook as she spoke. I'd never seen her this angry. "As for a crime, how about kidnapping? The county currently has both physical and legal custody of these girls. He has no right to any contact with Neisha and Kayla without the agency's permission."

Finley put his hand on Thill's shoulder. His grip tightened, keeping his client down. "Your Honor, this is highly unusual."

I raised my hands, cutting off the bickering. In the movies, a judge needed to pound a gavel to restore order, but in real life a simple hand gesture was quicker and easier. "Mr. Thill." I spoke in almost a whisper. "I don't want to put you in jail for contempt of court. I don't want to do that. But what I am saying is that you can no longer have any visitation with any of your children, supervised or unsupervised, until Neisha and Kayla are found."

I looked at Damien and little Bobby. Their eyes were wide, confused. "It's OK, boys," I said. "I'm not mad. I'm just going to move on to my other cases that I have scheduled for this morning." I turned to the others. "You all can go into one of the conference rooms and meet, and then I'll recall this matter when you're ready. Hopefully, Mr. Finley can talk with his client and his client can assist the county in locating his daughters."

I looked at Thill. "If sufficient progress is made, I'm not going to put you under oath, and everybody can go home. If you refuse to help, we'll see where that goes. Your attorney can advise you as to the risks."

Thill slammed his hand down on the table. "This is bull—"

"That's enough." I was direct but didn't raise my voice. "Mr. Thill, I'm going to pretend I didn't hear that."

◆ ◆ ◆

I worked through the remainder of the calendar. Two hours later, I recalled Thill and the rest of the parties into court. When they'd settled into their seats, I turned to Ms. Norgaard. "How are things going?"

She stood. "I think they are going pretty well, Your Honor. Mr. Thill contacted his daughters via Facebook, direct message. He then received a cell phone call from Neisha. He explained the situation, including his predicament. He then allowed the social worker to talk with them. Neisha would not provide her address, but she promised to meet the

social worker at a McDonald's tomorrow morning. Neisha also promised that Kayla would come with her."

I nodded, then looked at Thill. "That's progress. I appreciate that, Mr. Thill. I know that must've been hard, but it's the right thing to do." I looked at Damien and Bobby, then back at Peter Thill. "So I am not going to take any action. I want to see how things go tomorrow. In the meantime, however, I prohibit any direct or supervised visitation. That will continue until I issue a formal written order stating that it is allowed, even if Neisha and Kayla are back."

Peter Thill nodded, seemingly accepting the court's position. "Can I at least hug my boys goodbye?"

I'd never received a request like that, and I wasn't sure how to respond. I looked at Sylvia Norgaard for guidance, and she looked as surprised as I was. Then I looked at the guardian ad litem, Cherelle Williams. Williams also didn't have an opinion.

"That's fine," I said.

Thill got up and walked over to Damien and gave him a hug, patting him on the back. Then he did the same for little Bobby, except, when Thill was done with the hug, he shook Bobby's hand.

CHAPTER TWENTY-FOUR

Benji Metina was waiting for me in the hallway. I didn't want to spend my lunch break talking with her. I wanted to spend my time reading Harry's journals and figuring out how I had suddenly become a millionaire with the help of some obscure corporation that I'd never heard of.

She asked, "Did you see my article this morning?"

"No." I unlocked the door, and we both went inside. "Anything interesting?"

"I think it's pretty interesting," she said. "Front page, above the fold. Our website has gotten a lot of hits on it, too."

"Well, congratulations." I tried to keep it friendly. "Let me know when you win the Pulitzer, and I'll buy you a cup of coffee."

I was happy to see that my sandwich and chips from Ike's Place had already been delivered. I picked the bag up off Karen's desk, and we went back to my chambers, where I shut the door behind us.

"Please have a seat." I pointed at the chair and sat down behind my desk. "What did you want to talk to me about?" I opened the bag and took a few quick bites of my sandwich.

"This weekend I'm running a story about the relationship between Judge Meyer, Helen Vox, and Marshall Terry."

"Whether directly or indirectly, you pretty much told me that during our last conversation." I opened my bag of chips and offered them to Metina. "Help yourself."

She shook her head. "No thank you." She stayed focused. "I was wondering if you'd looked into it any further." Metina paused, allowing me to take another few bites of my sandwich. "Maybe now you'd like to give me your reaction on the record?"

"Please don't take offense," I said, "but I don't have anything to say." I clarified that we were off the record. "I talked to Helen Vox about it, and she said the county's given you everything they have about AFC Services and that they complied with all of the county rules and disclosure requirements. I asked Jarkowski about Marsh Terry and whether he could be involved in Harry's murder, and Jarkowski was, to put it mildly, very skeptical."

Since it was clear that I wasn't going to cooperate right away, Metina decided she'd try to educate me. "I have people who are willing to be quoted as saying that they complied with the letter of the law, but not the spirit," she said. "That the three of them colluded to manipulate the process. The first payments were part of multiple pilot programs. Marshall Terry created four different subsidiaries of AFC Services Inc. The amounts paid to each were just under the trigger that would've required a formal request for proposals. So they got going. Once they were established and Marshall Terry had relationships with the county, formal requests for proposal were issued and he was awarded even more lucrative contracts."

"But other people had an opportunity."

"Sort of," Metina said. "The criteria seemed pretty rigged to me, because the evaluators gave significant weight to applicants who have *demonstrated* experience and knowledge in the area of child protection proceedings."

"I don't think that sounds too out of line," I said.

"Even though the chair of the evaluation committee has been Helen Vox?"

I knew she was right, but I wasn't going to admit it. And, after learning about a money market account with a $6 million balance, I

wondered if Metina knew that it might be more than just friends helping friends. "So your theory is that Judge Meyer's girlfriend steered tax money to Judge Meyer's friend."

Metina nodded. "Pretty much. In addition to the fact that Judge Meyer presided over hearings and cases in which Helen Vox represented the county, which is such an obvious conflict of interest that I don't even need an expert opinion, and she's supervising the attorneys who appeared in front of Judge Meyer as well."

"You told me earlier that the contracts were worth millions, but I assume you have something more specific?"

"Well, that's hard to figure out." Metina was proud of her work, and she didn't mind showing off her knowledge. "There are about five hundred million dollars in community contracts. I know that Marshall Terry initially received three two-million-dollar contracts out of that fund and that in the last five years the contract amount has more than doubled to five million." Metina leaned forward. "I also know that Marshall Terry's company became a direct service provider. That's where you provide direct services to people receiving their health care through the county or on public assistance. That isn't a formal grant. There's no request for proposals. Once he became an in-network county provider, people could just come to him, but often it was a requirement of the court-approved case plan. If parents wanted to get their kids back and get the kids out of foster care, then Judge Meyer was ordering them to go to a Marshall Terry company to get the parenting evaluation or coaching that the plan required."

"Judges don't write the case plans," I said. "The social workers write the case plans."

"True." Metina shrugged. "But Helen Vox trains the social workers. She is the one who tells them what is legally required to be included in the case plan, and then Judge Meyer adopts the plan and makes it a requirement."

"And so what do you want me to say?"

"I want you to comment on it," Metina said. "I want to give you a chance to condemn it. As far as I can tell, this was all before your time. You can get on the right side of this story, maybe repair your reputation."

"I don't know. How long do I have until the story runs?"

Metina stood. "Probably going to do it this weekend. The editors published the story with all the statistics and outcome data today, so they'll probably want to publish the sexy stuff on Sunday when the circulation is higher. The affair between a judge and a prosecutor is going to be big news. The fact that Judge Meyer was murdered and there still haven't been any arrests makes it even bigger news."

"I'll think about going on the record and giving you a quote," I said. "I promise."

◆ ◆ ◆

After Benji Metina left, Karen stuck her head into my office. "You have about five minutes, Judge." She looked at my half-eaten sandwich. "I'm sorry you don't have longer, but we've got a full afternoon calendar."

"I understand."

Karen turned and left, and I looked at the journals that I'd brought from home. They were still untouched. Even though I was tempted to feign illness and cancel the afternoon, I knew I couldn't do that. The journals would have to wait for tonight, but I did have a few minutes to do some research.

I took two large bites of my sandwich, then pushed it aside. I pulled the PFC bank manager's sheet of paper from my pocket and typed the company name, Red Rock ABC-5555, into Google. Thousands of websites came up, ranging from radio stations to day care centers, but none of them were applicable.

"Red Rock" was too general, and if I was going to find it, I needed to be more precise. Since it was a corporation, I decided that I'd try the

California secretary of state's website. I typed the name into its search engine, but there were no listings for Red Rock ABC-5555.

Then I decided to do a national search. There were hundreds of websites available, each offering to query every government database for a small fee and return instant results. I picked one, logged on, and entered my credit card information.

After activating the account, I typed in the corporation's name and clicked the search button. The screen flashed, and information about Red Rock ABC-5555 filled the space.

It was incorporated in Florida a little over ten years ago, around the time that Mary Pat was placed in assisted living at the Walker and Marshall Terry got into the child protection business. Its president was Hector Benetiz, Esq., and the corporate secretary was Christine Benetiz, Esq. The corporation's address was a post office box in Miami.

I googled their names and got the website for Benetiz Law, which stated that the law firm was an affiliate of Morneau and Kapper LLC and openly touted its status as part of the *offshore magic circle*. The *magic circle* referred to its specialty in corporate finance and international banking. Morneau and Kapper had offices in Bermuda and the Cayman Islands, as well as alternate offices in the British Virgin Islands and Mauritius.

I thought about Benji Metina's story. She was going to write about cronyism, but, the way I saw it, the story was much bigger. If the money from Red Rock ABC-5555 was, in fact, from Marshall Terry to Judge Meyer in exchange for help securing government contracts, it wasn't cronyism. It was straight corruption.

When she had originally asked me if her stories had something to do with Harry's death, it seemed far-fetched, but now it didn't seem like such a big leap to go from corruption to murder. Especially if a person didn't want to go to prison.

The problem was that I was standing right in the middle of the storm.

CHAPTER TWENTY-FIVE

That night I sat on the couch reading Harry's journals. Nikki could tell I wasn't in the mood to talk, so she kept her distance after dinner. I think she thought I was upset about the new Benji Metina article that had appeared in the newspaper that morning. I still hadn't read it, but I'd rather Nikki think that I was depressed about that rather than know that my mentor was likely a criminal and I now had full control over a bank account filled with dirty money.

I didn't know what to do or say, so I lost myself in Harry's journals. Even though I hoped that they would contain the answer—at least something that I could take to Jarkowski to put everything behind me—there were no obvious revelations. No mention of secret bank accounts, Florida corporations, or other women. The person in the journals was the person I loved. The entries were clear and logical, and never afraid of being intellectual.

It was as if I had my old friend back.

In the beginning, everything was new to him. Harry was a voyeur. Those who circulated through the child protection system were outliers, unfamiliar. They fascinated him, but there wasn't much sympathy. They were animals in a zoo.

Harry's analysis of cases was simple at first. He made his observations, drew his conclusions, and then he was done. Quick to terminate

a parent's rights, Harry washed his hands of the decision and moved on to the next case. But as time went on, he began to see the nuance. The cases became more complicated, because he became more aware of the competing interests and contradictions.

He watched as the children left behind lingered in foster care with an attachment to nothing. Most bounced among ten to fifteen foster homes, some more as their behavior deteriorated. As the years passed, children became teenagers. There was no adoption, no happy ending, no Daddy Warbucks hugging Little Orphan Annie with fireworks in the background.

Harry wrote:

> In my first ten years, my law clerk has calculated that I have terminated the parental rights related to a thousand children. Most of the children's lives are arguably better off, not under the constant threat of violence or the grind of neglect. But I have not seen a rich family come into my courtroom, nor have I seen but a few middle-class families. The ones that sit down at the tables in front of me are poor, low functioning, and mostly some shade of brown. While addiction and mental illness are the threads that run through them all, certainly there are many wealthy people who suffer the same addictions and ailments. Yet I don't see them here in court. There is no movement to remove the children from the home of an attorney addicted to cocaine, a doctor who is an alcoholic, or a stay-at-home mother in the suburbs who is bipolar. Why is that? And if one concludes that those in my court are not all psychopaths, which I don't believe they all are (some, for certain, but not all), then what is going on?

> When reflecting upon my experience and looking at that experience through the lens of history, it is clear that the modern child protection system is merely a kinder and gentler modification of early government efforts to sterilize and eradicate the poor and undesirable. The modern child protection system arises out of the ashes of the 1920s eugenics movement. California was a leader in sterilizing the poor, retarded, and habitual criminals. I don't think it is a coincidence that as court-ordered sterilization waned, the child protection systems waxed. When government-sponsored sterilization programs were finally eliminated by federal regulations in 1978, Congress passed comprehensive laws related to the termination of parental rights and adoption procedures the same year. So now we don't sterilize these individuals, nor do we provide family planning services or access to birth control. Instead, we allow them to have children and then take them away, sometimes at the hospital immediately upon birth, but most often after years of abuse and neglect. Certainly, there has to be a better way.

The entries that followed reflected Harry's struggle to find that better way. He sought a balance as the pendulum swung from one extreme to the other, as social workers were accused of being *too lax* and then *too aggressive*. Often they were accused of being both, simultaneously. Whether true or not, it didn't matter. Both narratives fed into the conventional wisdom that all government agencies were incompetent and provided a justification for the reduction of funding.

As I turned the final page of the last journal, I thought about Benji Metina's newest article in the *San Francisco Chronicle* and the one she was going to be writing about Harry Meyer, Helen Vox, and Marshall

Terry. Metina was laying the groundwork for the governor's new task force. It was clear she had an agenda, a point to be made. The pendulum was swinging again. But this time it was coming through me.

◆ ◆ ◆

"You coming to bed tonight?" Nikki stood in the doorway. She wore one of my old Smiths concert T-shirts as a nightgown, revealing a considerable amount of leg.

"Be there soon."

I looked at the stack of journals, then at the four photographs I'd found. As I was reading the journal, all the entries had started to blur together, different variations of tragic. Not only had I not found any mention of corruption, I hadn't made any progress identifying the children in the photographs.

"So the real answer," Nikki said, "is that you're going to be up all night, reading sad stories."

"Not all night." I was a little too defensive. "I'm just going to go back and read the journal entries written at about the same time these kids would have been in the system." I looked at the photo of the three older kids holding the baby. "Has to be a reason Harry kept this."

Nikki nodded slowly. She'd heard it all before. "Well"—she turned away—"if you change your mind, you know where I'll be." With one smooth movement, the T-shirt came off, revealing a beautiful back. Her hand balled up the T-shirt and, without looking, she tossed it behind her as she walked toward the bedroom. "Our baby ain't gonna make itself, you know."

The T-shirt landed in my lap, and Augustus whimpered at me. The dog cocked his head, wondering what I was doing. He was right. *What was I doing?*

It was time to call it a night. Even a dog knew that a baby couldn't make itself.

◆ ◆ ◆

I was awake early the next morning. Nikki was still asleep in the Smiths T-shirt. I should've pecked her on the cheek as I crawled quietly out of bed, but I didn't want to wake her.

I returned to the living room after getting the coffee maker going in the kitchen. It felt a little like cheating on her, but I couldn't stop myself, and for that, I felt guilty. I should've been sleeping in with my wife. Instead I was drawn back to the journals, convinced they contained clues that nobody else could find.

The first pass through them was only a test. Now I needed to really study them.

Perhaps the pictures found in Harry's office were the secret. If only I could figure out who they were and why Harry had kept them hidden in a book, I'd understand. Harry would, in short, be restored to sainthood.

Google helped me date the T-shirt the older boy in the photograph wore. It was from one of the many superhero reboots, mid to late 1990s. A few minutes later, I'd located the journal that contained entries from the appropriate time period. Then I began skimming these entries for any case related to three kids and an infant.

When that didn't work, I expanded the scope of my search to journal entries related to any child that fit the description of any of the kids in the photograph, but each time I was unsuccessful. Just when I thought I was getting close, the ages, genders, or race didn't match the other children in the family.

Luckily, during my morning commute from home to the courthouse, I figured out a better way.

CHAPTER TWENTY-SIX

When I arrived, Karen was plugging away on some orders that were due in a few days. "Morning," I said, stopping at her desk. "Can I talk to you for a second about a new project?"

She stopped typing. "A project?" She found a notepad and picked up a pen.

"It's kind of a big, boring one," I said. "Sort of a research project."

She looked skeptical. "Like for a law review article?"

"Sure," I said, trying to come up with a plausible story. "Maybe a law review article or maybe just a personal remembrance of Judge Meyer for the bar association's magazine."

"OK." Karen nodded, pen at the ready. "What is it?"

"I want you to make a list of all of Harry Meyer's cases that he handled during the 1990s."

"All of them?" She didn't look too excited about the job.

"All of them," I repeated. "I want a spreadsheet: name of the case, case file number, and then all the kids involved, including their names and ages."

Karen squinted and pursed her lips, silently running some sort of calculation. When the math was completed, she said, "That's going to be like twenty-five hundred families, maybe more."

"I know." I took a long pause. I wasn't used to abusing my power, although I'd certainly seen other judges do it. "It's important. Talk to the tech folks. Maybe they can do something electronically. They run reports like this all the time."

"What's your time frame?"

"As soon as possible." I turned to walk to my desk. "Thank you, Karen."

I logged on to my computer to get a sense of how my day was going to go. At that moment, I felt pretty good. Surely my day would go much smoother than yesterday.

Unfortunately, my prediction was wrong.

My inbox was filled with over twenty e-mails, all marked urgent. The subject lines contained just one word: Thill. I held my breath as I clicked the first one, from the county social worker:

> I wanted to provide an update to the parties related to the status of the two older girls. They came to the McDonald's as promised. They are now back with their foster families. Unfortunately, the youngest boy, Bobby, stole his foster parent's car last night. He was stopped on the freeway. Although Mr. Thill has no permanent address, he had been staying at a house somewhere near Modesto. In Bobby's pocket there was a piece of paper with that address. I believe Bobby got that note from his father at the pretrial hearing and Bobby was trying to drive to Modesto.

It was that weird handshake at the end of the hearing, I thought as I clicked through the other e-mails, *that's when he passed the note.* I heard a knock on my door.

"What is it?" I asked, still scrolling through the e-mails.

Karen kept at a distance, choosing to remain in the doorway. "You got a call from that reporter."

"Benji Metina?"

"On hold right now." Karen glanced back at her phone as the other lines began to ring. "She says they picked up one of our kids on 580?"

"Yep, I know." I sank lower in my chair, but somehow my stomach sank even lower.

"She says the kid driving the car was eight years old."

"That's right."

"One of Tanya Neal and Peter Thill's kids."

"Correct."

"Do you want to talk to her?"

I closed my eyes, trying to avoid thinking about the next wave of public humiliation. "Refer her to the district's media guy," I said. "We don't comment on pending cases."

"OK," Karen said.

"No, don't," I said, my eyes still closed. "I'll pick up. I'll talk to her. What line?" I opened my eyes. Karen looked at me with such sympathy that I now felt incredibly guilty for forcing her to create a gigantic electronic spreadsheet based on a wild theory premised on four old photographs.

Karen nodded, ever polite. "On line one."

She turned and left, closing the door behind her as I picked up the phone. "Benji Metina," I said, trying hard not to sound ashamed and incompetent. "News travels fast."

"Especially this news," she said. "I need to post the story before everybody beats me to it."

"I thought we had a truce," I said. "I thought you were going to cut me a little slack while I weighed whether or not to give you a full interview and comment on how Alameda County does or does not choose appropriate people to provide services for families in the child protection system."

"This Thill guy sort of ruined that for you, Judge," Metina said. "I'm sorry about that. It illustrates how overwhelmed the system is and how unable it is to do its job." She paused. "Do you want to comment on this situation?"

"It's a pending case," I said. "You know I can't."

"OK," she said. "Then things are just going to fall where they fall, nothing personal."

◆ ◆ ◆

Metina posted an electronic version of her article at noon, and, as expected, the story broke the Internet. It was posted, reposted, shared, and tweeted. Although the article was brief and damning, the video was what everybody wanted to see. The whole thing was captured by a series of traffic cameras courtesy of the California Department of Transportation.

Although there were wars in the Middle East, rogue nations with nuclear weapons, and domestic and global economic problems, people had an insatiable appetite for a video of an eight-year-old driving a car and being slowly chased by a half dozen police cruisers. It was like an elementary school reenactment of O.J. Simpson's ill-fated escape in his white Bronco.

Only in America.

Chief Judge Karls summoned me to a meeting that afternoon. The moment I arrived, I knew it wasn't going to be good. It wasn't just Chief Karls. It was Nancy Johns and the entire executive committee. This included the assistant chief judge, the presiding judge of the civil division, the presiding judge of the criminal division, and the head of family and specialty courts.

"Judge Thompson." Chief Karls stood and pointed at an empty chair. "Please have a seat."

I nodded and tried to project calm as I walked to the empty chair and sat. All eyes were on me. The faces of the people assembled were somber, almost pitying. Clearly there had been a premeeting I wasn't invited to, and now I was here to simply learn my fate.

Chief Karls flipped through his notepad, and I waited. I suspected that at some point he was going to press a hidden button and an opening would appear in the floor beneath me. I would fall into a dark pit beneath the courthouse, never to be heard from again.

"Judge Meyer's passing has been very hard," he said. "And everyone here is sympathetic to your situation, but I got a call from the governor this afternoon as well as our chief justice. They are very concerned about the situation. The governor wants to see some action, doesn't care what. The chief justice is more supportive, but she's worried about the legislature. It's a budget year. The courts have many new initiatives, including a pay raise for all of us. She's concerned about how all this negative publicity is going to impact our budget proposal."

I stared at him, trying to read between the lines. "You're saying that if judges don't get a raise, it's going to be my fault?"

Chief Karls started to respond but stopped himself and decided to try a different approach. "I'm merely telling you what's happening, Jim. I'm also getting all sorts of phone calls and e-mails from people all over the world, wanting you fired."

"How is it my fault that this kid stole a car?"

"You're the judge, Jim. Everything is your fault."

The assistant chief, Tracy Fink, decided to chime in. "We have a situation where a boy died after you returned him home to his mother. Now we have a kid on a freeway, and I'm told there is going to be another, longer article posted shortly about how you're showing up late for hearings, and that the older sisters ran from foster care during court, right from under your nose, and you didn't do anything about it."

"That's not entirely true." I tried to defend myself, but a growl from the other side of the table interrupted me.

Judge F. Michael Christiansen folded his arms across his chest. "Why don't you just get these kids adopted by a good family?" His bald head and crooked teeth gave him the appearance of an angry Muppet. Judge Christiansen was the presiding judge of the district's civil division. He was obviously irritated that he had to be present for the meeting. I'd never really spoken to him, since he considered any judge who was not handling multimillion-dollar class actions to be below him in the hierarchy. The civil division was first. Criminal felonies was second. Criminal misdemeanors and gross misdemeanors were third. Family was fourth, and anything having to do with juveniles or children was last. Judge Christiansen was often heard saying, "We are not social workers. We are judges." And, clearly, I was not only a social worker; I was a bad social worker, too.

"There are rules and statutes I must follow, Judge Christiansen." I tried not to sound patronizing, but it was difficult. "Parents have due-process rights. Children have rights. There is a statutory procedure that I need to follow."

Judge Christiansen rolled his eyes. He started to respond, but Chief Karls interrupted. "Let's stay focused, shall we?"

The others around the table nodded in agreement. There was nothing uglier than a judge fight.

"We need to start cleaning some of these matters up," Judge Karls continued. "Nancy has an update related to your former law clerk." He looked over at Nancy Johns.

"Yes, Chief," she said. "We've made an offer to his attorney to resolve the matter for ten thousand dollars. That's much less than it would cost to fight in court, and the benefit is that Billy Pratt would be required to sign a confidentiality agreement. He would have to stop speaking to the press."

The mention of my former law clerk was a surprise. I hadn't really thought about Billy since Metina published her first article. I figured

he'd nicknamed me "The Kitten," given her a few quotes, and was done punishing me for letting him go. "Do you think he'll accept the offer?"

"The Executive Team authorized me to go up to twenty thousand dollars, if necessary." Nancy hated to spend the district's money on such things. It was evident by the look on her face, but Harry and I had put the district in a difficult position. "I'm confident he'll settle," she said. "An eviction notice was recently filed by his landlord. He needs the money."

"I don't see how we can enforce the confidentiality clause."

"I've thought about that." Nancy smiled. "He needs a new job, and that job is going to check his references. Part of the agreement is that you and the district merely confirm his dates of employment and salary. We make no comment regarding his performance or reasons for our separation."

"I guess I'm not following."

She leaned forward. "Billy Pratt, more than anything, needs a job. That settlement money is only going to last a limited period of time. If he breaks the agreement, then perhaps we are also not bound by the confidentiality clause."

I had my doubts, because it'd be foolish to disagree with Nancy Johns. My guess was that Billy Pratt would also know not to cross her. "When will you know?"

"His lawyer will get back to me in the next few days," she said. "It will hopefully be resolved soon."

Sensing the conclusion of that agenda item, Judge Karls cleared his throat and moved on to the next item of business. "As it relates to you, Judge Thompson." He put both of his hands on the conference table, as if bracing himself for impact. "I would like you to take a vacation for today, and maybe tomorrow as well. Stay away. Let this stuff die down."

"What if it doesn't?"

"It will."

"What if I don't want to?"

This time Chief Karls ignored my question. He wasn't going to engage in a back-and-forth. "I'm going to tell the governor and the chief justice that you are no longer assigned to the child dependency division. You are no longer going to handle cases involving children or juveniles." He took a heavy breath, the burden of leadership. "We had talked about this previously, Jim. I informed you of the possibility, and now it seems like the best course of action. The public wants to see that we are taking these criticisms seriously, and this will objectively show them that we are doing just that."

"What about my cases? I have motions pending and trials scheduled."

Chief Karls stayed calm. "Perhaps you should be quiet and listen now." He nodded, then continued. "I'm putting you on the criminal team, misdemeanors and gross misdemeanors, since that was your background before coming onto the court. But that, however, requires you to retain some cases so as not to disrupt or compromise the well-being of the children on your—"

"Nobody wants to do this job," I said. "Nobody understands it, and when they do, they're not going to come."

"They will go where I say." Chief Karls looked me in the eye and held it. "*You* will go where I say." He wasn't going to be pushed around.

"There are deadlines," I said. "With Harry gone and now me, there won't be anybody. We need two judges, not just one."

Chief Karls looked at Nancy Johns. "Let us worry about that," he said. "Although this announcement is being made and it is effective immediately, Ms. Johns will work with you to make sure the transition is smooth."

"I'm confused."

"Well," Chief Karls said, "since you obviously cannot understand anything remotely subtle, let me state it this way, and it is not to be repeated: I am announcing that you are assigned to the criminal division, effective immediately. But you know and I know, that is not

possible. When you return to the courthouse, you will handle a few nominal criminal calendars, but you will continue your current caseload until we find a permanent replacement."

"So the move isn't really effective immediately. You're just saying that?"

Chief Karls's face was a stone. "It depends on your definition of *immediate*. If you have questions, meet with Nancy. You two will figure it out."

It was clear that the conversation was over, and I was now on vacation just like Helen Vox.

CHAPTER TWENTY-SEVEN

When I got back to my chambers, Karen was talking to one of the tech guys and pointing at her computer screen. I'm sure I'd learned the tech guy's name at some point, but I couldn't remember. "Hello, Judge," Karen said. "We're talking about all that data you wanted about Judge Meyer's old cases."

The tech guy looked at me. "Big ask." Then he looked at the computer screen. "What do you need it for, anyway?"

Since I didn't want to tell him I was conducting my own murder investigation, I continued the lie that I had told Karen. "I'm writing a law review article. This is part of the research."

The tech guy nodded, as if it was perfectly normal, and then went back to fiddling with Karen's spreadsheet. I started to walk away but decided I better tell Karen what had happened before she heard the gossip.

"I don't mean to interrupt, Karen, but if I could talk to you for a moment, I'd appreciate it."

◆ ◆ ◆

"I just got out of a meeting with Chief Karls and the whole executive team," I said. "They're taking us out of child protection and putting us into criminal. It's more of a public relations move." I shrugged. "Not really sure what I think about it, actually."

Karen didn't say anything. I could tell the information took her by surprise, and she took a moment to comprehend that her job duties were going to change. Social workers would be replaced by probation officers. Foster care would be replaced by jail. "When?"

"They say it's immediate." I shook my head. "But that isn't possible. The truth is that I'm going to keep doing what I'm doing until they identify a replacement. If anybody asks, they're just going to say that I'm *finishing up* cases and that they were trying to *minimize the disruption to families*. It's just spin."

"So what do we do now?"

"Well," I said, "they say I'm on vacation for a few days. So talk to assignment and see what they want to do with my calendars. My guess is that they just want to keep me hidden, but I can do orders and handle administrative stuff. Officially, however, I'm not here."

"And the spreadsheet?"

"I still want it done as soon as possible." Even after discovering that Harry and Marsh and even Helen were likely doing something improper, I wasn't convinced that any of them would kill each other over it. Their histories and friendships were too deep, and, if Harry's murder wasn't connected to Marsh or Helen, then the kids in those photographs seemed to be one of the few loose ends.

◆ ◆ ◆

I found myself alone in a bar even though the sun was still shining and it was well before three in the afternoon. The Trappist was a cozy pub off Broadway that specialized in imported wheat beers with a ridiculous alcohol content.

I texted Nikki to meet me after her shift later that night. I spared her the details of my day, but I was pretty sure that she had seen the video of the boy on the freeway.

She texted me back. Stay there. Stay safe.

I will, I thought as I put the phone away. I had no intention of going anywhere. My plan was simply to get drunk as quickly as possible and eat as much half-price bar food as possible during happy hour.

Unfortunately, the soccer game on a large television in the corner finished before Nikki's shift was over. Bayern Munich had beaten Real Madrid 3–2, which the commentators found surprising. I, however, informed everyone around me that it should not have been surprising at all. I vaguely remember shouting in a slurred voice, "Bayern's been the top team in the German Bundesliga for more than a decade, you idiots."

Nobody appreciated my insight.

After six hours in the bar, I was done. The fact that the next event being broadcast after the soccer game was a stock car race live from Crawfordsville, Indiana, did not excite me, so I started searching my briefcase for my car keys.

◆ ◆ ◆

As I drove home, I felt myself getting more and more irritated. I hated being brought before the full executive team and having Chief Karls spin my transfer to placate the media and the governor. More than that, however, I hated the loss of control. My judicial assignment was simply a piece. I'd trusted Helen Vox, and I'd been slow to recognize that she wasn't telling me the whole truth.

I thought about her sitting on the edge of Harry's bed, crying. I comforted her, when she should've been confronted. Then we spent the evening together—going to dinner and playing pool—talking about Harry, but she never mentioned a multimillion-dollar bank account

or Florida corporation. Instead, she alluded to Harry remembering her in his will.

She was a fake.

Instead of ending up at home, I found myself across town at Helen's condo on Harrison Street. It was a four-story building, nice but nothing elaborate. I pushed the call button. It rang a few times, but nobody answered.

I pushed again, but the result wasn't any different. Helen wasn't home. I swore at her under my breath. In my mind, I had imagined a powerful confrontation. Despite my intoxication, I'd be strong and cunning. I'd ultimately extract the truth.

In hindsight, this self-delusion should have been recognized and resulted in me calling a cab. I instead wandered to my car, struggled to find the right key to unlock the door, and eventually got back behind the wheel.

As I turned the engine on, I saw a black Chevy Tahoe double-park near the front of Helen's building. The driver put the hazard lights on and then got out and ran around the front to the passenger side door.

He opened it and extended his hand, and a woman got out. It wasn't hard to identify her. She was thin with striking white hair. I knew, even from a distance and with a half dozen beers in my system, it was Helen Vox.

I watched the man walk her to the door. Helen removed her key from her purse, and the man pulled her toward him. They kissed, held each other close, then kissed again. There was a familiarity in the way that they said goodbye.

Helen Vox went into her building, and the man turned and walked back to the Tahoe. He stopped at the door, looked around, and got inside.

I laughed as the Chevy Tahoe drove away.

I couldn't believe what I'd seen, and I wondered how long Helen Vox and Marshall Terry had been romantically involved.

CHAPTER TWENTY-EIGHT

I pulled away from the curb and started toward my house. I thought I was doing great. The windows were open. The radio was off, and my hands were at ten and two. Every stop sign got a full and complete stop. Every lane change was signaled. Every traffic light was obeyed.

That was my recollection, anyway, but a police officer soon told me something different. I was two miles from Helen's condo when the lights flashed, blue and red. I'm not going to lie. I wanted to press the gas and flee. Marshaling every ounce of self-control that I had, I pulled the car over to the curb.

The squad car came up behind me, but the officer didn't get out.

As I waited, my heart pounded. He was probably running my license plate and vehicle registration, calling everything in to dispatch.

I contemplated whether or not I should hire a lawyer, and whether Nikki and I even had the money to hire a lawyer. I also imagined Benji Metina waiting for me as I left the jail. I thought about my mug shot on the front page of the *San Francisco Chronicle*. I was sure there would be a snarky headline, but at the moment I couldn't think of one.

It felt like I was in my car for an hour, but it was only a few minutes. The squad car's door opened. A patrol cop got out and swaggered toward me. The whole time his hand wasn't far from his gun.

"Can I get your license and insurance?"

I nodded, reached for my wallet, and retrieved the documents. As I passed them through the window, I saw my hand tremble.

"Know why I pulled you over, sir?"

In a soft voice, I told the truth. "I do not."

"OK." The patrol officer scanned the inside of my car, looking for open containers of alcohol or anything else that would justify my immediate arrest. Then he said, "Your headlights are not on."

I looked down at the dashboard, and it was true. I had forgotten to turn on my headlights.

"You were also driving about ten miles *under* the speed limit back there, and, at the intersection, you stopped about fifteen feet short of the crosswalk."

"Is that illegal?"

"Can be." The officer paused. "Have you had anything to drink tonight, sir?"

It was a standard question. The specific phrasing was taught at the police academy. The officer didn't ask whether I was drunk or driving under the influence, which would be immediately denied by the driver. The question, instead, was an objective one, and there was no good answer. If I refused to respond, I'd be deemed evasive and suspicious, providing the police officer with legal basis to continue his investigation. If I denied drinking any alcohol, which could easily be proven incorrect, then I'd be deemed a liar. If I told the truth, I was nearly certain to be placed under arrest for driving under the influence.

"A couple beers," I said, minimizing and being unoriginal.

The officer took a step back, still holding my driver's license and insurance. "Wait here for a moment." He turned and walked back to his squad car. I thought about calling Nikki but figured I'd only make her nervous. I also didn't want to be reaching for anything or having anything in my hand that the cop might think was a weapon.

Cars continued to flow past me. The drag from each one jiggled the Range Rover. Eventually the patrol cop returned. He handed me back my driver's license and insurance. "I'd like you to please step out of the car."

◆ ◆ ◆

I performed a series of field sobriety tests. Like a veteran drunk, I knew every one of them. I followed the cop's finger from left to right, as he performed the horizontal gaze nystagmus test. This is when a police officer watches the driver's pupil for smooth pursuit while tracking the movement of the finger as well as an involuntary shaking of the pupil when it is at maximum deviation. Maximum deviation is just a fancy way of saying when the finger is all the way over to one side.

I also did the walk-and-turn and the one-leg stand. I don't know whether I passed or not, but when these tests were done, the cop asked if I would blow into his portable breath test device. This was the moment of truth. I knew that, under the law, I really didn't have a choice. If I refused, the cop would still arrest me and take me to the station for testing on the BAC Datamaster. The station's machine was more sophisticated and arguably more accurate than the portable breath test, and the machine at the station would be the test that would be used for my criminal prosecution.

"Sure."

The cop nodded. He held up the little black box. "I need you to take a big breath and blow into this straw until you hear the beep."

I leaned in, put my lips around the plastic straw, and blew into the little black box.

He encouraged me. "Keep blowing. Keep blowing. Keep blowing." When three high-pitched beeps were emitted from the box, the cop patted me on the back. "Good."

He stepped away, and for a moment I thought he was going to let me go, but I was wrong.

"Can you come with me, Judge?"

When he called me *judge*, adrenaline shot through me. He knew who I was.

◆ ◆ ◆

I sat alone in the squad car, wondering why I hadn't been transported down to the police station. Enough time had now passed that the reality of my situation was undeniable. My legal career was over, and I began thinking about a life in Utah as a gym teacher. I could teach gym. I'd probably even like it, a little exercise every day and summers off. There were hospitals in Utah, too. Nikki could easily find a job. We could afford a nice house, decent schools.

Another squad car arrived. It was a taller cop, a little older. By their looks and gestures, they were obviously talking about me, but I couldn't hear them.

I waited as another ten minutes passed. I had to go to the bathroom, but I wasn't going to say anything or try to get their attention.

Nothing happened until a third car arrived. It was an unmarked Ford Crown Victoria, gray. The other cops walked up to the driver, words were exchanged, and then the patrol cop turned and walked toward me.

When he got to the squad, the patrol cop opened the door. "I apologize for the delay, Judge." He stepped aside. "We've got some staffing issues tonight that me and the night watch commander are trying to sort through." It was a peculiar statement, spoken in a tone more for the benefit of the squad's video recording device than for me. "Can you step out of the car?"

I did as I was told.

After sitting for so long, I almost lost my balance. The patrol cop led me over to the unmarked Crown Vic without conversation and opened the back door. I got inside.

When the door shut, the large man in the front seat turned and smiled. "Good evening, Judge Thompson." It was Detective Jarkowski. "I'm going to be transporting you downtown."

"I didn't know you investigated DUIs, Detective."

Jarkowski laughed. "Only when I get lucky."

Unlike a squad car, Jarkowski's Crown Vic was different. It didn't have a dashboard camera or any recording devices, which was probably why we weren't having this conversation in the squad. "What's going to happen downtown?"

"Well"—he rubbed his big nose, carefully choosing his words—"it's up to you, really. I'm taking you to the station no matter what, but, once we arrive, it's on you. I can have you immediately booked and arrested for DUI. Depending on your alcohol levels, you'll either be held in jail for the night or released to a sober friend or family member." He paused for a moment, and I kept quiet. "Or there is a possibility that you can be released without charge if you spend some time talking with me." He repeated his last words for emphasis. "Like really talking with me."

I picked up on the word *possibility*.

"If I heard you right," I said, "I think you're telling me that I could do whatever you want or answer whatever questions you had and you still may charge me with a DUI."

"It's a possibility," he said. "You could get charged with a DUI or maybe something more serious. It'd be up to the prosecutors. Believe it or not, I've had other people in this spot and they tell me they're going to cooperate and then they don't. So you'd be taking a chance, which, if I were you, I'd jump at this chance, Judge. You don't want to be in the news again."

I thought about Jarkowski's suggestion of being charged with *something more serious*, and I wondered if he knew about the photographs and the journals or Harry's will and Red Rock ABC-5555. It wouldn't be hard to satisfy probable cause to charge me with obstructing legal process for withholding that information from him.

An aggressive prosecutor could even charge me with murder, aiding and abetting after the fact, which was a fancy way of saying that I didn't help a person actually commit murder but I helped a person get away with murder by withholding important information from law enforcement.

I wasn't sure if there was enough evidence for a jury to find me guilty of either of those more serious charges, but I sure didn't want to find out.

"You're right." The back seat of Jarkowski's Crown Vic felt like it was getting smaller. I was trapped, and I had to work hard not to panic. A ruined legal career was nothing compared to fifteen years in prison. The lump in my throat made it difficult to continue, but I swallowed hard and told Jarkowski he had a deal. "I don't want to be in the news again."

He smiled and turned the key. The Crown Vic's engine roared to life. "But you can't hold back on me, Judge." Jarkowski put the car into gear. "Full disclosure. You need to be candid and frank. Because I know what you've been doing and who you've been talking to over the past few days. So this ain't a bluff."

"I'll be candid and frank," I said. "As long as you let me use the bathroom first."

CHAPTER TWENTY-NINE

I looked up at the corner of the interrogation room. A small camera recorded everything that was going on. Jarkowski was also probably sitting in another room watching the video feed. I knew what he was doing to me. He was *icing* the suspect, making sure that I understood that he was in control. I wasn't going to be set free unless he agreed. I needed to make him happy.

Almost an hour later, Jarkowski came into the room. He had a notepad and pen, as well as a folder. He sat down across from me and took a black digital recorder out of his pocket. He turned on the recorder. A small light went red.

Jarkowski identified himself, the date, and the time for the record, then removed a sheet of paper from his folder. "Judge Thompson, I know you've heard this before in your courtroom and that you know your rights, but I think it's always appropriate to follow standard procedures." Jarkowski looked down at the paper in front of him.

"Do you understand you have the right to remain silent and that anything you say can and will be used against you in a court of law?"

"I do."

Jarkowski nodded, then handed me the pen. "Then if you could initial next to that statement on this piece of paper, indicating that you

understand the right and you do not have any questions about that right."

I initialed in the appropriate place.

Jarkowski continued. "And do you understand that you have a right to have an attorney, and that, if you cannot afford an attorney, the court will appoint you an attorney?"

"I do."

We went through the signing ritual again. Then Jarkowski took the piece of paper, placed it back in the folder, and removed a longer document. "What I'm holding in my hand, Judge, is an agreement between you and the prosecuting attorney. They've agreed to classify you as a cooperating witness in the investigation of the murder of Judge Harry Meyer. This document does not grant you immunity from prosecution. The only guarantee is that they will take your cooperation into consideration as it relates to any charging or sentencing decision."

I read the document and signed the bottom. "I understand." Even though the actual phrasing used in the cooperating witness agreement sounded vague and not much of a promise at all, judges and lawyers knew the truth: the prosecutors were simply staying one step ahead of the defense attorneys.

After years of informants and adverse witnesses being destroyed on cross-examination because the prosecutor gave the witnesses immunity, a new, softer language developed. If I ever had to testify in a trial related to Harry's murder and a defense attorney questioned my motives or suggested I was merely testifying against their client to save myself, the agreement allowed a prosecutor to prove that I hadn't been granted immunity.

Jarkowski leaned over the table and retrieved the cooperating witness agreement. He read it quickly, making sure everything was in order, and then he began.

"First thing I want to do is show you this stuff. Get your reaction." He removed a series of photographs from the folder and placed them on the table.

Jarkowski pointed at the photograph of a shell casing. It was on the entryway floor. Near the casing, there was a yellow tent with the number thirty-three printed.

"The shell contains the gunpowder that rockets the bullet forward. When a pistol is fired, the casing or shell just falls out on the floor as the next one comes into the firing chamber."

He pointed at another photograph in the series. It was the same shell, but it was a close-up. Somebody on the forensic team had set the casing on its end so that the engraved markings were visible. Along the edge of the circle, it said 45 AUTO.

"We don't know, yet, because it's still at the lab, but we're figuring this casing will match the bullet that killed Judge Meyer." Then he put the photographs back in his folder and got out a picture of a black handgun. "You seen this before?"

"Assuming that's the one next to Harry's body, yes."

"No," Jarkowski said. "Like prior to that day. You ever see it before that day?"

I shook my head, confused. "Like where?"

"Like at his house or maybe at a shooting range or while camping." He watched me carefully, studying my reactions. "Did Harry ever show you his gun?"

"Harry didn't own a gun." I knew this. Harry hated guns. We had ridiculed judges who had conceal-and-carry permits, and Harry thought judges who carried firearms, on or off the bench, should lose their jobs. It disgusted him. He claimed it was a sign of "black robe disease"—paranoia and arrogance.

I looked back at the picture of the gun lying on the bloodied entryway floor. It wasn't even something I imagined Harry ever touching. It was compact, blunt, and crude. Harry was such an elegant man. If he were to ever own a firearm, which would be unlikely, I'd imagine him with a long silver gun with an ivory handle, like the Lone Ranger.

"This is a forty-five-caliber Smith & Wesson M&P Shield. It's light, concealable, and holds seven rounds. They're also not too expensive, about five hundred dollars, sometimes less." Jarkowski kept talking as he removed some more photographs and paper from his briefcase. "Because of the characteristics and the price, gun shops like to sell these to people who just want a little protection. It's not a gun for the guys that go to the firing range on the weekend for fun. It's for keeping in your nightstand next to the bed or people working late at night at a liquor store or people who want one in their car if they get jacked, something like that."

"That's not Harry." I was sure of myself. "He'd mention something like this to me." I folded my arms across my chest, agitated. "It isn't Harry's gun."

"You seem sure." Jarkowski raised his eyebrow and gave me a look. "Maybe I know things you don't know. You should consider that."

◆ ◆ ◆

According to talk radio, there was a gigantic database filled with the names, addresses, and personal information of every gun owner in the United States. A government agent could simply access the database and, in an instant, find the person who purchased a gun. This information is usually circulated as a precursor to conspiracy theories about the United Nations, Jewish bankers, and the left-wing media.

The Bureau of Alcohol, Tobacco, Firearms and Explosives, or ATF, however, was much more low-tech. In real life, tracing a firearm was cumbersome and often impossible. Jarkowski had to send information to a bureaucrat in a Washington, DC, cubicle. With the name of the manufacturer, model, caliber, and serial number, the bureaucrat personally contacted the manufacturer, got more information, and followed the distribution chain all the way down to the local gun dealer.

Once the dealer was identified, in this case, Jarkowski had to drive to a little gun shop in Castro Valley, about twenty minutes south of Oakland, and hope they kept decent records.

They did.

According to the six-page Firearm Transactions Record, often simply referred to as a 4473, Judge Harry Meyer purchased his handgun four weeks before he was killed. Jarkowski had a security video of the transaction as well as a credit card receipt.

I stared at the still images taken from the security video and Harry's signature at the bottom of the form, hoping to see some indication of fraud. After a few minutes of reading and rereading the 4473, I pushed them away.

Jarkowski was right and I was wrong, but he wasn't finished. "You been talking to Helen Vox, true?"

"I have." No point in denying it.

"She ever say anything about Harry's gun?"

"No. She told me he wasn't afraid. Nothing was different."

"Interesting." Jarkowski rubbed his chin. "You seem to want us to ignore Helen Vox."

"When we first talked, I couldn't imagine that she would be involved in Harry's death in any way." I thought about seeing her with Marshall Terry and about what Benji Metina had suggested about her possible involvement with the AFC Services kickback scheme. "Now I'm not so sure what to think."

Jarkowski floated a hypothetical. "Maybe there was an argument between her and Judge Meyer or something . . . maybe just an accident."

I thought about Helen asking about Harry's will, and then I thought about her telling me how much she loved Harry. But love seemed so inconsistent with what I'd seen.

I looked at Jarkowski. "I don't know. It's possible."

Jarkowski removed a final photograph from his folder. "This was taken from the security camera outside the gun shop." He handed the photograph to me. "I believe that's Helen Vox."

Jarkowski tapped the photograph with his thick finger, and I looked down at the woman in jeans. She was standing outside, next to Harry's car. Although she was wearing sunglasses, the image was clear. Helen Vox was there when he bought the gun. "She never mentioned that to me." I shook my head and handed the photograph back to Jarkowski. "And I doubt that she ever mentioned it to you."

Jarkowski didn't respond. "Why did you go to her condominium tonight?"

My eyes narrowed. "You were following me?"

He raised his hand. Jarkowski wasn't going to entertain any attitude. "Why did you go to her condominium tonight?"

"I talked to the reporter from the *San Francisco Chronicle*. She's writing a story about conflicts of interest and cronyism in the awarding of county child protection contracts. You already know about the affair between Helen Vox and Harry, as well as the relationship between Harry and Marsh."

"Did you know about Helen and Marshall Terry?"

I shook my head. "Not until I saw them together tonight. I had no idea."

"And you were going to confront her?"

"I was," I said. "A few days ago, I went out for dinner and drinks with Helen, and she'd mentioned Harry's will. When she raised the issue, it seemed sincere. At the time, I had only read an older copy of Harry's will, and so when I got a chance, I decided to see if there had been any additions or edits."

"Were there?"

"A few weeks before Harry was murdered, he had drafted a new personal addendum to the will. The addendum didn't include any mention or distributions to Helen, but there was one to me."

"Are you talking about the money market account at PFC?"

I nodded, wondering how Jarkowski knew about the account at Pacifica Financial Canyon Bank, but I wasn't worried. I signed an agreement that I was going to cooperate, and that was what I was going to do. "I was surprised by the amount of money in the account. I know Harry wasn't a big spender, but it seemed too large of a balance for somebody just setting aside a hundred dollars here and there."

"What was the balance?"

"Around six million dollars."

"Why'd you go to the branch office?"

"I wanted to know more about who was making the electronic deposits every month, where the money was coming from. There were also withdrawals made each month in much smaller amounts, and I wanted to know where that money was going."

Jarkowski checked his watch after I'd finished telling him about the Florida corporation and the cashier's checks. "It's getting late." He flipped through his notes, reviewing them. "I've got a few more questions, and then you can go. And I assume that you'd be willing to talk again when the need arises. True?"

"I have a trial coming up." I thought about Tanya Neal's four children. Kids that were so desperate to get out of the foster care system that they were willing to return to their father, a known predator. I brought myself back and assured Jarkowski that my cooperation would continue. "Even with a trial, I can make time if you give me a little notice."

"Good," Jarkowski said. "I guess my final question relates to your little visit to Judge Meyer's chambers the other night. From the security footage, it looked like you took some books."

"I didn't see any sign on the door that said I couldn't go into Harry's office."

"I never said you were trespassing." Jarkowski smiled coolly. "Never said you couldn't go in there. Just wondering what you were doing."

I held up my hand. "I understand." Then I glanced up at the small camera in the corner. It was easy to forget that you were watched. "At Harry's house, I found some old photographs. The pictures were of four children, three older kids and a baby. Harry had never mentioned them to me, and I was curious."

"Do you think they were involved in his murder?"

"I have no idea," I said, which was true. "But I doubt it. It was just something that caught my attention. I think during one of our first meetings you called it DKDK. I didn't know that I didn't know about these kids. It was strange, and I wanted to figure it out." I paused and corrected myself. "I still want to figure it out. It's a feeling."

"So what happened?"

"I showed the photographs to Helen Vox, and she told me that they were likely foster kids and that I might find information about them in Harry's journals. So at the end of the night, I went back into the courthouse and up to Harry's chambers and got them."

Jarkowski looked genuinely surprised. "There were journals in Judge Meyer's chambers? We didn't find any journals in his chambers."

"I did." Withholding the photographs was not good, but seeing the frustration in Jarkowski's face made it clear that taking the journals without telling him was even worse. "Harry built the little end table by the couch as a kid. The front panel comes off, and the journals were inside."

Jarkowski began massaging his scalp. "There was a secret compartment."

"It's not as if I really knew it all along," I said. "It was just this random story and I only remembered him telling me about building it once I was up there."

Jarkowski waved away his own frustration. "Any other reason you wanted the journals? Or was it just about the kids?"

"Threats," I said. "You had told me that you wanted names of people who had threatened Harry or who may hold a grudge. I also hoped that there would be something about the money. Those were other reasons to get the journals, but it was mostly about those photographs. It was mostly about finding out who those kids were."

"Did you figure it out?"

"Not yet."

CHAPTER THIRTY

Nikki picked me up from the station, and she did an excellent job at holding back her frustration. When she went to the bar to pick me up after her shift, I was already gone. When she called, it went to voice mail. When she texted me, I didn't respond.

Knowing that I had been drinking, she was worried and afraid. Now she was just mad.

Nikki drove me home in silence. My Range Rover had been towed, and it would have to be retrieved from the impound lot another day. I didn't even try and engage in a discussion. When Nikki wanted to talk, she'd talk.

◆ ◆ ◆

I changed out of my clothes and brushed my teeth. Nikki was waiting for me in bed. "Do you have something to say?" Her dark-brown eyes burned with anger. "I think I'm calm enough now to not hurt you."

I pulled back the sheet and got into bed. "I'm sorry. I know that's not enough. I know that I was stupid and reckless, and I'm sorry."

"You could've gotten into an accident and killed somebody," she said. "You could've died." She rubbed her forehead, then the back of her

neck. "I guess for me"—every muscle in her body seemed to tense—"it was just disrespectful and arrogant, and I never thought that I'd be married to a disrespectful and arrogant man. Everybody has flaws. Nobody is perfect, but this . . ." She shook her head. "I can't believe you'd do this."

"I've been under a lot of stress."

Nikki wasn't going to let me out of it that easily. "Do you think I don't know that? We're married. Of course I know that you are under a lot of stress. *I'm under a lot of stress.* I'm working overnights at a hospital. I'm dealing with everything from coughs to gunshot wounds in the emergency room, and then my husband is in the news being portrayed as an imbecile. Let's simply agree now that we are both under a lot of stress."

I'd never seen Nikki so fierce. I was sure she was going to kick me out of the house or ask for a divorce, and I wouldn't blame her.

"When you're under stress, you need to talk to me. We need to talk with each other. We need to work it out. You don't go get drunk and start driving around."

It was all true. "You're right," I said, and I let her rail against me for another hour before she ran out of steam.

◆ ◆ ◆

We both fell asleep after I told Nikki what had happened at the police station and what I'd told Jarkowski about the photographs, the journals, the will, and Helen Vox. Although we were now paper millionaires, Jarkowski had advised me not to touch the money in Harry's bank account. Given everything that had happened, it may be evidence of a crime. Using it would cause problems if it needed to be recouped, or worse.

When I woke up in the morning, she was in the kitchen.

"Good morning." I kissed Nikki on the back of her neck, then commandeered the carafe of coffee. "What're you making?"

"A little scrambled eggs," she said, still a little cool. "I thought I'd get some food in you before I went back to the hospital for another day."

"Thanks." I poured a cup and sat down at our little kitchen table. "When are you going to be back home?"

"Not until late again," she said. "Probably ten or eleven."

I wished she'd call in sick, but I knew not to ask. "I think I'll take Augustus for a walk and prepare for Peter Thill."

"And stay off the news sites." She was worried about me reading the stories about me and a child protection system *in chaos*.

I hesitated. "Maybe."

Nikki turned from the stove and pointed her spatula at me. "Don't do it. Don't read that stuff. Don't watch the videos."

"I'll try and be good."

◆ ◆ ◆

I lasted only thirty minutes by myself in the house. I gave Augustus a dog treat, promised to take him on a walk, and sat at the computer. With Nikki gone there was nobody there to stop me, so I played a Channel 3 news video.

The reporter, Sandy Ballero, was breathless as she recounted the *harrowing* chase down Interstate 580. The now-viral images were replayed once again, as well as the ending: the car slowly edging over to the shoulder, crossing the fog line, then easing toward the cement barricade that ran the length of the divided highway.

Its speed couldn't have been more than ten miles an hour, but that was part of why it was so compelling. The car was no doubt going to hit the barricade, but everything moved in slow motion. When it finally happened, there was almost a sense of relief.

Officers got out of their cruisers, slowly. They approached the car, crouched down, guns drawn. A door swung open. There was a pause. Nothing happened, and then there was a little foot, and then a little leg, and, finally, a boy. He emerged with his hands in the air.

One of the cops rushed over. Weighing about eighty pounds, the boy was picked up off the ground and carried away.

The breathless narration continued. Sandy Ballero's voice built to the big reveal, a Channel 3 exclusive. "This afternoon we sat down with Chief Judge Patrick Karls, and here's his reaction."

The video cut away to Chief Karls and Sandy Ballero at a conference table. Behind them were rows of dusty law books, an American flag, and the California state flag.

Chief Karls was, as always, impeccably dressed. No hair was out of place. His collar was crisp and sharp, and his tie was a conservative Harvard red and Yale blue.

"Chief Karls, I know that you are very busy, and I appreciate that you are willing to speak with us."

Chief Karls nodded his head solemnly. "It is hard, Ms. Ballero, but I wanted to take this opportunity to thank all of the law enforcement officers and first responders who showed such compassion and restraint with this very young man."

Sandy Ballero nodded. "Are you worried that people are losing faith in the child protection system?"

"Well, I can only speak generally," Chief Karls confessed, "but we need to support the governor's task force, and I personally guarantee the full cooperation of our court in providing whatever information or assistance the task force needs and the public needs to feel confident in our system and ensure our children are safe."

"And what about Judge James Thompson?" Her eyes narrowed. "First there was the death of Gregory Ports, and now you have another child on his caseload at risk and in the news."

"For several weeks we've been in discussion, even before this incident, and Judge Thompson has agreed to a reassignment to the criminal division. Of course he cares very deeply about all the families on his caseload, but Judge Thompson does not want to be a distraction. The focus should be on these very vulnerable children. The focus should not be on the judge making the decisions. He understands that."

The interview ended. The anchor made a comment about the story being *very powerful.* Then the news anchor and Sandy Ballero concluded the story by directing viewers to their tip line for any further information about Alameda County's child protection system or judge misconduct.

I shut down the computer. Augustus was ready for a walk, and so was I. Hearing other people publicly talk about you and what you are or are not doing was surreal. Maybe real politicians or celebrities got used to it, but it was new to me and oddly fascinating. When I had been appointed to be a Superior Court judge, there was a little puff piece on page three of the newspaper's metro section. There was certainly nothing that warranted television coverage.

Now I wasn't just in the news, I was the focus of the news. Sitting in my living room, I felt myself becoming a caricature. I wasn't real, and I had little, if any, control.

Augustus barked, encouraging me to move faster. He wagged his tail as I got his leash, attached it to his collar, and allowed him to lead us out the door. He knew our route by heart.

He sniffed his trees, barked at the poodle on the corner, and gave a quick inspection of items in yards or near the sidewalk that were not in their proper place. About halfway, we turned a corner, and I noticed that there was a dark-blue car about a half block behind us, driving slow.

It looked like an older, boxy, American car, but I couldn't figure out the make and model from such a distance.

I changed our route. I went right at the next block to see if the car would follow. Augustus looked up at me with a quizzical look, confused

by our change in direction. "It's OK, buddy." I bent down and patted his head. "Let's keep going."

About halfway down the block, I casually looked back to see if the car had followed us, and it had. Augustus and I continued. Sometimes I'd go faster, and then I'd walk more slowly. It didn't matter—the car remained the same distance away, following.

I cut over to a little neighborhood coffee shop and tied Augustus's leash to a fence post near the door. When I went inside, I saw a stack of newspapers at the counter. I glanced at the main headline across the top of the *Chronicle*:

> BOY IN FOSTER CARE LEADS POLICE ON HIGHWAY CHASE
>
> Controversial Judge Still Presiding Over Child Protection Cases

The newspaper had obviously gone to press before Channel 3 had aired Sandy Ballero's exclusive. From what I could tell, there was nothing about my reassignment and no comment from Chief Karls. Benji Metina was probably upset that I hadn't given her the exclusive regarding my own demise. At my most self-destructive, I toyed for a moment with calling her and apologizing.

I stopped reading when the barista was ready. As I ordered a latte, I looked at the shiny silver espresso machine, which reflected the cars on the street. Eventually the dark-blue car came into view.

It was the same car that had been following Augustus and me, an old Buick Regal. By the time I turned, it had passed, too late to identify the driver.

I waited for the car to return, but it never did. Then my name was called by the barista. I retrieved my drink and walked back outside.

Bending over to untie Augustus from the fence, I kept looking for the car, but the Buick Regal was gone.

◆ ◆ ◆

As Augustus and I walked home, I wondered who would be following me. Since Jarkowski had seemed to know everywhere I'd gone and everything I'd done since Harry's murder, I suspected that it was a police officer. That seemed to make the most sense, until I saw our front door.

It was wide open.

My heart raced as I walked up the sidewalk toward the house. At the front steps, I stopped. I studied the door—no damage. It didn't appear kicked open or pried apart. I peeked inside to look for movement. Nothing. No noise, either.

"Anybody home?" I took a tentative step inside. "Hello?"

I hoped that Nikki had found coverage at the hospital and come home early. I walked through the living room to the rolltop desk, looking for a note, but found nothing. It was just as I had left it. The computer, the journals, the papers, my notes—all undisturbed.

"Nikki, you here?" I waited for a response, but it didn't come.

I looked down the hallway toward the bathroom and bedroom, listening for some movement. I took a step, and then I caught a smell. Maybe I was imagining it, but it smelled like body odor and cheap cologne. Then it disappeared.

My hands were out, balled into fists. My heart pounded. I was ready to hit anything that came at me while Augustus, sensing that something was wrong, trailed behind, alert.

Nobody revealed themselves as I worked carefully through the bathroom and bedrooms. There was nobody behind the doors, in the closets, or hidden behind the shower curtain.

I went back down the hallway to the kitchen. I felt the cool breeze first, and I saw the back door second. Like the front door, it was wide open.

I examined the doorframe. No damage. Nothing broken. I looked around the house a second and third time. All the windows were shut and locked. Nothing was missing.

Maybe I had accidentally left one of the doors unlocked and ajar, but, even at my most distracted, I wouldn't have left both the front and back doors open.

Somebody had been inside.

CHAPTER THIRTY-ONE

I called Jarkowski to let him know what happened. He was concerned but skeptical. After I asked repeatedly, Jarkowski assured me that it wasn't the cops. He didn't deny that they were watching, but he promised, "We ain't got no cops following you in a Buick Regal and sneaking into your house."

I told him about Peter Thill's behavior and vague Internet threats. Jarkowski thought about it. "Do you know what kind of car he drives?"

"No," I said. "But you can look it up."

"I'll check it out." He promised to send a marked squad car past my house and through the neighborhood more regularly, and he also suggested that I get more sleep and stop drinking so much.

"Thanks." I hung up and looked at Augustus. The walk had worn him out, and he was now laying by the couch. "Time to get up, buddy. We got some work to do."

◆ ◆ ◆

Augustus and I went to Home Depot, and I bought new locks and a security system. The large kit had everything—cameras, motion detectors, door monitors—all ready to install. The cameras could even

live-stream to an app on my phone. The kit was marketed as *plug and play*, but it was a little more complicated than that.

I spent the rest of the day installing and activating the system, which was oddly satisfying and kept my mind occupied. I had never claimed to be handy around the house. My capacity for home improvement projects was often limited to those reliant more on brute force than any discernable skill, such as mowing the lawn, cleaning gutters, and applying a fresh coat of paint when needed. The security kit, however, was just a little more challenging.

I may have been the worst judge in California, but I could read directions and turn a screwdriver.

◆ ◆ ◆

I heard a noise at the front door, then the doorbell. I looked at my phone, and there was the image of Nikki standing on the front stoop in HD. The security camera I'd installed was working.

Perhaps I should have warned her about changing the locks, but I didn't want to worry her while she was at work. There was plenty of time to worry.

She knocked and rang the doorbell again. Augustus barked, and I hustled across the living room. "Coming." I unlocked the front door, and Nikki gave me a look of annoyance. "Is this like a passive-aggressive attempt to get a divorce?"

"Never." I kissed her on the cheek. "It's a long story."

◆ ◆ ◆

Our favorite Thai place was a hole-in-the-wall about three blocks from our house. Its facade was peeling. The sign on the outside, promising *authentic Thai cuisine*, was faded. Unless a person had been there before,

there was no indication from just passing by that the owners had built a cozy glass addition off the back.

By candlelight, a server hustled from the kitchen to the half dozen tables. After we placed our order, the server came back with a large glass of wine for Nikki. I stuck with just water. After what had happened the night before, I didn't think I was going to be drinking any more alcohol anytime soon.

While we waited for our food, I told Nikki about what had happened. I told her about the car that seemed to be following Augustus and me during our walk, then coming home to an open and unlocked house.

Nikki was a doctor. She was used to compartmentalizing. Every day she encountered overwhelming situations in the Oakland Medical Center emergency room. Like a judge, her job was to break the situation down, push the emotion aside, and solve the problem. I could tell that was exactly what she was trying to do now, but it was messy. Treating a man having a heart attack or a homeless woman with a knife wound was easier than the crisis in your own house.

"You're sure you didn't leave the door unlocked when you left?"

"You sound like Jarkowski," I said.

"Just checking." She took a sip of wine. "Do you think we should move?"

"Where?"

She shrugged, and we watched our waitress replace a set of tea lights that had gone out at the table next to ours. "If we're serious about a family, we'd need more space anyway."

"But we're broke." I didn't like the idea of moving. It felt a lot like running. "Things should calm down soon."

"Maybe." Nikki ran the calculations. "Maybe not. It doesn't feel like things are calming down."

Our waitress arrived with plates of cashew chicken for me and green curry for Nikki. When the waitress left, Nikki continued. "We don't

have to buy. We could rent someplace else, maybe closer to Berkeley. I feel like we need a fresh start."

I thought about what she was asking, and then I thought about starting the trial with Peter Thill next week and everything else that was swirling around me. I stared at my plate, suddenly feeling overwhelmed but unable to put anything into words.

I picked up my fork and started to eat, but, to my surprise, Nikki reached over and took my hand. I looked up at her, and she was on the verge of tears.

I had always been the emotional one in our relationship, impulsive. She was the planner, objective. But now, Nikki was on the verge of unraveling. The cool had melted away.

"I'm scared," she said. "After last night and this afternoon, I'm scared for you and for me. We're not doing well."

I nodded. "I know. But maybe after the trial . . . it might . . . I think it'll get back to normal."

"Normal?" Nikki shook her head. "I don't know what that is." Nikki took a breath. "I feel like somebody has been watching me, following me."

"Where?"

"At the hospital." Nikki stared down at the table. "It's stupid, because it isn't real. It's just a feeling . . . but I need it to go away."

CHAPTER THIRTY-TWO

I woke up for work early on Monday. I wanted to get to the courthouse before the crowds, avoid reporters, and minimize the likelihood of awkward conversations with attorneys and court staff. My return needed to be quiet, but Peter Thill wasn't going to make that easy.

The case was set for trial. Both sides had filed a series of last-minute motions. Bob Finley had filed a motion to dismiss and motions to exclude certain evidence. Sylvia Norgaard had filed motions for me to take judicial notice of thousands of court documents: certified convictions, medical records, video interviews, police reports, and transcripts.

Balancing the trial demands with my new criminal assignment would be difficult. Chief Karls and Nancy Johns decided that it would look dishonest if I didn't start hearing criminal cases immediately, so I had to spend my morning taking pleas and presiding over pretrial hearings for three dozen misdemeanor theft cases. The public schedule indicated that in the afternoon I would be the criminal signing judge. That meant that I'd be available to sign search warrants, set bail and conditions of release, and review criminal charging documents to ensure there was probable cause.

In the middle, I'd handle the pretrial motion hearing related to the State's petition to terminate Tanya Neal's and Peter Thill's parental

rights. My handling of this single hearing did not appear on any public court schedule. Although, if a person knew where to look, they could probably find it.

◆ ◆ ◆

When I heard Karen arrive, I got up and greeted her. "How are you holding up?"

She put on a brave face. "I'm doing OK." She put her purse underneath her desk and sat down. "We've got a full day today."

"Are you ready for criminal?"

She smiled. "I think so, Judge." She turned on her computer. "I've got everybody coming in on the pretrial at two o'clock. We've got a courtroom on the third floor. I'll monitor the requests that come through electronically, and I may have to ask you to take a break to review something if it is particularly urgent. I'll also put a sign on our door to notify any cops who come to get a warrant signed in person."

"You're the best," I said. "Any calls from reporters?"

"Quite a few," she said, "but Nancy Johns told me to send any inquiries to the media relations guy with State Court Administration. She also wanted you to call her about something else."

"Did she say what it was?"

"No," Karen said. "Something personnel related."

Billy Pratt, I thought. "And the database? How's that going?"

She hedged. "It's going. Slowly, but it's going. I think I'll get it done soon. The problem is that the data that was downloaded from the system is really raw. There's a lot of information that we don't want, and there are also a lot of duplicates." She took a breath. "But I'm working on it."

"Good." I went back to my office, shut the door, and called Nancy Johns. It was a quick conversation. Billy Pratt had settled for $17,000.

The agreement was signed, including the confidentiality clause, which hopefully meant one less source for Benji Metina.

◆ ◆ ◆

The morning criminal hearings were like riding a bike. I'd never handled criminal misdemeanor cases as a judge, but I'd prosecuted thousands of them in my early career at the Alameda County Attorney's Office. Misdemeanor theft cases, usually some type of shoplifting, weren't complex and offered few surprises.

I listened as one defendant after another pleaded guilty. I issued a sentence immediately, usually a fine with a little stayed jail time as an incentive for the defendant to stay out of trouble. If they didn't plead guilty, I sent the case on for another hearing in front of a different judge.

The whole morning calendar took less than two hours. I was stunned at the contrast between the sterility and simplicity of misdemeanors and the mess at the heart of every child protection case.

When I got to the door of my chambers, Benji Metina was waiting for me. "I heard you were back," she said. "How's life as a criminal judge?"

I needed to choose my words carefully. "Simpler. Not better or worse, just simpler."

"Good answer." She followed me, not asking if it was OK to enter my chambers. "I was surprised to hear that there was going to be a hearing this afternoon with Peter Thill." Metina shut the door behind her. "I was even more surprised to hear that you were going to be handling it."

"I am." I hung up my robe. "Unless Chief Karls asks me not to." I walked behind my desk and sat down. "It's part of the transition to criminal. There are just some cases that are too far along to transfer to a different judge, especially since the governor hasn't appointed a

replacement for Judge Meyer yet, and there aren't a lot of other judges excited about coming over."

"You know I'm going to write about this," she said. "It seems like the district isn't telling the truth."

"You're just doing your job." I wasn't going to argue about whether what cases I handled or didn't handle was newsworthy. It was Chief Karls's idea and decision to change my assignment, and I'd let him explain it.

"I also heard you spent some time down at the police station a couple nights ago."

That was a kick in the stomach. I tried to keep my expression neutral. "You must have sources everywhere."

"I do." She smiled. "Here's what I was told." She leaned forward. "You were pulled over, suspected drunk driving, and taken to the station. You were there about two or three hours, and then you were released. There's no record of your arrest, because I checked. There's no record that you were ever booked, because I checked. There's not even a police report."

There was nothing I could say. If I denied it, I'd be a liar. If I told the truth, I'd be in trouble.

We sat in silence for a minute, maybe longer. Then Metina made her move.

"If I were to write the story," she said, "it'd look very bad. I don't have the squad video yet, but it's coming. The video will probably show that you're intoxicated, and either you got the cop to let you go because you told the cop you were a judge, which is an abuse of power, or the cop knew you were a judge and let you go, which is preferential treatment."

"I thought we had a truce," I said. "I give you access. I tell you what I'm thinking, and you back off a little bit."

Metina softened slightly. "I like you, Judge. And I don't think you're incompetent." She paused, choosing her words and keeping it

professional. "But I can't ignore this, just like I can't ignore the fact that your boss is telling everybody that you're not handling child dependency cases anymore when, in truth, you are."

"I'm not going to argue with you," I said, "and I'm not going to tell you what you can or cannot write." Metina had made her move, and now it was my turn. I needed to take a chance. "What if I were to tell you that I'm a cooperating witness for the police in a criminal conspiracy case involving Harry Meyer, Helen Vox, and Marshall Terry? What if I were to tell you that I was talking with Detective Jarkowski for those three hours at the police station? We were working."

She leaned back and shook her head, skeptical.

"It isn't a conflict of interest with Vox and Marsh Terry," I said. "It's straight-up bribes."

She laughed. "Come on, Judge. That's a big leap. Do you have proof?"

"Not yet. But I'm getting there. I'm going to find it."

"And you want me to hold off on my drunk driving story while you go looking?"

"That's right."

Metina eventually agreed on a partial delay, but she made no promises.

◆ ◆ ◆

Peter Thill sat at the table next to his attorney. He had on jeans and a white dress shirt, no tie. He played with his pen while he stared at the attorney representing Alameda County's Child Protective Services Division.

This was likely the last time Sylvia Norgaard would handle a termination hearing. She'd been promoted, becoming the new Helen Vox. She stood, confident, wearing a new outfit and a fresh haircut. "Your

Honor," she said. "I ask that you preclude Mr. Thill's oldest children from the courtroom. Although the youngest boys have chosen not to attend, I know that Neisha and Kayla want to be present, but the testimony is going to be graphic, and I don't think it's appropriate for them to hear."

I looked beyond Norgaard to the gallery. Benji Metina sat on one side, taking notes. The two girls sat along the back wall on the other side. The one with blue hair was Neisha. Her ear had been pierced four times, and she had a ring in her nose. Kayla was the one with dyed blonde hair and was a little more preppy.

"How old are they again?" I knew they were in their early to mid-teens, but I couldn't remember.

Norgaard leaned over and looked at her notes, which were in four neat piles on the table. She picked a piece of paper off the second stack. "Sixteen and thirteen, Your Honor."

"Thank you."

Sylvia Norgaard sat down at the same time as Peter Thill's attorney, Bob Finley, got up.

Finley rolled his eyes at Norgaard. "These aren't kids, Judge. Whether we like it or not, they've seen it all and heard it all. Nothing is going to surprise them about their dad. They want to be here, and I see no reason why they shouldn't."

"They oppose the termination?"

"They all do, Judge. They all oppose termination." He was a brawler, and the county didn't pay him enough to be nice. "None of them want their dad's rights terminated."

Thill smiled. He loved the show.

Sophia Delgado—whose client, Tanya Neal, was still missing—also opposed the agency's motion to remove the children. Then the guardian ad litem, Cherelle Williams, said she didn't mind their presence, either.

After hearing the arguments, I denied the county's motion to prevent the girls from watching the proceedings. Neisha and Kayla could stay. They deserved to know the truth about their dad. They needed to know that he wasn't a victim of the government. They, at the very least, had to have the opportunity to hear why the government believed that their father was an unfit parent.

When I pronounced the ruling from the bench, the girls giggled, and I thought to myself, *What the hell?*

CHAPTER THIRTY-THREE

The next morning, I kissed Nikki goodbye. I got to the courthouse early again, but Karen was already there. She was hunched over her computer, finishing up the spreadsheet. She had her earbuds on and a tall coffee nearby. I knew better than to interrupt her.

I went back to my office and held my breath as I clicked onto the *San Francisco Chronicle*'s website. The main story related to the never-ending dream to redevelop San Francisco's old Pier 70, and the next covered the debate about whether there should be a limit to the number of marijuana dispensary permits issued in the city.

The absence of a story about my night at Oakland police headquarters came as a relief. Maybe Benji Metina was laying off after all.

◆ ◆ ◆

The trial started at 9:30 a.m. "Good morning, everybody." I looked at Karen and nodded, signaling that it was now OK for her to leave. There was no need for her to sit next to me for the whole trial. I'd rather she finish the database.

"We are on the record *In the matter of the children of Peter Thill and Tanya Neal.* Before we go any further, I'd like those present to note their appearances."

The attorneys and their clients were all seated around the table, and one by one, each stood and introduced themselves. Afterward I asked, "Is there anything that any of the attorneys would like to put on the record before we begin?"

Norgaard stood. "At this time, the agency would ask that Tanya Neal's parental rights be terminated by default. She had notice of this trial. She was supposed to be here, but she is not present and has not made the county aware of any legal excuse for her absence."

Since Bob Finley represented the father, Peter Thill, and not the mother, he didn't raise any objections or make any arguments against the motion. That was Sophia Delgado's job.

She stood. "Your Honor, you've been patient over the past few weeks. Each time this Court could've found my client, Ms. Tanya Neal, in default. We waited for trial, and here we are. We are ready to start, but Ms. Neal is not present and she hasn't contacted me or the court. I do not believe I have a legal basis to oppose the motion to find her in default."

"Thank you," I said as Delgado sat down. "The Court now finds that Ms. Neal has waived her right to contest the termination of her parental rights as to the four children in this case. She had proper notice of this hearing and is not present. Therefore, Ms. Neal's parental rights are hereby terminated."

Just like that, Ms. Neal's parental status disappeared. Her name would no longer appear on any of the children's birth certificates. She had no right to visit her children or have any further contact. If she won the lottery and later died, the children would have no right to inherit any of the money.

"Is there anything else?" I asked as the back door to the courtroom opened. Norgaard and Finley heard the noise and turned. All of us half expected to see the children's mother, Tanya Neal. It'd happened

before in other cases: a long-absent parent stumbled into the courtroom moments after the court found them in default. It created a scramble and a complete legal mess.

This morning, however, it wasn't Tanya Neal. It was Benji Metina. She made eye contact with me and smiled. Then she found a seat in the back row.

"Your Honor." Peter Thill stood, playing to Metina in the back of the courtroom. "I have a motion."

◆ ◆ ◆

We took a break so that Bob Finley could talk to his client. Finley was a veteran. He'd seen it all, and he had little patience for clients who embarrassed him in court. He was the lawyer. They were the clients. I could hear him scolding Thill as I exited the courtroom.

The fifteen-minute break turned into an hour.

Karen gaveled court to order, and I took my seat behind the bench and acted as if nothing unusual was happening.

"Please be seated, everybody." I looked at the attorneys. "Can you both approach?"

Norgaard and Finley walked up to the bench. I covered the microphone with my hand and leaned over. "What's going on?"

Finley shook his head. "My client wants you to recuse yourself. He also doesn't want me to be his attorney."

"Why's that?"

Finley smiled. "Well, I can't tell you exactly because it would violate attorney-client privilege, but let's just say I told him his odds of prevailing and he didn't like my advice."

"And then what?"

"He told me to fuck off, and I told him that I'd be glad to." Finley chuckled.

Norgaard's lips pursed. "Your language, Bob. Watch your language in court."

Finley rolled his eyes. "You want to go to trial with this clown representing himself?"

"Well . . ." Norgaard looked flustered. "Of course not."

"Then chill out."

I sent them back to their seats. "Just let him make the motion, and we'll take it one step at a time."

The attorneys retreated. Norgaard sat down, but Finley remained standing. "I spoke with my client, and he feels very strongly that you should not be the judge in this matter. He believes that you are biased against him, and it was also his understanding that you were no longer assigned to hear child protection matters due to your lack of experience and questions about your legal knowledge in this area."

Finley was playing it straight, but he was careful to distance himself from every allegation. He was merely parroting what his client believed.

"It's true," I said. "I'm transitioning to the criminal division, but the legal deadlines to resolve child protection matters in a timely manner are very clear." I looked at the back row. Metina was writing down every word. "It is inappropriate to delay these proceedings. Do you agree, Ms. Norgaard?"

Sylvia Norgaard stood. "That is absolutely correct, Your Honor. We have witnesses that are prepared to testify, having rearranged their busy schedules. It is not fair to the children to delay any further. Even if this is a legitimate motion, which I do not believe it is, then it should have been filed, in writing, prior to today. It is not timely, and I believe it is just an attempt by Mr. Finley and his client to manipulate these proceedings and delay a resolution."

"I agree." I watched Metina, who appeared thoroughly entertained, scribble notes. Even though there wasn't an article today, I was pretty sure there would be one tomorrow with or without our agreement. "The motion to recuse is denied. We'll break for an early lunch and start testimony this afternoon."

CHAPTER THIRTY-FOUR

Lunch was a granola bar and a Diet Coke in between phone calls and e-mails. Nikki offered to pick up whatever I wanted for dinner, and criminal assignment was pressuring me to break up the Thill trial. They wanted me to handle at least one half-day criminal calendar each day or a full-day criminal calendar every other day.

I was politely refusing their offer when Karen appeared in my doorway. "Detective Jarkowski is here to see you."

I nodded, then told criminal assignment that I had to go when Jarkowski stepped into the room and closed the door.

"How's it going, Judge?"

"It's been better." I looked at my watch but decided to ignore the time. I wanted to know what Jarkowski had found.

"I've got a little information for you." Jarkowski took a seat. "We've been doing research on that Florida corporation."

"Have you figured out where its money is coming from?"

He passed me a packet of paper. "Some of it. The corporation owns a house in Sedona, Arizona."

The packet's first few pages were simply advertisements of the house as a vacation rental: $570 per night. The rest were photographs.

"We called a cop down there to go check it out." The detective took the packet back. "The cop knocked on the door and a guy answered. He said he was renting the place for a month, and then the cop talked to the neighbors. The neighbors say they rarely saw anybody coming and going. The fact that there was currently a renter was unusual. The place is nice, they say, but it isn't five-hundred-seventy-dollars-per-night nice."

"I know Harry liked Sedona," I said. "I know he went there on vacation pretty regularly, but he never said anything about owning a piece of property over there."

"That's what I wanted to know." He stood up. "And you've never been there?"

"No."

"And you never heard Helen Vox talk about it?"

"Never."

"It ain't a bad scam, though."

"You think they laundered money through this vacation rental?"

"Pretty easy when you think about it," he said. "If somebody wants to swing some money your way, they just rent this house for a week or even a few months. The owner is in complete control of the price. Judge Meyer can charge whatever he wants to charge, and nobody is around to verify anything."

◆ ◆ ◆

"I believe that I represent the father, Peter Thill," Bob Finley said. He looked down at his client. "Is that true, sir? Do you want me to represent you in this trial?"

Thill did not respond. He looked up at Finley, then at me. I almost prompted him to answer, but Finley beat me to it.

"Mr. Thill, you understand that I have been appointed to represent you, true?"

There was a pause, then a slow response. "Sure." He rolled his eyes. "If that's what you call it."

"In private, I tell you what I think. In the courtroom, I'm your advocate. I'm not paid to be your friend or your cheerleader." Finley put his hands on his hips, and I noticed Benji Metina watching intently.

I thought what he was doing was great. Finley was building a record, making sure that we were all protected on appeal. Although a lawyer was there to advise his or her client, they were not a puppet. Legally, a lawyer didn't simply do whatever the client wanted. Tactics were within a lawyer's discretion. Finley wanted to make that clear.

"Now, Mr. Thill, you are not happy with my advice, but you understand that I am your court-appointed attorney, and if you don't like me, you have two choices. First, you can represent yourself, which no lawyer or judge would advise. Second, you can hire somebody else."

"But I can't afford somebody else."

"That's not my issue, Mr. Thill. You cannot shop around for a court-appointed attorney. You get who is appointed to you, unless there is something that I have done that mandates my discharge from this case."

There was silence. Finley crossed his arms and pouted.

"Mr. Thill, what is your choice?"

He mumbled something under his breath, and Finley leaned over to him. "Mr. Thill, you need to state that clearly for the record."

"I'm ready to go."

Finley folded his arms over his chest and pouted out his lower lip. "Ready to go, how?" Finley wasn't going to let it go. He wanted to eliminate the ambiguity, and I was perfectly content letting him do it.

"Ready to go with you."

"As your lawyer?" Finley glanced my way with a wry smile.

"Yes." Thill slammed his hands down on the table, and his daughters giggled in the back. Their immaturity was starting to make me rethink my decision to allow them to stay. "I want to continue with you as my lawyer, OK?"

"Sounds good." Finley put his hand on Thill's shoulder, and he gave it a hard squeeze. "That's all, Your Honor. The respondent is ready to proceed."

◆ ◆ ◆

There were no opening statements, because there was no jury. It was a bench trial, and since we were already behind, Sylvia Norgaard wanted to get started. "Your Honor, the State calls Peter Thill to the stand."

"Very well." I gestured at Thill and directed him to the witness chair. It was an aggressive move, but I didn't blame Norgaard. Depending on how much he admitted, Thill's testimony could make many of her other witnesses unnecessary.

Benji Metina looked a little confused, but she probably didn't understand that child protection proceedings were civil. The rules were different. Everybody who watched a cop show knew that in a criminal proceeding you had the right to remain silent, and your silence could not be used against you. In a civil trial, there was no general right to remain silent; if a witness refused to answer a question, the fact finder could use that silence against the person invoking their right to remain silent. Norgaard was just doing her job, and I was following the law by allowing her to proceed.

I held my hand in the air. "Mr. Thill, can you raise your right hand?" Thill did as I instructed. "Do you swear to tell the whole truth and nothing but the truth?"

"I always do."

"Thank you," I said. "Please have a seat."

As soon as Thill sat down in the witness chair, Norgaard came after him.

"You're a sex offender, isn't that right, Mr. Thill?"

"I suppose," he said. "That's what they say."

"That's what they say." Norgaard looked bemused. "Meaning that twenty years ago you were convicted of kidnapping and raping an eighteen-year-old girl."

Thill shifted in his seat. "That was a misunderstanding."

Norgaard picked up the old police reports and began to summarize. "You befriended a homeless girl. You eventually got her in your car. You put duct tape over her eyes. You drove her to an abandoned house and raped her. Isn't that correct?"

"That's not what happened."

"You pled guilty to those charges, kidnapping and rape."

"Upon the advice of my lawyer." Thill pursed his lips and looked at his two daughters in the gallery. "Should've never tried to help her. She was a disturbed girl. Lots of mental problems, you know?"

Norgaard ignored the question, moving on. "Ten years later, you're out of prison. Within a few months, you became a suspect in an attempted kidnapping. Isn't that right?"

"I'm always a suspect." He held his head high. "Harassment is a better term for what them cops do."

"A young woman, sixteen years old, a runaway, is lured into a car by a man offering her some marijuana. She gets in the car. The man punches her three times in the head. She loses consciousness and then wakes up in an abandoned house—alone, naked, with duct tape on her eyes. The door is locked, but she escapes through a window and gets help. Do you remember that?"

"I do not," Thill said. "Wasn't me."

"Sounds like you."

He shook his head. "Wasn't me."

"Do you remember the police searching your apartment?"

"I do. The pigs trashed it. Flipped everything over. Took everything out of my drawers."

"Do you remember what you had in a storage trunk underneath your bed?"

"Nope." He looked at me. He wanted me to stop the questioning, but Norgaard was well within her rights to make a record of his background.

"You don't remember having a collection of pornography in this trunk?"

"Nope."

"The pornography featured bondage, torture of women. Really, they weren't pornos so much as video recordings of sexual assault, wouldn't you agree?"

"When was this?"

Norgaard ignored his question. "Also in the storage trunk were newspaper clippings. Did you cut out those newspaper stories?"

"I don't recall. Long time ago."

"They were newspaper stories about missing children, mostly young women. You don't remember having this collection in your apartment in your storage trunk?"

"I don't remember. Sounds like stuff that cops would plant on me, trying to get me in trouble. They always be harassing me."

"You were never charged for that crime, but seven months later you were charged with another crime. It was the attempted kidnapping of a twenty-year-old waitress. It was the end of her shift. She was taking garbage out to the dumpster in the back of the bar, and you grabbed her and tried to force her into your car. One of the bartenders heard the noise, rushed outside, and he subdued you until the police arrived."

"They stole my money. Bitch was flirting with me all night, asks if I want a blow job. Tells me to meet her behind the bar after close. Then the bartender jumps me, takes all my money, and tells the cops this story."

"You were convicted of attempted kidnapping, true?"

Thill didn't answer.

"You were charged with this crime, and ultimately you pled guilty to attempted kidnapping."

"It wasn't going to make a difference what I said. The prosecutors and the cops and the judges, they all got my number. They were going to send me away for life unless I pled."

"That night," Norgaard said. "The one with the waitress and the bartender, the police searched your car, correct?"

"Don't know." He sighed, as if simultaneously annoyed and bored with the proceedings. "Are we almost done?"

"When I'm done, we're done," Norgaard said. "And I'm not done." She looked at her notes again, finding her place. "So as I was asking you, the police searched your car the night of your arrest and they found a roll of duct tape, rubber gloves, and condoms. Is that correct?"

"It wasn't mine."

"You think the police planted those items in your car as well?"

"I have no doubt."

"And now let's talk about what happened a year ago." Norgaard picked up a file from the table and flipped it open. "You are out of prison for approximately three months. And you're working as a dishwasher at a restaurant. A woman you work with, who is nineteen, agreed to party with you at a hotel. She tells you that she's got a friend. And you meet up at this hotel room later that night. You asked her how old her friend was, and she says sixteen."

"That's not true. I'm not talking about any more of these lies."

At this point, Finley probably should have objected, but he didn't. I was going to allow it. The testimony was relevant to whether Peter Thill's children were safe, and I wanted Benji Metina to hear about his background.

"You got to the hotel room. They wanted marijuana and alcohol, and you agreed to give it to them if the sixteen-year-old stripped for you. Isn't that true?"

"Nope." Thill remained defiant.

"You asked her to masturbate for you?"

"Never happened," he said. "That's why them charges were dropped, because it wasn't true."

"No," Norgaard said. "The charges were dropped because the victim wouldn't cooperate with the prosecution."

"They was dropped because the police made it up."

◆ ◆ ◆

Norgaard pressed Thill regarding his criminal history for another forty minutes, and then she transitioned to Thill's treatment at Nexus Addiction Center. "You received cognitive treatment for your sex addiction and violent thinking, isn't that right?"

"Probation made me go." Thill's eyes narrowed and he shifted in his seat. "I ain't got no problems."

"You received this treatment from Dr. Nigel Paul, is that correct?"

"Can't remember his name." Thill blew it off. "If you say so, then that's his name."

"Maybe this would be a good time, Your Honor, to admit the records of Mr. Thill's treatment at Nexus Addiction." Norgaard picked up a stack of paper, approximately three inches thick. "At this time, I'd like to admit Exhibits 114 through 160, previously stipulated to by the parties."

I looked at Finley, but he didn't look up. He was writing something down on his notepad, trying to avoid eye contact with his client. "We already objected to all of these therapy documents in a pretrial motion. The court ruled against us, but my objection remains."

The documents were admitted, and Norgaard pushed forward. "I want to direct the court's attention to Exhibit 132." Norgaard removed an exhibit from her own stack of copies and glanced over it, confirming that the exhibit was the one she wanted. "This is a dream journal that you wrote, true?"

"I don't know."

"May I approach, Your Honor?" I waved her forward, and she walked up to the witness stand. Thill was working hard to contain his anger. "This is your handwriting, Mr. Thill, correct?" She held the exhibit in front of him.

"I suppose."

Norgaard put her hand on her hip. "You don't recognize your own handwriting?"

Thill clinched his jaw, and he ultimately agreed.

"And in this dream journal you were encouraged to write about your dreams and fantasies, and then you could discuss them with the therapist and address the thinking and values behind them, true?"

"They made me write that stuff," Thill said. "The doctor said I would be discharged from the program unless I wrote some stuff, and so I made it up because I didn't want to get in trouble with probation."

"In the dream journal, you talked about your family, isn't that true?"

"I don't want to do this anymore." Thill started to get up from the witness chair, but I directed him to sit back down. He looked at me as if he was going to spit, and then he turned back to Norgaard. "I wrote what I wrote."

"You referred to your sons as homosexuals, and that you needed to show them how to be real men, isn't that right? You wrote, if you couldn't set them straight, then they'd have to be culled. You said that some branches of the family tree need to be trimmed."

"I made all that up for the doctor so that he could think he was teaching me something."

"And you also told the doctor that your daughters were almost *ripe*, isn't that true?"

"You're blowing it way out." Thill looked away. "It's all a game. This whole therapy, mental health, corrections, courts, lawyers, it's just money, people trying to make money off me."

"Mr. Thill, you blame your wife for being here, don't you?"

"Damn right." Thill puffed out his chest. "She babied them boys, made them into sissies. Let the girls run wild, and then couldn't keep herself clean. I got no reason to be here. Now, you want to take me away from my kids. Kids that love me and want to be with me. They know the truth about you."

Thill turned and looked at me. "How'd you feel if I took someone away from you?" he asked. "What if that wife of yours disappeared?"

I stared at Thill and thought about Nikki and how she'd felt like somebody had been watching her at work. Then I thought about Thill's Facebook posts. Thill had posted pictures of a gun, a box of bullets, and a roll of duct tape. The bailiff had tried to warn me, but I'd shrugged it off. Now my skin crawled. "That's enough." I forced myself to focus. I needed to do the trial and move on.

Norgaard shook her head, and Finley remained silent. She was nearing the end of her examination. "Let's go back to your wife," she said. "You met her between your early stints in prison, true?"

"That's right."

"She was seventeen when you met her."

"When I met her, she was seventeen," Thill said. "Nineteen when we got married."

"You like young women, don't you?"

The question caught Thill for a moment, but he recovered. "I did." He looked at me, then turned back to Norgaard. "But now as an older man"—Thill stared at her, his voice a pitch lower, each word spoken with deliberation—"I find the young ones don't do it for me as much anymore, you know?" With his eyes locked on Norgaard, Thill ran his tongue across his lip. "I now find myself fantasizing more about older women."

The room went cold and silent as Norgaard stuttered to a close.

CHAPTER THIRTY-FIVE

Karen had stayed at work, determined to get the spreadsheet done. She eventually e-mailed me a copy after dinner, and while Nikki sat on the couch and read her book, I began to play with the data.

It was everything I had requested. The database contained all of Judge Meyer's cases during the 1990s. The file was big, but not as big as I had thought. Karen had predicted twenty-five hundred cases. There were just under nine hundred, but Karen's e-mail stated that she narrowed the query's scope by excluding families that had appeared before Judge Meyer only once or resolved their cases quickly.

I looked at the old photographs again, then set them aside.

I planned on sifting through the data line by line, but I quickly learned that my approach was not as straightforward as I had thought.

The spreadsheet did not include the children's race or gender. Sometimes I could guess the race by last name, but not always. The gender might be clear if the child's name was Matthew or Ella, but even that wasn't simple.

Age was an entirely different problem. Karen had included the age of each child, but I wasn't exactly sure which ages I was looking for.

All I had were the photographs, and the photographs didn't have any of that information. I wasn't even sure whether the photo was taken

near the time that the child protection matter had started. The fact that I was creating an age range for not just one child, but four, made it seem like guesswork.

There were too many variables.

◆ ◆ ◆

I went over to the couch and sat next to Nikki. She closed her book and put her arm around me. "What's the problem?"

I explained what I was trying to do, and she listened patiently. "Do you want me to listen or try and help you solve it?"

That was easy. "Solve it?"

"OK," she said. "Your problem is that you are analyzing every data point for every family. You need to work backward. Instead of trying to find families that meet all of your criteria, go through and find the families that don't as quickly as possible."

I sat up a little straighter.

"Start with family size," she said. "Just go through and eliminate every family that has the wrong number of kids. Then maybe focus on gender or race—whatever eliminates the biggest number the fastest. Then you can refine the search criteria when the numbers are smaller and more manageable."

I kissed her. "You're a genius."

Nikki smiled. "And sexy?"

"Yes." I kissed her again. "The sexiest genius I know."

I went back to the computer and started again. This time I switched my approach. Rather than trying to be inclusive, searching case by case for a family that met all my criteria, I became exclusive. I focused my energy on eliminating cases, narrowing the pool.

By the time we went to bed, I had the list of nine hundred families down to twenty. I looked at the photograph of the three kids and the baby.

I was getting close.

CHAPTER THIRTY-SIX

When I got onto the elevator at the courthouse the next morning, I didn't push the button to take me up to my chambers. I had an errand to run first. I needed to see the file clerk in the basement.

The basement hallway was empty. I walked down the corridor to the Records Department, then up to the counter. A lonely file clerk was in the back shuffling paper, and I went unnoticed.

I tapped the button on a small nickel-plated call bell. A clear, steady ring got the clerk's attention, and she came to the counter. When she recognized me, she looked like she'd seen a ghost. "Judge Thompson." The clerk forced a smile. Even in the dark, windowless basement, I'm sure she'd heard the rumors of my demise. "I don't see many judges down here."

"Well," I said, "I'm not like most judges." It was meant as a joke, but the clerk wasn't sure whether or not she should laugh. An awkward silence followed, and I decided I should be the one to break it. "Can you get these files for me?" I took a folded piece of paper from my pocket and placed it on the counter. It was a list of the twenty cases I'd narrowed down from the spreadsheet. "They're old cases, before everything got scanned."

The clerk looked at the list of names and file numbers. Child protection and adoption records often fell into a gray area. The statute governing whether these files were confidential was complicated, but I wasn't a reporter. I was a judge, and the court clerks were repeatedly instructed to give a judge whatever he or she wanted.

Eventually she nodded. "I can pull them."

"Good." I looked at my watch. "About how long will it take?"

She thought about it. "Depends on what archive they got sent to. If they're still stored here, it'd only take a day or two. If they were sent to the warehouses, it could take longer."

I wanted to get a better time frame. "Like a week?"

The clerk didn't want to commit. "Maybe, maybe longer. There's one warehouse in Fremont, and another in Livermore. Fremont is usually faster."

"OK." I gave her my card with my cell phone number written on the back. "Call me when you've got them. I'll pick them up myself."

"Are you sure?" Few, if any, judges had probably ever spoken directly to her, and certainly no judges had ever given her their personal cell phone number.

"I'm sure."

CHAPTER THIRTY-SEVEN

In re the Honorable James Thompson
California State Board on Judicial Standards
Inquiry Transcript, Excerpt

BOARD MEMBER GREEN: Isn't it true that you ordered your law clerk to compile a large database related to Judge Meyer's old cases?
THOMPSON: I'm not sure that I ordered her to do anything, but I did ask her if she would assist me with some research.
BOARD MEMBER GREEN: But it wasn't really legal research, was it? You wanted to find the children that were in one of Judge Meyer's photographs, true?
THOMPSON: That was part of my research. I thought it would be a nice hook for whatever article I was going to write.
BOARD MEMBER GREEN: And you also thought that one of those kids was responsible for Judge Meyer's death?
THOMPSON: It was a hunch, but that was Detective Jarkowski's job.
BOARD MEMBER GREEN: And as part of your purported research, you directed someone from the district's IT department to assist your law clerk, true?

THOMPSON: My law clerk wanted some help, and she reached out to the IT department. I didn't have anything to do with it. I certainly didn't order anybody to help her.
BOARD MEMBER GREEN: And then you personally directed a document clerk to contact the district's archives and pull approximately twenty files out of the warehouse and transport them to the main courthouse, is that correct?
THOMPSON: Yes. I wanted to read them.
BOARD MEMBER GREEN: And who gave you permission to access this information and use district resources in this manner?
[Pause]
THOMPSON: I don't need permission.
BOARD MEMBER GREEN: Because you're a judge?
THOMPSON: Because it's public information.

This was the portion of the board's inquiry that focused on an abuse of power, misusing an individual's status as a judge for personal purposes. I saw the records in front of Nick Green. Even from across the table, I could see he had everything. There were two dozen exhibits, including e-mails from my law clerk, Karen, to the IT Department as well as the various forms that the records clerk needed to fill out in order to access the county's archive.

"We've gone around and around about this, Judge Thompson, and it seems apparent that you are not being candid with the panel." After sitting at the table all day, it was the first thing Judge Pamela Nitz had said in several hours.

I turned to her. It was late, and I was tired. It was getting harder to keep up the fight, but there was something in her tone that kept me going. "I'm being candid, Judge Nitz." I wasn't going to fold. "Let me try and be clear."

I raised my voice and looked at the court reporter. "Under oath and for the record, I was doing a research project. I wasn't sure, maybe it was

going to be a law review article with statistics or maybe a remembrance article for the bar association's magazine. I wasn't sure where my research on Judge Meyer's career was going to take me. And, of course, I was also looking into things for Detective Jarkowski."

"But he didn't specifically ask you to do this, right?"

"He didn't expressly ask me to do it," I said, "but that was the impression he gave me."

"But you initially withheld your discovery of the photographs and the journals from him, true?" Nick Green retook control. He didn't like the other members of the panel interrupting his line of questioning.

"I shared all of the information with Detective Jarkowski," I said. "But I waited. I wanted to make sure it was relevant. He's busy, and I didn't want to waste his time."

"And this law review article? Have you ever written it?" Judge Feldman asked.

I shook my head. "No."

"And why not?"

I laughed. "Because this investigation and doing my actual job has taken up a lot of my time."

CHAPTER THIRTY-EIGHT

When court began, Peter Thill's daughters hadn't returned. They may have heard enough. Benji Metina was also gone, and I wondered what was happening. Perhaps she'd come for the afternoon.

It was just the usual players. Bob Finley and Thill had come to an uneasy peace, and I didn't expect any surprises. Thill was still agitated, but the emotion was dialed back. The electricity of the first day was gone.

Foster parents, doctors, and social workers would be called. Medical records, police reports, and certified copies of criminal convictions would be offered into evidence, hundreds of pages. It was a guaranteed tedious slog for the rest of the week, as Sylvia Norgaard had to establish each statutory element required to terminate Thill's parental rights.

She had the information and the documents, but it would take time.

"Are you ready to call your next witness?"

Norgaard stood. Today she was wearing an expensive black suit, a white silk blouse, and an impressive pearl necklace. If I didn't know the truth, I would have thought she could have passed for one of the venture capitalists who lunched at places like Il Fornaio and La Bodeguita.

"Your Honor, the agency would like to call Dr. Neville Wiess. He's the psychiatrist for Peter Thill's youngest son."

When I got back to my chambers for the noon recess, there was a voice mail from Benji Metina. She wanted me to call her as soon as possible.

Metina answered on the second ring. "Judge." She sounded excited. "Where are you right now?"

"I'm at the courthouse, of course. Where are you?"

"About six blocks away. You've gotta come down here."

"Why's that?"

"The cops and the FBI," she said. "They're raiding Marshall Terry's offices. It's total chaos. Employees are out on the street. Some people are crying. Law enforcement is loading up these big moving vans with boxes of files and computers."

"What about your story?"

"It's already up on the website," she said. "It'll be printed tomorrow, but I wanted to break the news first. Thank you for your help on it. I had it ready to go, and then this happened." It was the happiest that I'd ever heard her. "Couple quick additions and I was done."

◆ ◆ ◆

I told Karen I was going to go for a walk. It took about ten minutes to get to Marshall Terry's offices, but I didn't mind. The fresh air and the exercise felt good after sitting all morning.

AFC Services Inc. was housed in a dark stone building across from Snow Park on Harrison Street. The fifteen-story office tower was considered fancy when it was first built, but its modern curves hadn't aged well.

I found a park bench across the street and watched the show from a distance. Although there were no longer as many people standing

around, the number of cops and FBI agents seemed to be growing. As soon as one moving truck was filled with documents, files, and computers, another one arrived.

"What do you think of all this?"

I turned and saw Jarkowski. "I didn't know the feds were involved."

Jarkowski nodded. "The offshore stuff and the theory that Terry was funneling money through the Arizona vacation property—all that crosses state lines and makes it federal."

"So you're not involved anymore?"

"I'm just a detective." He smiled. "I'm hoping Helen Vox sees the light, takes a deal, and tells us what happened to Judge Meyer." He shrugged. "I don't think it matters much, since they're all going to prison for quite some time, but it'd be nice to know for sure."

"Where is she?" I asked.

"Both Vox and Terry are at the federal courthouse being arraigned right now, but I figure they'll be home in a few hours, probably placed on electronic home monitoring or something." He put his hand on my shoulder. "Appreciate your help on this."

◆ ◆ ◆

The afternoon's testimony was much like the morning's. Each witness called by Norgaard talked about how Peter Thill was an unfit parent, unprepared and incapable of raising his four children. He was forced to sit there and listen.

Although Thill spent most of the time with his head down, writing in a notepad, I could tell he was becoming increasingly agitated. When Norgaard finished with one of Kayla's therapists and was ready to call a teacher, I decided we'd heard enough for the day.

Karen gaveled the court session to a close, and I left the courtroom just as Thill began arguing with his attorney. "Why aren't you stopping this? You're not fighting for me."

◆ ◆ ◆

I didn't have to go to Harry's house, but I wanted to go. The little Craftsman in the middle of that quaint leafy neighborhood had always been a place of stability and calm. With the stress of the trial and everything else, I needed that house. If I could just recapture a fraction of what it represented, I'd feel better, even though the Harry that I thought I knew was not what he seemed.

I listened to KQED while driving over. *All Things Considered* reported on national and world events, but the raid of AFC Services and the indictment of Marshall Terry and Helen Vox dominated the local news.

As I pulled up to the house, I found it difficult to believe that Harry was involved in such a scheme. What would have happened if he hadn't died? What would I have done if he and Marsh Terry would've invited me to play, too?

I was certain that was their plan. It had to be. Would I have taken the money, somehow rationalizing the greed? Is that what Helen had done?

Helen Vox was a woman I had consoled when she was grieving, a woman I had trusted enough to call when I needed answers. We drank beers and played pool together. Now, like Harry, she had become someone foreign. News of her arrest had stirred every emotion on the spectrum, but, in the end, I was left numb.

As I walked up the driveway, a neighbor emerged from her front door, waved, and came over with a stack of mail.

"Hoping I'd see you." Lucille was a plump woman, recently retired from Pacific Gas & Electric. "Been piling up. Glad you came by."

I smiled, thanked her for collecting Harry's mail, and apologized for not coming by on a more regular basis. "Anything interesting?"

"Mostly junk, but I didn't throw any of it away." She held the stack of different-size envelopes up as if to prove it. "Figured you can sort it out."

"Appreciate that." I expected her to go back to her house, but she remained. Lucille was on a mission.

"Any plans for the house yet?" She kept it casual, but it was obvious she wouldn't accept vague pleasantries. Whenever an owner-occupied house goes up for sale in Berkeley, neighbors go on high alert, fearful that it's going to be turned into a rental or torn down to build a completely out-of-scale McMansion that casts its neighbors in shadow.

"That's one of the reasons why I'm here." I tried to reassure her. "I need to check it out, then figure out a plan to start boxing things up, moving them out, and preparing it for sale."

"So you're selling it?" Her eyes narrowed in order to better study each facial tick and expression. Lucille wanted the truth.

"Don't have much of a choice," I said. "Harry's wife, Mary Pat, isn't going to get better, unfortunately, and I can't just let it sit empty."

Lucille tried to be understanding, even though letting it sit empty sounded pretty good to her. "Well, I hope you have a good night." She took a few steps away, then, as if it were an afterthought, asked, "Any time frame?"

"Not sure. Probably a few months."

◆ ◆ ◆

I closed the front door behind me. I put the stack of mail on the kitchen island, then walked from room to room, opening windows.

When I was done, I went back to the kitchen and reached into the fridge for one of the beers Nikki and I had brought to the house. It'd been a long week, but I promised myself I'd have only one.

As I sat down on a stool, I began to sift through the pile of mail.

Remarkably, little of it was worth keeping. I sorted through the different gradations of junk mail until I found something that might actually be important. The return address was from Alliant Credit Union.

I opened the envelope and removed a bank statement. This surprised me, because Alliant Credit Union was not on the list of bank accounts, retirement funds, and credit cards in Harry's files.

The balance was $40,375, but the three-month activity summary below the balance was much more interesting. At the end of each month, it appeared as though Harry deposited a relatively small amount and then withdrew a couple of thousand in cash.

The amounts Harry had deposited looked consistent with the amount of cashier's checks he was obtaining from PFC.

I took out my phone and called Jarkowski. I told him about the bank account at Alliant, and he told me that the feds had already figured that out. "They talked to the clerks, who said Harry would get the cash and leave. Sometimes there'd be a person with him that looked shady—whatever that means—but the bank couldn't come up with any video. So we're out of luck."

I thought about the nine hundred families on Karen's spreadsheet. "Do you think the money was for foster kids?" My thoughts went from the spreadsheet to the photographs I'd found in Harry's office. "Like Harry had some kids he was taking care of?"

"That's quite a theory," he said. "Not sure how we'd track them down."

"You're right. Thanks for talking about it with me."

"You ain't planning on doing any more freelance crap with this, are you?"

"No," I said. "I might try and talk to Mary Pat tomorrow, but you know how that's going to go."

"I do," Jarkowski said. "Because I've tried having the same conversation with her a dozen times, and I get nothing."

"Maybe we're just not doing it right."

CHAPTER THIRTY-NINE

The final witness, guardian ad litem Cherelle Williams, was called on Thursday afternoon. The guardian always testified last, because he or she would render an opinion. Based on all the evidence presented, as well as on knowledge acquired over the course of the case, the guardian would state whether it was in the child's best interest to terminate the parent's legal and custodial rights.

This conclusion was every case's final and overriding requirement.

Ms. Williams approached the witness stand with pride along with a good deal of grief. She'd been a guardian ad litem for twenty years. She'd seen it all but hadn't become ambivalent or worn down over the years. When she was sworn in and stated and spelled her name for the record, she commanded the room. Her husband was a prominent African American pastor, conducting a service for eight hundred worshippers every Sunday morning, and she'd been known to take the pulpit herself from time to time. She wasn't afraid to take center stage.

Sylvia Norgaard smiled. "Good morning, Ms. Williams."

"Good morning."

"Let's begin with the basics. When were you assigned to this case?"

"About a year ago," she said. "All cases are randomly assigned, and I was notified that an emergency motion had been filed to grant the

county's child protective services to take the children into emergency protective care."

"And why was that?"

"My understanding was that they were living alone in an apartment. The apartment was rented to Ms. Tanya Neal. She had been evicted for nonpayment of the rent. When the landlord came to evict her, he discovered the four kids. When he asked where the mother was, they said they didn't know. When he asked how long she'd been gone, they said about a month. Then the landlord asked if she had a cell phone number or something else to reach her, and the eldest daughter, Neisha, gave him a number."

"And did the landlord try that number?"

"Yes."

"And did the mother answer?"

"No," Ms. Williams said. "The phone was disconnected. Later, we were told that it was a prepaid phone. The mom was out of minutes. Couldn't afford more."

◆ ◆ ◆

Norgaard continued to guide Williams through the case's legal history, her conversations with the four children, and then to her final opinion. "You've been present for all the testimony that has been provided in this trial?"

"I have."

"And have you formed an opinion in this case as to whether Peter Thill's parental rights should be terminated related to each of his four children?"

"I have." Williams looked at Peter Thill, then turned to face me. "I believe that termination is in their best interest. Peter Thill is a dangerous man. In the past twenty-five years, I don't think he has been in the community more than a year or two before he's suspected, caught, or

charged in some sort of kidnapping, sexual assault, or predatory behavior. The children aren't safe with him in their lives."

Williams looked at Thill, and her eyes narrowed. She was fearless. "We all heard the testimony about his plan, and I believe those dream journals reflect Mr. Thill's true beliefs. He only wants the children back because he has a plan. It's a plan that only makes sense in his mind, and we'll never understand where those urges come from." She looked at me. "As for the children"—Williams sighed—"I think it's desperation. I know the kids want to be back with him, but it isn't in their best interest. He's made them believe in something that isn't real. It's not possible. Unfortunately, I've seen it all too often. Therefore, I support going forward with the termination."

Norgaard pushed her notepad aside and leaned back in her chair. "Thank you, Ms. Williams." She looked at me. "I have no further questions at this time."

"Mr. Finley." I checked my watch for the time and instructed Bob Finley to begin his cross-examination.

It didn't take long for Finley to work through the preliminary questions and start to score points.

"How many cases do you have on your caseload, Ms. Williams?"

Williams braced herself. She'd been around long enough to know exactly what was coming at her. "I have about a hundred on my caseload, but only sixty cases that are particularly active."

"So let's just go with the lower number, sixty cases. You'd say it's on average two kids per case?"

"Probably closer to three, tough to say."

"Three times sixty, that's a hundred and eighty children," Finley said. "That right?"

"That's right."

"And they're not all in the same foster home, true? That'd be ideal, but often the agency has to split brothers and sisters up, right?"

"That's right."

"Must be hard to keep track of all those kids?"

Williams paused, then seemed to choose her words carefully. "It's challenging."

"So challenging that there are people that you don't meet with, true?"

"I *try* to meet with everybody, but sometimes that's not possible."

"Did you meet with the two eldest children? The two girls, Neisha and Kayla."

"I tried."

"How'd you try?"

"I called them and left messages. They didn't call me back."

"In the past year, how many times did you leave a message?"

"Probably once every two months, about the time I was writing my court report." Williams looked at me. "The social worker assigned to the case and I talked. I knew they opposed termination and loved their father. I didn't see much that would be gained."

Finley scoffed and barked, "Perhaps what could be gained was perspective." A smile widened across Thill's face. He loved the show. He loved the fight. He'd waited for a few days for someone to fight for him. "You're recommending that the parental rights be terminated, and you disregard their feelings entirely. Don't even talk to them."

Williams shook her head. She was mad but worked to contain her emotions. "Sometimes adults have to make the tough decisions. Of course a child loves their parent. Of course they don't want their father's parental rights to be terminated, but it is up to us in this room to weigh the facts versus the emotion and determine whether the value of that continuing relationship is outweighed by other factors."

I had assumed Finley would move on to the other, younger children. He was an experienced attorney, but he was caught up in the emotion. He made the ultimate mistake: he asked one too many questions.

"Other factors." Finley shook his head, dismissing the idea. "Like what?"

Williams's eyes brightened. The door was opened. "Based upon Mr. Thill's history and conversations with the mental health professionals in this case, I believe he was grooming his daughters for sexual abuse and exploitation. He encouraged—"

Finley recognized his mistake and tried to interrupt. "Your Honor, this answer goes beyond the scope of my question. It's a narrative response. So I object and would like to instruct the witness to not provide narrative answers."

Norgaard stood. "I believe he asked 'Like what?' and the witness is trying to answer that very broad question. Usually a lawyer doesn't object to their own question." She smirked. "Even if the lawyer doesn't like the answer."

"Thank you," I said. "I'll allow the witness to continue, but please keep it succinct. The attorneys will surely follow up."

Williams nodded. "Like I was saying, he was grooming the girls. He'd encourage them to bully their younger brothers. Although the reports are vague, I think he also encouraged them to physically abuse the brothers when they were small and couldn't really fight back. He wanted to show the girls that they were his favorites. He spoiled them. He let them do whatever they wanted, provided them with alcohol and drugs. And now that they have hit puberty, I think it is only a matter of time before he sexually abuses them or uses them to lure other young women to him."

◆ ◆ ◆

The questioning of the guardian ad litem went back and forth between Finley and Norgaard for the rest of the morning and into the early afternoon. Finley scored a few points, but there was little doubt that Williams knew the law and her role, and she had solid reasons for her opinions.

Norgaard stood. "We have no further witnesses at this time, Your Honor."

I looked at the clock at the back of the courtroom. "Mr. Finley, are you prepared to go forward with witnesses or closing arguments?"

Finley stood. "Your Honor, I want to review the testimony and evidence that's been presented over the past several days with my client. I want him to advise me as to how we should proceed."

"How long do you need?"

"Ideally, Your Honor, I'd like to come back in the morning. I've got some obligations at four today, a medical appointment, and I'd rather not miss it."

I looked at Norgaard, and she shrugged.

"No objections to this, Ms. Norgaard?"

"No," she said. "The extra time to prepare my closing will actually be appreciated."

"Very well," I said. "We'll recess until tomorrow morning at nine."

CHAPTER FORTY

As I got into my car, the phone rang. I hoped it was Jarkowski with an update on Helen Vox. She now had an attorney, and they seemed close to a plea deal.

But it was Nikki. "Where are you?"

"I'm done with court," I said. "Pulling out of my parking space now."

"Are you coming home?"

I looked at my watch. "Soon, but I want to go visit Mary Pat."

"Why?" Nikki was probably suspicious. She knew I didn't like to visit Mary Pat. It wasn't that I didn't love her. It wasn't that I didn't appreciate all that she had done for me. I didn't like visiting Mary Pat because it was so hard to see her locked up in the hospital. Mary Pat didn't understand what was going on, but she was smart enough to know that there was more to life. She just couldn't remember it.

"I want to talk to her about Harry," I said. "Jarkowski's done it a number of times and hasn't had much success. I thought I could try."

There was silence, and then Nikki agreed. "I only wish I was there with you."

"I would like that, too. Next time we'll go together. I just want to get this done."

◆ ◆ ◆

I arrived at the Walker Assisted Living and Memory Care facility at dinnertime. Large stainless steel food carts zipped through its various hallways. I followed one toward the secure area where Mary Pat had lived for the past ten years.

I checked in and went toward her room. As I walked in the door, a nurse delivering dinner was walking out. "Glad you're here tonight," she said. "Ms. Meyer has been pretty naughty lately." The nurse pointed to a box on the wall. "It's a wander alarm. She's been getting up in the middle of the night."

"Has she done that before?"

"Periodically," the nurse said. "Comes and goes. Been worse lately, though."

"Wish you would have called."

She tilted her head and put her hand on my shoulder. "Not much you can do about it." She retrieved two more trays from the dinner cart and went to the next rooms.

"Hello, Mary Pat." I smiled and kept my hands visible. Mary Pat turned her attention away from the television mounted on the ceiling and looked at me. I thought I saw a flicker of recognition, but then it was gone.

"Can I help you?"

"It's me," I said. "Jim Thompson." I remembered the last conversation we'd had. "You remember, don't you? Little Jimmy Thompson, now all grown up."

Mary Pat shook her head. "I'm afraid I don't." She looked back at the television—*Jeopardy!*—and played along. *How could a woman who didn't recognize me identify world capitals and Broadway musicals?*

I sat down in a wooden chair near the window as the game broke for commercials. I figured it was now an appropriate time to talk.

"I was wondering how you're feeling," I said.

Mary Pat looked away from an image of a woman running through a field due to a new prescription medication. "Are you my new doctor?"

"I'm not. I'm Jim Thompson. Your husband was a friend of my father's. We spent a lot of time together growing up."

"My husband?" Her eyes grew wide. "You've talked with my husband."

I paused. I didn't want to lie, but I also didn't want to upset her.

"Not recently," I said as the game show started again, and the host introduced the contestants. "But he was a good man."

She gave me a look of indifference, and then turned her attention back to the television screen and mumbled along with the category "1776." I left her alone. As the show continued, I looked out the window, wondering whether I should just leave. After another five minutes and questions related to "X Marks the Spot" and "Exotic Soups," a new series of commercials began.

I decided to take a chance. I had nothing to lose.

"I saw your husband at the bank the other day," I said. "Seemed like he was withdrawing quite a bit of money."

This got her attention. "It's his money," she said, but she was annoyed.

As the commercial for erectile dysfunction ended and a commercial for replacement windows began, I decided I'd push a little more. "I know he *earned* the money, but you're married. You should have a say."

She shook her head. "I have said many things." She folded her arms across her chest. "But he doesn't listen. Harry can't let it go. I tell him that it wasn't his fault, but he doesn't listen. He says he signed the order, but that's nonsense."

My heart skipped. I realized that Mary Pat was talking about the case that I had been trying to find. After hours reading the journals and sifting through Karen's spreadsheet, I was sure that it was somehow connected to Harry's murder.

Questions filled my head. I almost blurted one out, but I caught myself. I had to remain calm. Mary Pat was fragile, and I didn't want her

to lose the thread as I'd seen so often over the past ten years. I needed to allow her to lead, until the time was right.

"You can only make the best decision you can based on the information you've got," I said. "Nobody can predict the future."

"Exactly." Mary Pat shushed me as the categories for Double Jeopardy were announced, and a librarian from Oklahoma began working her way through the board. I couldn't wait for another commercial. I had to ask.

"Mary Pat," I said. "Do you know how they get the money?"

"Through that lawyer." She answered without looking at me, still focused on the game. "Harry gives the money to her, and she gives it to them. The government lawyer. I don't trust her."

Only one government lawyer I knew of could have matched the timeline in Mary Pat's memory. "Helen Vox?"

Mary Pat finally looked at me, angered. Her nostrils flared. "That's the one." She shook her head. "I don't trust her."

I pushed my luck. "I keep forgetting their names. Do you remember?"

"The kids?" She laughed. "How could I forget?"

◆ ◆ ◆

A small pad of paper with the Walker logo printed on the top sat near the telephone. I took out my pen and wrote down the name: Plank. Although it was odd to suddenly stop a conversation, jump out of your seat, and scribble something down on a random piece of paper, Mary Pat didn't seem to mind. It was now Final Jeopardy, after all.

I politely folded the piece of paper in half and said my goodbyes. Tomorrow, I doubted that Mary Pat would remember me or anything she had said.

I drove home as if I had a winning lottery ticket in my pocket.

By the time I got home, Nikki had already eaten without me. I went into the kitchen and kissed her quickly on the cheek, and then I walked straight to the computer and pulled up the list of twenty names that I had culled from Karen's spreadsheet.

It was there. A little more than halfway down the list was the name: Jennifer Plank.

I screamed so loud that Nikki dropped the dish she was drying. It shattered on the kitchen floor, and Augustus scrambled into the bedroom. "I found it."

Nikki looked out at me from the kitchen. "Are you OK?"

I looked at the pictures on the corner of the desk. "I think I found them."

CHAPTER FORTY-ONE

The first thing I did in the morning was call the file clerk. The twenty files still hadn't arrived from archives, and I wanted to let her know that I hadn't forgotten. Then I called Benji Metina. She was still glowing about her exposé. "Are you calling to buy me that cup of coffee?"

"You haven't won the Pulitzer yet." I put her on speakerphone and took a tie out of my briefcase. "I believe that was what I promised. First the Pulitzer, then coffee. You don't get the coffee first." I walked over to a small mirror.

"Well, I have a place on my shelf just waiting for that gold medal."

I had missed a spot on my neck while shaving, but there was nothing that I could do. I buttoned the top button of my shirt and lifted the collar. "Are you coming to the end of the Thill trial, closing arguments?"

"That's my plan, although things are pretty hectic over here. The editor has put together a whole investigative team."

"All the more reason to see the end of the trial." I put the tie around my neck, looped it over and under, and pulled it up. "I have a favor to ask you."

"I now see the real reason for your call." Metina laughed. "What is it?"

"I'm still working on those photographs I found in Judge Meyer's home," I said. "Could you run a name through your database? I don't know where it fits in, but it could be interesting."

"What name?"

"Plank," I said. "Like the piece of wood. First name Jennifer." I heard a knock on my door, and the deputy undersheriff poked his head into my chambers to see if I was in. I held up my finger, walked over to the phone, and turned it off speaker. "Somebody's here. I've got to go." I hung up and turned to the deputy. "Good morning."

"Can I talk to you, Judge?" Deputy Ben Kasper was in charge of courthouse security, and I would've been stupid to say no.

"Sure."

"This shouldn't take long, Judge." Deputy Kasper closed the door. "Just want to let you know that there was a loud argument this morning up by the courtrooms. It was Finley and that guy Thill. Some of our deputies overheard, and we're putting extra security up there. Seems like Peter Thill is more fired up than usual. He went through our screens, so we know he doesn't have a weapon, but just so you're aware."

I nodded. "Thanks for telling me."

"You need anything, just let us know." The undersheriff stood. "Remember that the bench is bulletproof. Got a two-inch-thick piece of steel behind that fancy wood."

"Good to know."

"And press that panic button if you think it's appropriate. That's what it's there for."

◆ ◆ ◆

Finley stood an arm's length away from his client. "We're ready to proceed, Your Honor." Peter Thill remained seated, shaking his head. He was obviously frustrated but was working hard not to do anything that would allow the three deputies in the courtroom to take him into custody.

I knew better than to ask any questions. I wanted to keep this part of the record clean and didn't want to create issues on appeal. I didn't want Thill to claim that his attorney was ineffective or that he wasn't acting as a zealous advocate. By not admonishing Thill's behavior or seeking a detailed waiver of his rights, the transcript would never reflect what Thill did with his head, his facial expressions, or his sighs. The appellate court would never know.

I looked at Norgaard, then back at Finley. "My understanding, then, is that the respondent will not be calling any witnesses, and so we will then proceed with closing arguments."

"That's correct, Your Honor." Finley sat down, and Norgaard stood just as Benji Metina entered the courtroom and sat in the back row.

"Thank you." Norgaard grabbed a small wooden podium and brought it near where she had been seated during trial, then opened a folder and began her closing arguments.

"Your Honor, may it please the court, this is a sad case. It's never easy to terminate a parent's rights, but the law is clear. And there is no doubt that Peter Thill is an unfit parent. The law states that anyone convicted of criminal sexual conduct *shall* have their parental rights terminated. Peter Thill has been convicted of such a crime and has further demonstrated that he is not done. I don't think Peter Thill or his attorney will argue that some of the statutory requirements have been satisfied, while others are in dispute."

She took a step away from the podium. "And so we then turn to whether it is in the children's best interests to see Mr. Thill's parental rights terminated."

◆ ◆ ◆

By the time Norgaard sat down, she had provided a detailed summary of all the evidence against Thill and had outlined the danger to his

daughters, the psychological damage inflicted on his sons, and the risk to his children's friends.

Bob Finley looked at his notepad, then tossed it on the table. I knew Finley was about to let it rip. "Your Honor, my client isn't a good guy," he said. "He's done horrible things, terrible . . . but that isn't a legal basis for the government to take such an extreme action. Terminating a parent's rights is, in my opinion, far more significant than locking somebody up in prison. It's altering an individual's family tree. It's taking a kid and telling that kid that their dad is not their dad, their mom is not their mom."

Finley looked at Thill, then back at me. "It has to be in the best interests of the children, and, in this case, the children love their dad—however flawed he may be. None of the children want the court to take this action, and they are old enough to understand what is going on. They are old enough to understand that their dad's been to prison. The girls were even present when the state outlined every criminal act committed by Mr. Thill. Yet they do not want his parental rights to be terminated. They want him to be their dad."

Finley shook his head. "My client is not a man who has ever hurt his children. There are no allegations that he ever physically or sexually abused them. This court and I have known parents who have done heinous things to their children, but not Mr. Thill. There is no evidence he is into incest. There is no evidence he harmed any of their friends. There is no evidence that he so much as spanked these kids, and yet here we are."

Finley put his hands on his hips. "What does the future hold for these kids in foster care? Who's going to adopt two teenage girls or two boys with mental health and behavioral issues? We both know where that path leads. So why not let Mr. Thill continue to be their dad? I'm not saying he's going to be father of the year, but he is going to be a father, which is more than these kids will have if you terminate his

parental rights. There is absolutely no way that the foster care system is better. It's arrogance."

Finley picked up his notepad and flipped through his notes. "Again, Your Honor, our job is to look at this without passion or favor. Terminating an individual's parental rights is not and should not be a mere extension of the criminal punishment that has already been meted out by the court."

It was a good argument, and hopefully it would be enough to calm Peter Thill.

"Thank you," I said as Finley sat down. "I'll take this matter under advisement and issue my order shortly." The clerk gaveled the court to a close. I heard Thill as I walked out the back door.

"That's it? He ain't gonna decide now?"

◆ ◆ ◆

Benji Metina and I decided to meet for a late breakfast at the Tin Cup, the place I was supposed to meet Harry the morning he was killed. I invited Jarkowski, too. It was Friday. My trial had just ended, and I needed to get away. My guess was that Metina and Jarkowski wanted an excuse to get away and have a stack of pancakes as well.

We easily found a booth near the back. The diner was an early-morning breakfast place, so it was practically empty now.

The waitress brought out three cups of bottomless coffee and took our orders. Afterward I asked Metina if she'd found anything.

"It didn't take too long," she said. "Our archivist pulled up this story. It's a puff piece about National Adoption Day." She gave one copy to me and another to Jarkowski. "Recognize anything?"

Just below the article's headline was a large photograph, the same one I'd found in Harry's office: the three children holding the baby.

"That's it," I said. "That's them."

"I knew you'd be happy," Metina said. "The article doesn't get into details, but it says that the adoption of the baby, Jeffrey Plank, was a happy ending to a *difficult* case. Doesn't say what happened to the other three."

"If you got the names," Jarkowski said, "I can track them down."

"I can get you the names." I thought about Karen's spreadsheet. "It shouldn't take long, a couple clicks."

"Good," Jarkowski said as our waitress walked our way. "Then I'll find them. Might be nice for the feds, too, allows them to follow the money to the end."

"Speaking of the feds . . ." I paused as the waitress delivered our plates and left. "Has Helen Vox reached a deal yet?"

Jarkowski picked up his fork. "No. Since she's home in her comfy condo, I don't think she's in a rush anymore." He stabbed a piece of sausage and put it in his mouth. "They tell me she's ready to talk about Harry the moment the plea deal is signed."

"Do you think she did it?" Metina asked.

"What I think and what she says might be two different things." Jarkowski chased his sausage with a splash of coffee. "I don't think she's going to confess or anything."

"But you still think she did it?" I asked.

Jarkowski smirked. "And after all this, you still think she didn't?"

CHAPTER FORTY-TWO

I didn't tell Jarkowski or Metina I was going to pay Helen Vox a visit. The last time I'd gone to her condo, I ended up in jail. I also knew that Jarkowski would expressly tell me to stay away, and I'd much rather ask for forgiveness later than be denied the opportunity.

Since Helen was represented by an attorney, I knew that Jarkowski and any other law enforcement was prohibited from having direct or third-party contact with her. The only exception was if her lawyer consented, which her lawyer never would. I technically wasn't law enforcement, so keeping Jarkowski out of the loop also protected the investigation.

That was how I rationalized my own recklessness, anyway.

I pushed the call button, seeking closure and hoping to find something redeeming in what Harry had done. Although the feds didn't care, I wanted to know why. Perhaps if Harry was trying to care for Mary Pat or help pay for a better life for Jennifer Plank's children, his involvement with the conspiracy would not have been driven entirely by greed. That was important to me.

I rang the buzzer a few more times before Helen answered. "Yes."

"This is Jim," I said. "I need to talk to you."

There was a hesitation. I figured Helen would want to ask a few questions herself, but I didn't ask.

The door clicked as the magnetic lock released.

I went through the small lobby, past a row of mailboxes, and got on the elevator to the third floor. I had a copy of the photograph and the newspaper article. As the elevator doors slid open and I walked out into the hallway, I had second thoughts. It wasn't too late to turn around.

The door to Helen's condo opened, and she stepped out. She wore a soft black sweater and a pair of designer jeans. Near her ankle was a bulge—the electronic monitoring bracelet. She looked sad and as hesitant as I was about meeting. She looked lonely, too.

Helen turned, and I followed her inside.

Helen had decorated her one-bedroom, open-layout condo well, but simply. Obviously there were no children to mess up the pillows, clutter the tabletops, or dirty the white furniture.

As we crossed to the kitchen, she pointed at the open bottle of wine on her counter. "Can I get you a glass?"

"Too early for me, but thank you."

Helen went around the granite island and refilled her wineglass. "I can't talk about the case. And I won't."

"I'm not here to talk about you and Marsh." I put the photograph and the old newspaper article on the counter. I watched as she looked at both. Her eyes narrowed. Her hand trembled slightly as I slid the article closer to her.

Eventually she looked up at me, her face oddly bemused. "The road to hell . . ."

CHAPTER FORTY-THREE

Some cases stick, even when you try to push them out of your mind. According to Helen Vox, *In the matter of the children of Jennifer Plank* was a case that Harry could never leave alone. He kept picking at it, a scab he never allowed to heal.

Harry never found peace, convinced that he should've found the right answer.

He was a younger judge when the case was filed. The child protection division was smaller back then, too. Helen wasn't a supervisor. She worked in the courtroom every day, pushing files through the system as a dedicated soldier in the fight against child abuse and neglect.

Their affair came much later.

A doctor at Highland Hospital met Jennifer Plank in the emergency room. Her baby, Jeffrey, was fussy, and he'd been suffering from a runny nose and cough for weeks. Her pediatrician examined the baby just days before and instructed her to rest and do her best to comfort Jeffrey with warm baths. The older children could take care of themselves with microwave dinners and television.

The baby's father was unknown, a product of too much alcohol and bad luck. The older children's dad had left seven years prior, seeking

freedom in the Texas oil fields. Jennifer Plank didn't mind. She figured that they were better off, less drama.

She was a single mom, working as a secretary for a shipping company at the Port of Oakland. As thousands of steel containers arrived from China, she managed the paperwork. It wasn't a high-paying job, but it was decent: regular hours and benefits.

After the doctor listened to the baby's breathing with his stethoscope, he asked to do a chest X-ray. It probably wasn't necessary, but he had stated that he wanted to be thorough. Jennifer Plank agreed, and that was it.

She didn't know it at the time, but that was the last decision she would ever make as a mother.

The X-ray revealed a broken clavicle. It wasn't uncommon for a collarbone to fracture during childbirth. Given the healing that had occurred, it was unclear when it had been broken. So that injury alone was not sufficient to prompt a report to Alameda County's child protection unit to remove the children.

It was, however, the myriad of other broken bones that ethically mandated the doctor to disclose what he had found.

The radiologist noticed six rib fractures, mirroring one another on the front and back. Given the angles and symmetry, it was impossible for the fractures to have occurred from a car accident, fall, or baseball bat. It could have occurred only by gripping an infant with both hands, squeezing and shaking vigorously for an extended period of time.

The combination of the clavicle and rib fractures prompted the radiologist to obtain further X-rays. Those revealed two additional fractures, one in the left femur and one in the right femur.

An infant's bones were like green branches on a tree, pliable and hard to break. It was incredibly rare for an infant's bone to fracture, absent a clear and logical explanation. One fracture would be suspicious. Baby Jeffrey had nine.

◆ ◆ ◆

"If she would've admitted it, maybe something would've been different." Helen examined her small rack of wine and pulled out another bottle. "We're required to make reasonable efforts, but therapy and treatment don't make any sense or do any good if the parent doesn't admit that there is something to treat."

"What about babysitters or relatives?"

"She denied that there had ever been a babysitter. Also said that she'd never left the baby alone with her kids or a relative." Although the case was close to twenty-five years old, Helen answered the questions like it had happened yesterday. It haunted her in the same way that it had haunted Harry.

"You said she worked at the port," I said. "Somebody had to watch the baby while she worked."

She shook her head as she removed a corkscrew from the drawer and began to remove the foil from the top of the wine bottle. "Maternity leave." She lined up the corkscrew on the top of the bottle and started twisting. "She wasn't going to go back to work for another month, combination of paid leave and accrued sick time." The cork came out with a hollow pop.

◆ ◆ ◆

We sat on the couch as Helen continued drinking wine. It was as if talking about abused and neglected children was perfectly normal. She recalled the bitter hearing, the trial, and ultimately Harry's decision. "He terminated Plank's parental rights. Of course that was the agency's position, but I'd be lying if I said we didn't have doubts. But the medical experts were clear. There was no bone disease, no vitamin deficiency, no rickets, nothing medical that could have caused Jeffrey's bones to fracture or break. It was child abuse."

Helen took another sip of wine, then refilled her glass. I wondered when, and if, she was going to stop drinking.

"Then the question was whether Harry should terminate her parental rights to the older kids as well," she went on. "Keep in mind, there was no abuse alleged against them. Nothing that would indicate that they had ever been harmed, but Harry terminated her parental rights to those kids, too." She looked away. "It was hard."

"He drew a bright line," I said.

"Exactly. If you accept the science and the testimony as true, then the mother did that to her newborn child. And, if the mother did it, then she wasn't a fit parent for any child. That was Harry's logic, setting all sympathy aside."

"And he bore the guilt from that decision for the rest of his life."

"Right again." Helen got up and walked to the kitchen. "It tore him up."

I turned on the couch and watched her open the refrigerator and remove a package of sliced cheese.

"Of course, Plank appealed," Helen said. "And on appeal, her story changed. This time she was ready to admit that she was involved with a man. Her affidavit said that she had a boyfriend that she had met on the docks, and that Jeffrey was probably his kid." She removed some crusty bread from a drawer and cut off a slice. "She admitted that she sometimes let the boyfriend watch the kids, just to give her a break. But it was too late. The termination was done. The county's position—my position—was that you can't undo it, and her new story wasn't credible, because she still refused to reveal the name of the boyfriend."

◆ ◆ ◆

The adoption of baby Jeffrey to a new family was a happy day, but the older kids didn't fare as well. The two oldest, Tina and Brooke, were placed together, and they refused to be adopted. Some people were interested, but the girls wouldn't consent. They wouldn't go on visits.

They wouldn't give adoption a chance. They kept saying they wanted to go home to their mother, which the court wasn't going to approve.

The girls had three foster care placements in two years, and then, finally, they got one of the ghosts.

"Ghosts?"

Helen nodded. "Foster care parents in name only. They just cash the check for providing foster care, even though the kids are coming and going as they please, if they come home at all. The agency knows what's going on, but it's easier to let it be. No questions. Just let the kids turn eighteen and wash our hands of them."

Then there was Jeffrey's older brother, Mitchell Plank. He was the boy in the photograph with brown hair and a gap between his two large front teeth. Mitchell was already a handful, but the termination made his behavior much worse. A young couple was set to adopt him. As the adoption paperwork slowly made its way through the bureaucracy, the couple got increasingly nervous. They wanted more money, more resources. The state denied it, so they backed out.

Mitchell had been living with them for over a year when he was suddenly shifted to another foster care home, and then another, and then another.

"So Harry gave them money?"

Helen looked at me for a moment. Then she put down her glass of wine, took a deep breath, and straightened her back. "I don't think I should talk about that."

"Did one of them come to Harry's house on the morning he was shot?"

Helen pursed her lips and sighed. "I think you should go."

CHAPTER FORTY-FOUR

I called Jarkowski, but he didn't answer. It was one of the few times that I'd ever been grateful for voice mail. I left a message about my conversation with Helen Vox, and, given her reluctance to say whether any of the Plank children were at Harry's house the morning that he was murdered, finding them had taken on an even greater importance.

Pushing the investigation back onto Jarkowski was a relief, and I slept better than I had slept in over a month. The next morning, I woke up gradually and spent a fair amount of time staring at the ceiling and looking at Nikki still sound asleep beside me. A lightness came from clarity, and I thought I'd found it.

I didn't have all the answers, but I was on the path. The Thill trial was over. I was confident that Helen Vox and Marsh Terry would now become the focus of the governor's task force and Benji Metina's articles, which would dig deeper into the corruption and conflicts of interests within the child protective services department as well as the county. The spotlight would finally be off me and the death of Gregory Ports.

I was even at peace with Judge Karls and Nancy Johns. If they wanted me to continue working on child dependency cases, that would be fine. On the other hand, a permanent transfer to the criminal division also seemed like a vacation by comparison, and I needed a vacation.

I walked to the bathroom, grabbed a towel off the shelf, and put it on the hook next to the shower. I turned the water on hot and drowned myself for thirty minutes.

When I got out, the lightness remained. Morning sun poured in through the windows. It'd been weeks since we'd seen the sun, and Augustus was ready to play. He wagged his tail as I let him go out into the backyard while I made some coffee.

As the water heated and beautiful brown liquid began to drip, I went to the computer and checked my e-mail.

That was my mistake.

I should've waited for the coffee to be done before I did anything requiring intellectual functioning. There were at least fifteen e-mails marked urgent, each one more desperate and tragic than the last.

CHAPTER FORTY-FIVE

In re the Honorable James Thompson
California State Board on Judicial Standards
Inquiry Transcript, Excerpt

BOARD MEMBER GREEN: Let's talk about the matter involving Tanya Neal and Peter Thill.
THOMPSON: I don't have anything to say. There's a written record of the case, and that record speaks for itself.
BOARD MEMBER GREEN: Certainly you feel some responsibility for what happened?
THOMPSON: I feel responsible for what happens in all of my cases, Nick, but I'm a judge. I'm not a fortune teller. I can't predict the future. Nobody could have predicted what happened.
BOARD MEMBER GREEN: But there were indications that this was not going to end well, correct?
THOMPSON: There's a written record of the case. If there is something that I did wrong, legally, then there's a process to appeal it. I believe I followed and applied the law to the best of my ability.
BOARD MEMBER GREEN: Do you think you had an ethical obligation to step down as the judge?

[Pause]
THOMPSON: No.
BOARD MEMBER GREEN: And you also suspected that Thill broke into your house?
THOMPSON: I suspected it, but I don't know.
BOARD MEMBER GREEN: But you were worried enough to buy a security system with alarms, motion sensors, and cameras?
THOMPSON: I bought a security system, yes.
BOARD MEMBER GREEN: And prior to trial, you did not disclose these incidents to the attorneys or the parties, correct?
THOMPSON: The record speaks for itself.
BOARD MEMBER GREEN: And if the record indicates that you never disclosed these incidents, either on the record or off the record, you don't have any reason to dispute it?
THOMPSON: I do not.

He was excited. I could tell, and I'm sure Judge Feldman and Judge Nitz could, too. For the first time, Nick Green was scoring some serious points. I wasn't going to make it easy for him, but I had to admit that his line of questioning wasn't unreasonable. He may have found a way for the board to get me, and he wasn't going to let it go.

Green leaned in. "You'd agree, Judge Thompson"—he looked over at the court reporter in the corner, wanting to confirm that she was documenting every question and answer—"that the rules on judicial conduct require a judge to recuse himself for *actual bias* as well as the *appearance of bias*, correct?"

"That's what the rule states."

"And wouldn't you also agree that your interactions with Peter Thill were such that an outsider could conclude that you were incapable of keeping an open mind, even if you, in fact, had no actual bias against Mr. Thill and believed that you could handle his case fairly?"

"I was and am aware of the rule, and I believe that the record speaks for itself."

I wished Green would've stopped there, but he kept going. "And the record indicates that you went forward with the trial despite all that had happened?"

"I went forward," I said. "That's correct."

"And by the end of the trial, Peter Thill was quite agitated, right?"

"He was agitated, but he wasn't disruptive to the court or out of control."

"Do you think your decision to not recuse yourself and push forward with the trial may have contributed to Peter Thill's behavior? That the trial caused him to snap?"

"I think that question calls for speculation." I pushed my chair back from the table. "I'm not going to speculate."

CHAPTER FORTY-SIX

The tragedy of Peter Thill began after court on Friday afternoon, while I was with Helen Vox. Although I wasn't there, I'd read every report. After that barrage of urgent e-mails, I spoke with the social workers and the foster parents and met with the police officers who investigated the incident.

There was no dispute about what happened, and I was not even sure there was a dispute about why it happened. I can picture it all, and I understand exactly how it unfolded the way it did.

Turns out the older girls hadn't returned to the foster home after school. That wasn't unusual behavior for Neisha and Kayla, and it wasn't reported to the police or anybody else. The foster parents figured the two sisters would be back late at night, and they'd deal with the consequences in the morning. After dinner, the foster parents got a call from the social worker. That's when everybody grew concerned.

The oldest boy, Damien, hadn't come home from school, either, and Peter Thill had been seen at his youngest son's school that afternoon. Bobby was waiting in line with the other kids. As the school buses idled, waiting for all the children to be released from class, Bobby recognized his dad's car parked across the street.

Bobby's teacher reported that he'd turned to her, excited. "That's my dad." He didn't hesitate. He ran through the crowd of other kids and across the street. Bobby got into the car and was gone before the teacher figured out what was going on.

Now all four children had gone missing.

◆ ◆ ◆

After hours of searching without success, the social worker contacted the police around ten o'clock. A missing person report was filed, and the social worker outlined Peter Thill's history and her concern. The children were at risk, and the police decided that they needed to get a trap and trace warrant.

Few people outside of law enforcement and the courts had ever heard of a trap and trace warrant, but, as technology improved over the past fifteen years, it had become an essential law enforcement tool. Within minutes of the signed warrant, Neisha and Kayla's cellular phone company had identified their location by pinging a signal off nearby cell phone towers.

The address came back as an abandoned house on Twenty-Eighth Street in Oakland's Hoover-Foster neighborhood. Police were dispatched to that location.

◆ ◆ ◆

Four cops arrived at the house. One went around to the back, just in case somebody tried to escape from the rear. One stayed with the squad cars, keeping in contact with dispatch and watching the sides of the house. The remaining two went through the front with a flashlight in one hand and a gun in the other.

The cops didn't wait for a warrant. They broke through the door. Wood splintered as they came into the dilapidated bungalow. There was

a small propane lantern in the corner. It was on, surrounded by garbage and a moldy sleeping bag.

Somebody was there. Maybe it was just squatters, maybe not.

"Police. Police." The cops moved in tandem through the abandoned living room and cleared it before checking the kitchen in the back and clearing it, too. "Police. Police. Police." They relayed their status and positions in the house to dispatch, who then relayed the information to those outside the house. "Entering the first bedroom, front."

One cop swung the door open and shone his light into the front bedroom. The other cop stayed behind. He stood in the living room, watching the doors to the basement and the back bedroom. If somebody came out with a gun, he'd be in a position to take them out.

"Front bedroom clear."

The two cops switched positions. The one who had been in the front bedroom held watch, while the other cop moved toward the door to the second bedroom. To dispatch he said, "Now entering back bedroom."

He swung the door open and took a step inside. The cop later said he smelled it before he saw it—a raw, musty odor of blood. A small boy was on the floor in the corner. His throat was slit so deeply that his head was nearly cut all the way off. An older boy was in the far corner, half sitting against the wall, his shirt ripped and darkened, stabbed a dozen times in the chest and stomach.

"We got two down. Two down." The transcript of the police officer's search, as relayed to dispatch, captured every moment. "Get an ambulance here. I repeat, two down."

The cop confirmed that there was no pulse and backed out of the room with as few steps as possible. He didn't want to disturb the scene. Instead, he walked toward the closet. He took a step back and shone the light inside.

Nothing.

"Going upstairs." In the distance came the sound of sirens—EMTs and more cops came to secure the scene. The two inside moved up the narrow staircase to the attic. There was no handrail. The old wooden steps creaked with each step. If somebody was waiting, there'd be no surprise. "Police. Police. Police."

At the top, the beam of the flashlight scanned the room, side to side. The floor was plywood and cardboard. There were four soiled mattresses, a camping stove, and discarded food as well as a pile of empty plastic water bottles. To dispatch: "The attic is clear." They backed down the steep stairs. Dispatch informed them that the paramedics had arrived and would be entering the house shortly.

The lead cop inside told dispatch to hold off a minute. "Let's clear the basement."

Once again positions switched. The lead for the attic now followed behind his partner as they descended the basement steps. The smell of mold and human waste grew strong. "Police. Police. Police," the first cop shouted as he reached the bottom step. He heard a grunt in the corner. Then there was a whimper. "Police. Get on the ground and get your hands where I can see them."

The cop crouched down, repeating his instruction over and over. He pointed his flashlight at the sounds, then stopped. He was frozen. "What the . . . ?"

His partner followed, and then he saw it, too.

Two girls were chained to the pipes. They were both naked, duct tape over their eyes. They were panicked, trying to get free, kicking at any sound, real or imagined. Their clothes and cell phones lay in a messy stack nearby.

To dispatch: "Found the girls." He scanned the rest of the basement with his flashlight. There was a battered chest freezer in the corner. It was unplugged. Its bulk had likely prevented it from being stripped and stolen like everything else in the house.

With a quick movement, he lifted the lid. "Christ almighty." Inside the chest freezer and packed in ice was the dismembered body of Tanya Neal. To dispatch: "We got another one."

He closed the freezer lid and scanned the rest of the basement with his flashlight. "Rest of the basement is clear."

Peter Thill was gone.

CHAPTER FORTY-SEVEN

The rest of Saturday and Sunday were a bust. Benji Metina kept calling, but I ignored her phone calls. Nikki and I tried to keep ourselves busy. We cleaned our house. We went to a movie. We walked Augustus and ran a few errands.

We designed each activity to help us avoid news coverage about what had happened to four children whom I was supposed to have protected from harm. I had failed again.

Nikki was worried about me. She knew that, if left alone, I'd drift over to the computer, turn on the television, or check my cell phone for e-mails and updates. She wouldn't allow it. She called the hospital and rearranged her schedule so that I wouldn't be left alone.

On Sunday night, we lay next to each other in bed. Nikki snuggled up against me. "It's not your fault."

I told her I knew it wasn't my fault, but as I lay in the darkness, trying to fall asleep, I didn't feel without fault.

If the judge wasn't responsible, who was?

Every state and local law enforcement officer in the area was on duty. It was one of the largest manhunts in the history of California. Forty-eight hours after Peter Thill killed his sons and tortured his daughters, he had still not been found.

◆ ◆ ◆

On Monday morning, I scheduled an emergency hearing about Peter Thill. Although I knew what had happened, nothing was on the record. A judge was limited by the rules to consider only the evidence that had been presented at a trial.

That's why Sylvia Norgaard filed an emergency motion to reopen the evidence in the termination proceeding. She wanted to submit supplementary reports and, perhaps, recall witnesses to testify. She believed that the new information was important. Norgaard wanted it to be taken into account, but Bob Finley disagreed just as strongly.

If this had been a criminal proceeding, Finley would have been right to disagree. Double jeopardy attached the moment a jury was empaneled, meaning that the government could not try a defendant more than once for the same crime. After all the evidence was presented, the trial was over. Even if a defendant jumped up on a table, danced a jig, and confessed to the crime after the jury left the room, that information would never be given to them. Once the jury was sent to deliberate guilt, no new evidence would be considered, not even a confession.

Child dependency proceedings, however, were civil. It was merely a family case, no different from a divorce. Although Peter Thill had a constitutional right to due process, many of the protections given to criminal defendants did not apply to him.

Nikki was still asleep when I left. She'd managed to get Monday and Tuesday off, but then she'd be working seven days in a row. I didn't understand it, but that's how hospitals were run.

I fiddled with the radio, trying to find some decent music, but it seemed like all the stations had coordinated with one another to have a commercial break at exactly the same time. I turned the radio off and wondered how many reporters would be waiting and how I was going to handle the proceeding itself. Logistically, I needed to decide

if I was going to accept written evidence, like affidavits, or take additional live testimony. Then I'd need to decide whether I'd issue an oral ruling or take the matter under advisement, issuing a written order at a later date.

I'd driven this route so many times that I was on autopilot. I wasn't paying attention. If I had been more aware, I may have seen Peter Thill drive past me. He was going in the opposite direction, headed toward my house in his dark-blue Buick Regal.

◆ ◆ ◆

My cell phone rang about halfway to work—Jarkowski. When I stopped at a red light, I picked up the phone and answered.

There were no pleasantries.

"Where are you?"

"I'm in my car." A stream of traffic passed in front of me. "What's going on?"

"Where's your wife?"

"Home. She's sleeping in."

"Why isn't she answering her phone?"

Jarkowski's tone scared me. I didn't bother asking why or how the police had my wife's cell phone number. "What's going on?"

"We're tracking Thill, talking to anybody who knows him," he said. "We talked to a guy he used to work with this morning, a dishwasher. He says Thill was saying lots of stuff about your wife, Judge. Like he knew way too much stuff about her. It might be nothing, but I don't think it's good now that Thill's running."

"Hang on." The light turned green. I crossed the intersection and pulled into a parking lot. I tapped the new security app installed on my phone. Up popped a menu. I tapped the "Camera One" button, and an image of our backyard appeared on-screen. Nothing to see.

I tapped the "Camera Two" button, and an image of our side yard appeared. Nobody there, either. I tried "Camera Three"—also clear. Finally, I tapped the "Camera Four" button. The front stoop appeared. Nobody was at the door, but in the distance I saw the car across the street. I recognized it right away as the one that had followed me on the day my house was broken into, but I couldn't tell whether Thill was inside.

I couldn't tell where he was.

"He's there!" I shouted at Jarkowski. "He's at my house right now."

CHAPTER FORTY-EIGHT

I don't remember whether I said anything more or what Jarkowski said in response. I was focused on speed. As I rounded the final corner toward my house, everything came into focus. I saw Thill's car.

I pressed the gas pedal, accelerating even more. Then I cranked the wheel hard to the right at over eighty miles per hour, hoping he was still inside.

The collision was a quick burst of thunder filled with bent metal, snapped plastic, and broken glass. The impact pushed Thill's car into the curb, turned it on its side, and then lifted Thill's car up into mine so that the two vehicles wedged together.

The airbags deployed on impact, blowing out while the right corner of the Range Rover collapsed into itself. I turned my head away. The bag hit the side of my face and felt like a massive hand slapping my ear. My head rang. For a moment, the only sound was a high-pitched bell.

I groped for the door handle, pulled, and fell to the ground.

The coarse street cut through my pants and scraped my knees and hands. I lifted my head. That's when I saw him. Thill stood in my doorway, looking at me.

The ringing in my head became softer, replaced by the sound of sirens in the distance. Thill must've heard them, too, because he turned and disappeared back into the house. I pulled myself up and ran across the street. I stumbled at first but kept going.

I was at the door within seconds, charging into the house. As soon as I crossed the threshold, something knocked me to the ground. My breath left me. I rolled over just as a baseball bat came down, missing my head by an inch and glancing off my shoulder.

I kept rolling, trying to get far enough away to get back on my feet. Thill, however, stayed on me, wildly swinging the bat. As I continued to roll, the far wall got closer. I was almost out of space when Thill tripped on the carpet.

That was my chance.

It was less than a second, but it was enough. As he stumbled, I pulled myself up and ran past him toward the closet. Even with a cloudy head and diminished hearing, I recognized his bark. Thill had put Augustus in the closet. This was my only move.

I opened the door. Augustus bolted out. I'd never trained the dog to attack. He'd never bitten me or anybody else, not even a hint of aggression, but Augustus went at Thill with pure fury.

The dog jumped. His teeth exposed. His eyes wide. Thill took a step back, raising his forearms in defense. Then Augustus bit down. Thill shouted at the dog, kicking at him, but Augustus wasn't done.

As soon as he landed, Augustus circled back. This time he attacked the leg. I saw Thill raise the bat and I leaped. Instead of striking Augustus, the bat came down flat across my back.

Both Thill and I fell to the floor. Augustus jumped off, barking and growling, then went at Thill's face. I rolled over, saw the bat, and ripped it out of Thill's hand. Augustus continued to bite.

I stood up. Augustus had moved from Thill's head and taken hold of his forearm. When Thill tried to push Augustus away, the

dog clamped down harder. Augustus had a solid grip, and he wasn't going to let go.

"Away. Augustus, enough."

The dog heard my voice. It broke the trance he'd been in since I had opened the closet door. He released Thill's arm. As the dog jumped off, I brought the bat down on Thill's head.

CHAPTER FORTY-NINE

Police came through the front door. Their guns were drawn, but their demeanor changed when they saw Thill on the floor, his head cracked and encircled by a pool of blood. "Is anyone else here?"

I stared at them. I heard the words, but I was unable to speak.

"Can you put the bat down, Judge?"

The bat—it took a few seconds for it to register. I looked down at the baseball bat in my hand, part of it red with blood. I dropped it, and Augustus barked.

"Can you step over to the kitchen, Judge?" The officer's voice was calm. "Just step over there so we can talk to you. You're going to be OK."

I nodded, doing as I was told.

"We're gonna get some doctors in here to take a look at you." He pointed at my forehead. "Looks like you got some cuts."

I lifted my hand. I touched my forehead, then the side of my head. I pulled my hands away and noticed my fingers were red. I went to the sink and began to wash my hands clean.

When I reached for a towel, I saw them—Peter Thill's tools. Knife, rope, duct tape, rubber gloves, and a package of condoms. He must've been in the kitchen when he had heard me crash into his car.

I guessed that Thill went to the door, saw me coming, and grabbed my old baseball bat.

"Nikki." The daze was gone. I panicked. "Where is Nikki?" I ran out of the kitchen, through the living room, and down the hallway. I pushed past a police officer and ran into our bedroom.

Nikki was on the bed, clutching a pillow across her chest. She was scared but otherwise unharmed.

◆ ◆ ◆

I sat with her as she told the police what happened.

Nikki had woken up and heard somebody at the front door. She thought that maybe I'd forgotten my cell phone, so she got out of bed to see if I needed any help.

When she got to the living room, however, I wasn't there. She looked out the front window, and she didn't see my car. Then she heard Augustus barking at the back door, and that's when she saw Peter Thill. He was staring at her, hungry for her.

Nikki knew what was going on. She turned and ran back to the bedroom as he broke in. Once inside the bedroom, Nikki managed to lock the door just in time.

In the hallway, she heard Augustus barking and Thill screaming at the dog. It was enough of a delay for her to push the dresser in front of the door, blocking it. Maybe Thill could've gotten inside, but he never had an opportunity to try. There was the sound of the cars crashing, and then the fight, and then it was over.

CHAPTER FIFTY

We never went back to that house. I found a temporary rental across town, a three bedroom, if you counted a windowless storage room in the basement as a bedroom. Located a block off Peralta Street, it was available, priced right, and better than staying where we were or living in a hotel.

I rented a truck, and I loaded it with the bed and some essentials. Movers packed the rest, and cleaners took care of our old place when everything was out. I didn't need to see it. I just needed a phone call to let me know when to mail the landlord a final payment and the keys.

Nikki and I retreated up the coast to avoid the media and unplug for a week. They'd keep asking their questions, but I wasn't going to be there to answer them. Peter Thill was now gone, and there wasn't anything more to say.

When Sunday came, we reluctantly returned to Oakland, and the next morning I dug a suit and tie out of one of our many boxes, got dressed, and went to work. My move to criminal was complete, without any further discussion. No more transitioning or split calendars. I wouldn't see another child protection case for the foreseeable future, and I was fine with that.

I walked into my office and placed a large bouquet of flowers on Karen's desk with a note of thanks. Then I hung up my jacket and went back to my chambers. On my desk were four tall stacks of files, and a few stacks on the floor. They were the twenty child dependency files that I'd asked the records department to retrieve from the court archives.

I thumbed through the stacks until I found the file related to Jennifer Plank. I separated it from the others and sat down. I flipped the file open and read the first few pages, then closed it.

Maybe later. I was burned out. It took incredible effort to just get out of bed in the morning, and I had little drive to do much of anything. After talking with Helen, I also felt like I already knew what had happened to them. I didn't need to read the file. I also figured that Jarkowski would call me when the kids were found. He had the names, and, unlike me, he had the badge. And that was exactly what happened.

◆ ◆ ◆

A week later, the telephone rang. "Hey, Judge." Jarkowski's voice was brisk. "Been trying to give you some space; hope you don't mind."

"I don't mind." I sat up straighter, suddenly interested. "What's going on?"

"Been following up on those Plank kids."

"And?"

"The first one I found was Mitchell. He was the boy in the superhero T-shirt. He's had a rough life, Judge, but he also has a pretty solid alibi. Works the overnights at an office-supply warehouse. His employer is getting me the timesheets.

"I found the middle girl, Brooke. She turned out pretty good. She isn't a brain surgeon or anything, but doing OK, got kids and a husband and all that."

"What about the money?" I asked. "Did they admit to taking Harry's money?"

"They did." Jarkowski laughed. "I gotta admit that I didn't think much of your theory, Judge, but you were right. Brooke took the judge's money, just like her brother, but I can't see her being desperate enough to kill him over it or anything. She also had an alibi. She was getting breakfast and running the kids off to school that morning."

"What about the oldest sister?"

"That's what I'm calling about, Judge," Jarkowski said. "Wondering if you got that file from the archives yet?"

I looked at the Jennifer Plank file that was now sitting in the corner of my office with the others. "Yeah," I said. "I finally got it from the warehouse."

"It'd be great if you could look up that social security number for me. Turns out we got four Tina Planks in California, and I want to narrow it down."

"I'll take a look and get back to you," I said. "It should only take me a few minutes." Then, as an afterthought, "What about the baby, Jeffrey Plank?"

"That was a weird one," Jarkowski said. "Didn't find anything."

◆ ◆ ◆

After hanging up the phone, I got the Jennifer Plank file and brought it back to my desk. I opened the first set of documents and paged through the various attorney filings and court orders. I found the social security number for the oldest child fairly quickly and wrote it down before checking the time.

I had another five minutes, probably more, before I needed to return to the courtroom. On a whim, I continued skimming the documents. My phone rang as I reached the end. "This is Judge Thompson."

Karen told me that the parties were ready to proceed.

"Be there in a few minutes." I hung up and looked at the last piece of paper in the file, a court order signed by Judge Harry Meyer

approving and certifying the baby's adoption. Before seeing the record, I hadn't thought too much about the baby. I had always focused on the other three children in the picture. They were the ones who had lost their mother, a mother who loved them. Everybody agreed that Jennifer Plank had never hurt or neglected the three older kids.

I read through the waivers and admissions, then the conclusions of law. The final paragraph of the adoption order made my heart sink. Everything made sense.

CHAPTER FIFTY-ONE

When the hearings were done, I had time to make multiple copies of Jeffrey Plank's birth certificate. I also made multiple copies of Harry's final order in the Jennifer Plank child dependency case, which had granted Jeffrey's adoption. I took one set of both documents to Karen and asked her to put them in a safe place, and then I took another set of both documents and instructed her to scan and e-mail them to me.

While Karen worked, I went back to my chambers and shut the door. Cell phone in hand, I walked over to the big window overlooking the park, deciding what I should do next.

I could call Nikki first and get her advice, but I didn't want to get her involved. She didn't deserve to get in trouble.

Eventually I called Benji Metina, and she answered right away. "Judge Thompson, I was beginning to think you didn't like me anymore."

"I like you, Ms. Metina," I said. "I just needed a break."

"To what do I owe the pleasure?"

"I was wondering whether you still wanted that full interview. On the record."

"No limits."

"I can't talk about pending cases, but, of course, I'm not handling child protection cases anymore. I'm on the criminal rotation now, and all of my old files have been reassigned."

She was quiet. "So everything we've already talked about, like our conversation about Gregory Ports, would go on the record."

"Everything."

"What about Judge Meyer, Helen Vox, and Marshall Terry?"

"The same," I said. "I'll tell you what I know, the good and bad."

"And Peter Thill?"

"Yes." I looked down at the pigeons in the park. They'd gathered once again around the garbage can. The wind had blown a half-eaten bag of potato chips to the ground, and its remaining contents had spilled. "Like I said, you can ask whatever you want. It'll be exclusive. I won't follow up with an interview with a television station or anything like that."

"I have to tell you, Judge . . . I'm surprised. Are you sure you want to do this?"

I turned away from the window. "I'm sure, but I have a condition."

"What's the condition?"

"I need to know the name of one of your sources."

"Reporters don't reveal the names of their sources, Judge. If that's the condition, then I don't think this is going to work."

"What if they're in danger, like their life is at risk?" I asked. "Isn't there an exception?"

CHAPTER FIFTY-TWO

At the end of the day, I convinced Karen to take care of Augustus for the weekend. She would come over to the house, check on the dog, and take him for a walk. I expected to be back, but I didn't know what was going to happen. Things could go horribly wrong, and I wanted to make sure that the dog was taken care of. Karen could tell that I was nervous, but she didn't ask too many questions. The ridiculous amount of money that I offered helped assuage any of her reservations. Nikki was working a double shift at the hospital, and she wouldn't be home until Sunday morning.

There should be plenty of time.

Our plan was relatively straightforward. Benji Metina and I would fly from San Francisco to Phoenix at six in the morning. We'd arrive two hours later, rent a car, then drive I-17 north from Phoenix to Sedona.

We'd spend the day in Sedona and drive back to Phoenix to catch the nine o'clock flight home that night. It'd be a one-day trip, there and back. Pursuant to our agreement, Benji Metina could interview me the entire time we were in the car. It would be on the record, and she'd be recording our conversation. I'd have no right to retract anything that I said or later claim that I had misspoken.

Metina intended to e-mail a copy of the exclusive story before getting on the flight home. It'd run in the Sunday newspaper—her editors were reserving a place for it.

◆ ◆ ◆

I gave Nikki an extra hug and kiss when she left for work Friday evening, and I promised myself that this would be the last secret that I would ever keep from her. I didn't sleep at all Friday night. My mind was racing, and I was trying to figure out all the different ways that things could go wrong.

At four in the morning I got up, poured some dog food into Augustus's bowl, and went over to my computer. I pulled up the electronic copies of Jeffrey Plank's birth certificate and Judge Meyer's final adoption order, then e-mailed the documents to Jarkowski with a note telling him where I was going and what I was doing. I concluded the e-mail with a request: If something happens, let Nikki know that I love her.

Then I put a hard copy of the documents as well as the four photographs in my briefcase, and I was ready to go.

◆ ◆ ◆

I fell asleep on the flight, but when we landed, I knew I had to fulfill my end of the bargain. Metina had pages of notes and questions she wanted to ask, and she turned on her digital recorder as soon as I drove us onto the interstate.

We went back and forth. I don't know if I sounded coherent or crazy, but it felt good to unpack everything that had been compartmentalized and shoved away. The two-hour drive felt much faster as we went through the tan foothills and red canyons of the Southwest.

When we arrived in Sedona, I took out my copy of the vacation rental listing and gave it to Metina. At the bottom was a map, instructions, and an address. She read the instructions to me and guided us to the house.

In front, I stopped. "Here we are. We made it."

"Are you sure you want me to record this?"

"I'm sure."

Metina rang the doorbell, and I stood behind her and off to the side. When Billy Pratt came to the door, he looked pleasantly surprised. "Benji," he said. Then he saw me, and his expression changed. "Judge Thompson." He looked from me to Benji, then back again. "How'd you find me here?"

"I think you're in trouble, Billy," I said. "Can we come inside and talk?"

Billy reluctantly agreed, and he led us through the living room and into the backyard. There was a nice patio, grill, and pool.

We sat around the table, and I took the lead. "Do you know what's been going on with Helen and Marshall Terry?"

Billy looked at Benji and nodded. "I've been following it." His eyes shifted from side to side, nervous.

"Do they know you're here?"

"No." His shoulders slumped. "I didn't have anyplace else to go. I didn't have any money for rent, so I'd have been evicted if I didn't leave. I didn't have a job. My credit cards were maxed. And I knew this place just sat empty all the time, so why not use it?"

"But you know who owns this place and what it's been used for?"

He shifted in his seat. "I know it sits empty. That's all I know."

"I don't think that's true, Billy," I said. "I talked to Benji, and she said that you had information about Judge Meyer and that you'd sell it to her."

Billy rolled his eyes. "Maybe. I had to do something to keep going after you fired me."

"But I think that when Benji told you that she wasn't going to pay you, you switched tactics and started harassing Harry for money, and he probably gave you some."

Billy didn't admit or deny. He could've gotten up and left, but he clearly wanted to know what I knew.

"That's blackmail," I said. "Extortion, and there's a bank clerk that I think would recognize your face." I bluffed. "She remembers you going there with Harry to get the money, and my guess is that if we started to dig, we'd find evidence about where and when you received payments from Harry."

"You can't prove anything." Billy pushed back from the table. "I didn't do anything except talk to this reporter and tell her how you screwed up and that boy died."

"It upset you, because it wasn't the first time the system made a mistake, right?" I opened my briefcase and took one of the photographs out. "I found this in a book in Harry's house." I handed the photograph to Billy. "It took me a while to figure out who all these kids were."

I waited for Billy to say something. When he didn't, I continued. "It was a family. A case handled by Judge Meyer over twenty years ago. The mother's name was Jennifer Plank." I paused, then pushed further. "You see, the oldest girl is Tina." I pointed at her, then at her younger sister. "And that girl right there is Brooke, and she lives with her husband and kids out in the suburbs. And that boy, right there, his name is Mitchell. He's struggled, but he's hanging tough and working at a warehouse. And then there's this baby." I pointed at the little child in the center of the picture. "The mom named him Jeffrey, but you already knew that. Right?"

He shook his head. Tears formed in his eyes, but he still hadn't said a word.

"I know who you are, Billy," I said. "I know that you're that baby, and that you were adopted, and that your adoptive parents changed your name. I got the file. I saw the adoption order that Judge Meyer signed. I also know that he was giving your brother and your sisters money over the years, and"—I paused, deciding to shade the truth—"I talked to Helen today, and she's reached a deal with the prosecutors. She's going to tell them about the morning Harry died."

"He screwed up," Billy said. "And he knew it. He should've never terminated my mother's parental rights. He should've never broken up our family."

"Your mother didn't tell the truth."

Billy got angry. "At first, but she came clean. She eventually told the truth about who hurt me, but Judge Meyer was too proud. He couldn't admit that he made a mistake, that the system doesn't work."

"Harry knew the system didn't work all the time."

"Then why didn't he fix it?" Billy shook his head. "I'm a lawyer, remember? Maybe a drunk one, but I graduated law school. I've studied the rules, and you cannot tell me that Judge Meyer didn't have the authority to make things right. This wasn't a hit-and-run lawsuit. This was a family, and he let my mom go and it destroyed her."

"He tried to help."

"He gave us a little money here and there." Billy was crying now. "That's true. He gave me an externship during law school, convinced you to hire me. That's true. But none of that makes up for his decision to split me and my brother and sisters apart."

"So you killed him?"

He leaned over and put his hands over his face. "I didn't mean to do it . . . it was an accident, a misunderstanding. I went there to get money. At that point, I knew all about how he was paying for his wife's treatment, and I knew all about his affair with Ms. Vox, and I knew all about the kickbacks from his buddy Marshall Terry, and I

told him I'd tell everyone everything if he didn't pay me . . . and that scared him."

He sat up, wiped the tears from his face, and told us how it ended.

"I came to collect. I called a couple times. I don't remember pieces of it, honestly, because I was drunk, but I know I made some threats—serious threats. Then I told him I was coming over, and when I showed up, Judge Meyer had a gun. I couldn't believe it. I looked at it, and I started screaming at him. 'You gonna shoot me? You gonna shoot me?' I kept yelling that at him. Part of me wanted him to. Suicide sounded good. To die, that sounded really good to me."

He closed his eyes. "I reached for the gun. We struggled, and as Judge Meyer pulled away, the gun went off." He shook his head. "I watched him fall to the floor. Then I looked up, and Helen Vox was standing there, watching me. She had been in the other room, screaming at Harry to shoot me, the whole time. She'd seen the whole thing. That's when I turned and ran."

CHAPTER FIFTY-THREE

"I don't want to go to prison." Billy's shoulders slumped, weighed down with pity and guilt. "I can't go to prison, Judge. I just can't. I can't do it."

"It's not my call." I looked at Benji Metina, then pushed back my chair and stood up. "I'm sorry."

Billy's face stretched long, pleading. "Sure it is, Judge. You don't have to tell anybody. You don't have to say anything." Then he looked at Metina. "Tell him he doesn't have to do this. Tell him."

"Goodbye, Billy." I turned and walked back through the house and out the front door, Metina right behind me. When we were outside and at the car, I asked her if she would e-mail a copy of the digital recording of our conversation with Billy to Jarkowski.

"I will," she said. "And it's OK if all of this goes in the story?"

"That was the deal."

CHAPTER FIFTY-FOUR

In re the Honorable James Thompson
California State Board on Judicial Standards
Inquiry Transcript, Excerpt

BOARD MEMBER GREEN: When did you hire Billy Pratt?
THOMPSON: Shortly after I was appointed to the bench.
BOARD MEMBER GREEN: And did you check his references?
THOMPSON: Of course.
BOARD MEMBER GREEN: And who were his references?
THOMPSON: I don't remember all of them, but Judge Meyer was one.
BOARD MEMBER GREEN: Billy Pratt did an externship with Judge Meyer, correct?
THOMPSON: Correct, for course credit.
BOARD MEMBER GREEN: And did Judge Meyer ever disclose or discuss his relationship to Billy Pratt?
[Pause]
THOMPSON: No. I didn't have any idea.
BOARD MEMBER GREEN: And, eventually, you figured out that Billy Pratt had known Judge Meyer his entire life, and that Judge Meyer

was the person who terminated the biological mother's parental rights and oversaw the adoption.

THOMPSON: I learned that after Billy was terminated.

BOARD MEMBER GREEN: As a judge, do you think it was appropriate to conduct your own investigation into Harry Meyer's death?

THOMPSON: I was grieving. I was looking for answers. [Pause] I don't know if I should have done anything differently.

I looked across the table at Nick Green, then at Judges Feldman and Nitz. "I have to be honest with you," I said. "I didn't want to punish Billy Pratt; I only wanted the truth." I shook my head. "Maybe Harry Meyer would've done that. He'd bent the rules because he thought that the purpose justified the means. But that wouldn't be the right thing to do. I, alone, shouldn't have the power to do that."

I took a deep breath, and it felt good to say something out loud that had been kicking around in my head for so long. "Hiding evidence to manipulate an outcome is inappropriate behavior for a judge or anybody, and I wasn't going to do that. We gave the recording to Detective Jarkowski, and the criminal system is going to do whatever it does. It's not in my control."

For the first time Nick Green didn't have anything to say, and neither did Judges Nitz and Feldman. I'd been there all day, and I wondered whether it was finally done.

"I don't think we have any further questions," Judge Feldman said. "Is there anything further you'd like to say?"

"No."

CHAPTER FIFTY-FIVE

On the Saturday before Thanksgiving, families had gathered at the courthouse. Some girls wore fancy dresses. Some boys wore suits with small clip-on ties. The waiting area outside the courtrooms—normally a place of frustration and boredom—overflowed with balloons. People snapped pictures, dined on cake and punch, and laughed.

It was National Adoption Day.

Karen Fields ordered everyone to rise when I entered the courtroom. As I sat down, I scanned all the faces. They were smiling. They were happy. Their families were about to grow.

"Good morning, everybody," I said. "It's a great day, and I'm so honored to be here for you." I thought about the governor's press conference in Sacramento, where he'd announced his task force's recommendations. I wished he and the other task force members were in my courtroom instead so that they could see the success stories. Despite the system's flaws, many had better lives because of it.

"We have every courtroom in this building filled. As we speak, a dozen families are in the process of being reborn in a dramatic way with the addition of a child . . . or two or, in this case, three." I asked the parents, as well as the social worker and guardian ad litem, to introduce themselves for the record.

From the pages in the blue binder before me, I worked through the statutorily required questions. One by one, the parents answered under oath. They denied that they had ever been convicted of a serious crime. They recited their own family history and confirmed that the social worker had given them information about the children and the ongoing financial support that they may be eligible to obtain.

After they had answered all these questions, I got to the end. "Do you promise to love and care for these children to the best of your ability? Do you promise to provide for these children emotionally, financially, and with the best education?"

Both parents agreed, and I announced that I was granting the petition for adoption. As I signed the written order and gave it to Karen, I looked out at the people gathered. I smiled. "Now's the moment when you all get to clap."

And the courtroom erupted in cheers and applause.

After taking pictures with the children and the family, I returned to my chambers and sat down. Ten minutes later, Karen knocked on the doorframe, then came into my office.

"There are some reporters outside in the hallway," she said. "They were wondering whether you wanted to talk to them about National Adoption Day or the task force's recommendations."

"Not really."

"Nothing?"

"Tell them I'm on the criminal assignment now," I said. "They should talk to Judge Perillo. He's in charge of the child dependency courts now. I just came back for the day."

◆ ◆ ◆

Nikki waited for me outside the courthouse. Her belly had now grown large as the due date approached. "You were fabulous."

"Thank you." I kissed her and gave her a hug. "I've decided I'm going to do this every year, regardless of what assignment I'm on."

"Sounds like a plan." Nikki opened her purse and removed an envelope made of heavy paper, off-white. In the corner, printed in dark blue, was the name and return address for the Board on Judicial Standards.

Although I didn't know when exactly the decision was going to be made, I had known it was coming.

After an ethics violation is investigated, the lower panel makes factual findings as well as a recommendation to the full board. Then every member of the California State Board on Judicial Standards meets in private and decides whether to accept, reject, or modify the lower panel's finding and recommendation.

"Do you want to sit down?" she asked.

I nodded, and we walked to a park bench, the one I could see from my window. The one always surrounded by pigeons pecking away at something fallen from the nearby garbage can.

I sat on the bench, then carefully slid my index finger underneath the seal along the top. The tear followed the edge, and the envelope opened. I had a lump in my throat. I was sure that this was going to be the end. This was the moment when Nick Green won. I was sure that the Board on Judicial Standards was going to remove me from office.

It only seemed reasonable, given all that I'd done.

I reached inside and pulled out the folded pieces of paper.

The first page was a brief cover letter. Attached was a six-page decision by the board. Along the top, it stated, "In the matter of Judge James Thompson." Then, in bold type:

PRIVATE REPRIMAND

I read the words again. Then I skimmed the findings of fact and flipped to the end of the decision:

Based on the foregoing Findings and Conclusions, the Board hereby issues the following private reprimand and conditions:

1. You are hereby privately reprimanded for the foregoing misconduct.
2. You will comply with the following conditions:

1. You will determine the causes of the misconduct set forth above and take the actions necessary to ensure that the misconduct is discontinued and not repeated.

2. You will attend the National Judicial College in Reno, Nevada, and successfully complete coursework in Judicial Ethics, Enhancing Judicial Bench Skills, and Courtroom Management.

3. You will attend and successfully complete the weeklong Child Abuse and Neglect Institute sponsored by the National Council of Juvenile and Family Court Judges.

4. The Chief Judge shall appoint you a judicial mentor, and you shall meet with your mentor at least once per month for two years.

That was it. There were four things the Board on Judicial Standards could have done. First, they could dismiss the complaint. Second, they could remove me from office. Third, they could issue a public admonishment. Fourth, they could issue a private admonishment.

I flipped back to the first page of the board's decision. I reread it, confirming that the decision was private. Confirming that there wasn't going to be another newspaper article about "The Kitten."

I kissed Nikki and whispered, "It's over. We can move on." And then I kissed her again.

ACKNOWLEDGMENTS

Many thanks to Megha Parekh and the entire team at Thomas & Mercer for their patience and support of this story. Child abuse and neglect is not an easy topic. In addition to writing a compelling mystery, my goal was to highlight the many people impacted by this issue as well as those in the system—social workers, foster parents, attorneys, and judges—who are trying to make the best decisions they can under enormous time constraints, with limited resources and limited choices. They deserve our thanks and understanding.

ABOUT THE AUTHOR

Photo © 2016 Gwen Kosiak

Award-winning author J.D. Trafford, described as a "writer of merit" by *Mystery Scene* magazine, has topped numerous Amazon bestseller lists, including reaching #1 on the Legal Thrillers list. IndieReader selected his debut novel, *No Time to Run*, as a bestselling pick and *Little Boy Lost* was an Amazon Charts bestseller. Trafford graduated with honors from a top-twenty law school and has worked as a civil and criminal prosecutor, as an associate at a large national law firm, and as a nonprofit attorney. He's handled issues related to housing, education, and poverty in communities of color. Prior to law school, he worked in Washington, DC, and lived in Saint Louis, Missouri. He now lives with his wife and children in the Midwest and bikes whenever possible.